Jeffrey Si————————————————————————————sylvania.
He practi————————————————————————————1d, while
there, serv————————————————————————p responsible for reporting on New York City's prison conditions. He
left Wall S——————————————————————————
and continued as one of its name partners until giving it all
up to write full-time among the people, life, and politics of
his beloved Mykonos, his adopted home of twenty-five years,
and spear fish in its Aegean waters. When he's not in Greece,
he enjoys his other home, a farm outside New York City. *Murder
in Mykonos*, the first in his Chief Inspector Andreas Kaldis
series, was the number one best selling English-language novel
in Greece, and his second in the series, *Assassins of Athens*, is
also a bestseller. The Greek press has described him as a
'prognosticator' of Greece's societal unrest and attitudes.

For more information log on to www.jeffreysiger.com

Praise for Jeffrey Siger:

'This is international police procedural writing at its best'
Booklist

'With ten million Greeks, half of who think they are
writers, how come we had to wait for a foreigner to
come along to write such a book!'
Esquire Magazine (Greece)

'The must-read book of the week!'
OK! (Greece)

Also by Jeffrey Siger:

Murder in Mykonos

ASSASSINS

of

ATHENS

Jeffrey Siger

piatkus

PIATKUS

First published in the United States in 2010 by Poisoned Pen Press
First published in Great Britain as a paperback original in 2010 by Piatkus

A CIP catalogue record for this book
is available from the British Library.

ISBN 978-0-7499-5226-6

Typeset in Plantin by Palimpsest Book Production Limited,
Falkirk, Stirlingshire
Printed and bound in Great Britain by Clays Ltd, St Ives plc

Papers used by Piatkus are natural, renewable and recyclable
products sourced from well-managed forests and certified
in accordance with the rules of the Forest Stewardship Council.

Mixed Sources
Product group from well-managed
forests and other controlled sources
FSC www.fsc.org Cert no. SGS-COC-004081
© 1996 Forest Stewardship Council

Piatkus
An imprint of
Little, Brown Book Group
100 Victoria Embankment
London EC4Y 0DY

An Hachette UK Company
www.hachette.co.uk

www.piatkus.co.uk

To my brother, Alan. None better.

Acknowledgments

Petros Alafasos and Georgia Toli; Mihalis and Roz Apostolou; Olga Balafa; Tonino Cacace; Nikos Christodoulakis and Jody Duncan; Giannis Dimotsis; Lori Estes-Markari; Andreas and Aleka Fiorentinos; Nikos Ipiotis; Nikos Karahalios; Panos Kelaidis; Artemis Kohas; Alexandros Kontogouris; Dimitris and Elsa Kordalis; Nicholas and Sonia Kotopoulos; Manos Kounenakis; Ilias, Lila, Demetra, Maria, and Ioanna Lalaounis; Giancarlo and Diamara Leone; Sharon Lock-Sikinioti; Angelo Lyberopoulos; Ilias and Laoura Macropoulos Lalaounis; Linda Marshall; Roberto Mendes-Coelho and Edward Prendergast; Nikos Nazos; Nikos and Georgia Nomikos; Lambros Panagiotakopoulos; Barbara G. Peters and Robert Rosenwald; Eraldo, Antonella, and Camilla Prini; Christos Psallidas; Theodore, Manos, and Irini Rousounelous; Eileen Salzig; Antonia Sapounakis; Christine Schnitzer-Smith; Deppy Sigala; Alan and Patricia Siger; Jonathan, Jennifer,

Azriel, and Gavriella Siger; Karen Siger; George and Efi Sirinakis; Ed Stackler; George and Theodore Stamoulis; Maggie Taylor; Pavlos Tiftikidis; Jessica Tribble; Sotiris Varotsis; Miltiadis Varvitziotis; Zanni Vasilakis.

And, of course, Aikaterini Lalaouni.

Author's Note

Athens is the cradle of Europe. Six thousand years of history still alive in one place, crammed with sources of Western man's intellectual thought and artistic expression. It stands as a symbol to the world, a source of infinite pride of Greece and endless wonder to its visitors.

But, like every great city, it has its dark side: places where a civilization's worst practice their values, or lack thereof, and where cops do battle every day. Those places no more define the soul and life of Athens than do their counterparts in Paris, London, or New York. But they do exist. And that is where stories such as this are told.

Alexandras

28th Oktovriou (Patission)

Polytechnic University

Exarchia

Omonia

Pireos

Athinas

Kolonaki

Ermou

Vass. Sofias

Parliament

Plaka

 Acropolis

 Hadrian's Arch

Royal Residence

Kifissia

Piraeus

Panathinaikon Stadium

1

Andreas Kaldis once read or heard somewhere that the chatter never stopped in Athens. Not even at sunrise, when the earth itself seemed to pause to draw a breath. Like its people, the city always had something to say, whether you were in the mood to listen or not. Sun-up simply shifted the style of conversation from high-pitched shouts of an Athens at play to the anonymous din of a city at work.

That's what Andreas was doing now, working. 'Turn off the damn siren, no one's listening.' He was in a foul mood. 'The body's going nowhere. Just like us in this goddamn coming-home-from-partying morning traffic.'

Police officer Yianni Kouros said nothing, just did what his boss told him to do. That's why Andreas liked him: he listened.

Andreas stared out the passenger-side window at a hodge-podge of neglected private and graffiti-covered government buildings. This section of Pireos Street, a formerly elegant avenue, began west of the Acropolis, ran northeast through the trendy, late-night bar and club area of Gazi, and ended with a name change amidst the around-the-clock drug and hooker trade by Omonia Square. What remained of its once-treasured three-and four-story buildings were now warrens of ground-level check cashers, bars, small-time retail shops, and cheap, foreign restaurants. It seemed every immigrant group in Greece had set up shop in this part of town. Truth was, they were everywhere; well, almost.

'I remember when I was a kid my dad used to bring me down here for sweets on Sundays. Especially this time of year. He loved late spring.'

'Bet he wouldn't bring you here today, Chief.'

Andreas nodded. 'God bless him, he'd sit by the edge of the park at Omonia—' gesturing up ahead with his left hand, 'having coffee with friends while I'd play. Everyone liked him. I thought that came with being a cop. I should have known better.'

They were locked in traffic packed solid up to an intersection about one hundred yards ahead. The traffic light at the corner was red and, when a gap opened in oncoming traffic all the way back to the light, Kouros pulled the unmarked car into the empty lane and raced toward the intersection.

'Christ, Yianni, at least turn on the lights.'

'Never turned them off, only the siren.' Another reason Andreas liked Kouros: he listened but was no fool.

Kouros reached the intersection just as the light turned green. He swerved across the front of their lane and shot up the street to the right, narrowly missing the rear wheel of a motorcyclist who'd jumped the light.

2

Andreas turned his head and stared at Kouros. He knew there must be a grin breaking out somewhere on the other side of that face. Andreas was a dozen years older than Kouros but, except for the few tinges of gray streaking Andreas' slightly too long dark hair, you'd think they were the same age, perhaps because Kouros' boot-camp style haircut and compact, bull-like build made him look older than he was, or because Andreas' hard work at keeping his six-foot two-inch athletic frame in shape paid off.

Kouros weaved through a series of far-from-fancy back streets running roughly parallel to Pireos. Just before Omonia he turned left and cut back across the road. 'It's only a couple blocks from here.'

Andreas watched a hooker lean out from a doorway marked by a single white light above it, the local signal for 'hookers here.'

'Great neighborhood.'

'Yeah, probably another drug deal gone bad.'

'Don't know yet, but something tied to drugs would be my guess. Dawn on a Sunday morning, this neighborhood, a foreign-looking young male in a dumpster, no money, no ID, no witnesses, no one with him, and no one looking for him. At least not so far.' Andreas shrugged. 'We'll see.'

Two minutes later Kouros pulled up to a uniformed officer leaning against the hood of a marked blue and white Athens police car. It blocked anyone from going down a narrow, alley-size street just south of where Saint Constantino Avenue ran into Karaiskai Square. 'It's Chief Inspector Andreas Kaldis, Special Crimes Division, Athens Headquarters,' said Kouros.

Even a year and a half after his promotion, Andreas still

3

marveled that he was the guy with that fancy title. It posed no such problem for Kouros; he'd only known Andreas as 'chief.' First, as newly appointed chief of police for the Aegean island of Mykonos and, six months later, by his current title dating from when Andreas returned to Athens – bringing Kouros with him – to assume command of the same unit he'd been forced to leave for doing too good a job at catching politically connected bad guys. But Andreas' political allies proved to be a hell of a lot tougher than theirs, something Andreas reminded them of every chance he got.

They drove the hundred yards or so to where the cop said to go. There were no yards or open spaces along the way, only the back doors of buildings lining both sides. The buildings to the right fronted on a main street running back into Karaiskaki Square and were commercial; the ones to the left were a mix of smaller businesses and apartment buildings facing onto a side street. Everything was rundown, typical for this neighborhood. Kouros stopped at a thirty-foot-wide break on the left, an open lot that went through to the side street, or would have but for a row of weather-beaten plywood fencing it off at the edge of the street. Some of it had been kicked in, probably by junkies and street-hooker trade looking for a place to do their business.

An ambulance from the coroner's office and two marked cars from the Saint Constantino police precinct were parked ahead of them on the other side of the break. This part of town fell under their jurisdiction, until now.

Andreas' unit was in charge of all murder investigations and any other crimes he considered serious enough to warrant special attention. It was a unique position in a politically sensitive department, one that many envied, but far more feared. He was not someone to fuck with.

'So, what do we have, Manos?' he said to the man in plainclothes hurrying toward him.

'Morning, sir. A white male, late teens, early twenties, about six feet, 160 pounds. Dead about five hours. Appears to be strangled.'

'Did anyone touch the body?'

A man from the coroner's office standing next to a forensic technician gestured 'no' with his head. 'We were waiting for you, Chief.'

Manos hesitated.

'Did anyone touch the body?' Andreas said in a slightly sharper tone looking straight at Manos.

'Yes, sir. The officer who responded to the call was a rookie and—'

'Is he here?'

'Yes.'

'Call him over.' Andreas knew from the initial report of 'no wallet or ID' that someone must have touched the body, but there was a point to be made to the rookie and his supervisor.

The young cop looked almost as white as the corpse. No doubt he was wondering to what worse precinct he possibly could be banished for this screw-up.

Andreas leveled his steel-gray eyes on him. 'You were the first one on the scene?'

'Yes, sir,' he answered nervously.

'What did you see?'

'A body in that dumpster over there.' He pointed to a partially green, partially rusted, commercial-size bin against the wall across the lot from where they stood. It was close to the street.

'Anything else?'

'No, sir.'

'And what was the first fucking thing you did, strip-search him?' Andreas' voice was rising, driving home his point.

'I thought it important to know who he was. I only touched pockets I could reach without moving the body.' His voice was about to crack.

Andreas was not pleased with the answer, and his tone showed it. 'It's a damn lot more important to know *who killed him*. That's why you're trained and—' turning his eyes on Manos, '*supposedly* reminded by your shift commanders *NEVER* to touch a body unless told otherwise by someone from homicide. Understand?' He said the last word softly, his eyes moving between the two men.

'Yes, sir.' The words came from both men in two-part harmony.

Andreas walked over to the dumpster and peered inside. Without looking back he said, 'Was the lid up when you got here?'

'No, sir,' said the rookie.

'How did you open it?'

'With my baton.' Again his voice was shaky.

'Good.' Andreas believed in praising the good along with damning the bad.

The container was nearly full, packed with commercial-size black garbage bags. The body was on top: face up, eyes closed. Andreas always dreaded these first moments staring at the face of a once-living, unique being now reduced to

6

the ubiquitous status of victim. Andreas felt a shiver. This was not the face of a man. It was a boy.

'You didn't close his eyes by chance did you?'

'No, sir, I never touched the body, only his clothes.' He almost barked his answer.

Andreas looked at the man from the coroner's office. 'Can you tell me if he died like that, or someone closed his eyes for him?'

'I'd guess someone did it for him.'

'I can guess on my own, Spiros. I want to know if you can tell me for sure.'

'Probably not.'

'So, whose garbage is this?'

'Belongs to that bar over there.' Manos pointed to the back door of a building directly across from the lot. 'It's a notorious late-hours gay bar, lot of drugs in there. Our guess is that the victim was in the wrong place at the wrong time, looking for the wrong thing.'

'And just how did he happen to end up in the dumpster?'

Manos seemed surprised at the question. 'Whoever killed him hid the body there to make time to get away before someone found it. This part of the street gets pretty busy late at night, especially just before sunrise when the bar closes.' He finished the last part with a smirk.

'I bet it does.' Andreas again looked in the dumpster. 'So, where's last night's garbage?' Manos again looked puzzled. 'What do you mean? It's in the dumpster.'

'I see, so when the bar closed last night, probably around sunrise from what you said, whoever dumped the garbage carefully placed it around the body or pulled him out, put

7

the bags in, and then tossed him back on top?' Manos' face was beet-red. Andreas didn't wait for an answer.

'Have you spoken with anyone from the bar?'

'No one's there yet.'

'When you talk to the guy who dumped the garbage, I'm sure he'll swear there was no body in the dumpster when he did. But that corpse has been dead a lot longer than since sunrise.' Andreas shook his head. 'I don't think this is the murder scene. Somebody picked this place to dump the body.'

He gestured for Kouros to get a camera from the car. 'We've got a lot more going on here than just some kid in the wrong place at the wrong time. And who said he's foreign?'

The rookie raised his hand. 'He looks a lot like the Eastern Europeans living around here.'

'With all the intermarriages, so do a lot of Greeks. This kid could be Greek, and if I get a better look at the ring on his finger I might know for sure.' The coroner started toward the body.

Andreas put out his hand to stop him. 'No, Spiros, don't. I want everything videotaped exactly as it is before anyone touches the body. I'll get what I need from this.' He took the camera from Kouros, leaned back in and took a few pictures.

'So, let's see what we have.'

He brought one of the photos up onto the screen on the back of the camera and zoomed in on what he wanted to see.

'Damn handy, these things.' He stared for a moment; everyone was quiet. 'Gotcha!' He practically shouted the word.

8

Manos and Kouros moved in for a closer look at the screen. It was a blurry image of a crest from a ring, but distinct enough to make out the emblem of Athens Academy, the most prestigious private school in all of Greece: the place where the richest and most powerful sent their children to study and, more important, to network a life for themselves and, on occasion, for their parents. Next to the crest was the year of graduation: one year from now.

'He's just a boy, and I bet he's no foreigner,' said Andreas. He'd also bet, but didn't say aloud, that a media circus was about to begin. He looked up from the image of the ring and over to the dumpster, then to the backdoor of perhaps the seediest gay bar in the seediest section of Athens. What more could the press ask for? It was a story they could run with forever.

Whoever set this up knew that, too. Anyway you looked at it, Andreas sensed this was going to get real messy, real fast. He looked at Manos. 'What did the guy who called your precinct say? That he'd found the body while rummaging through dumpsters?'

'Something like that. Sounded like a bum, wouldn't leave a name.'

Andreas shook his head. 'Whoever set this up wanted the body to be found here. He wouldn't leave that to chance. Find your caller and we find our killer. Trace that call ASAP.'

Manos almost seemed to snicker. 'We're way ahead of you, Chief. Already did the trace. It gave us nothing. We even called the number and no one answered. It's for one of those disposable cell phones you can buy anywhere. This one was activated last night.'

9

Andreas shook his head. 'Gave you nothing, huh? Like a fucking destitute bum rummaging through garbage bins would buy a cell phone to call in a dead body. Yianni, let's get out of here. We've got some catching up to do. Someone *definitely* is way ahead of us.' He stared at Manos long enough to get the point across without saying the words, *but it's not you.*

2

Zanni Kostopoulos looked at his watch. It was still early. His assistant wasn't due in for another half-hour. Things weren't going as planned and he worried the media might turn on him. They would for sure if they ever found out. He tried not to think about it.

Zanni wasn't an easy man to get to know, and an even tougher one to like. He'd achieved his wealth the old fashioned way: stolen, bribed, and laundered for it. And, if the truth to rumor could be measured by its persistence, he'd killed for it more than once. Today, though, the Kostopoulos name was 'a pillar of Athenian society.' At least that's what his third wife paid several publicists to get virtually every society reporter in Greece to repeat *ad nauseam*. If you linked 'respected international businessman' and 'philanthropist' to a name long enough, people started believing it. Or so went the theory.

Mrs Kostopoulos' plan certainly had worked on her

husband; Zanni was intoxicated with himself, never missing a word uttered about him in the media, and bothered to no end when the press did not grasp that his vast fortune made him right in all things and deserving of public esteem equivalent to his wealth. Each morning, the assistant he'd hired solely for the purpose of keeping track of his fame gave him a folio containing clippings and tapes of every recorded mention of his name in the past twenty-four hours. His mood for the next twenty-four depended upon the size of the package she handed him.

Where is she? Zanni stepped away from his desk and paced around the room. He'd experienced the media turning on him before and didn't like it one bit. That last run-in was what got him into this current mess. At least that was his take on it. He still bristled at the memory of his public battle with the owner of Athens' most popular soccer team. As Zanni saw it, the owner was no different than he – both had returned from family exile in the former Soviet bloc to amass vast, newly-minted Greek fortunes – and yet, Zanni was forever in the other man's shadow. Zanni's decision to attempt wresting control of the team away from his rival wasn't made for business reasons; he did it because he believed the team was the source of the other's prominence.

Two such famous boys fighting over a nationally popular toy had every headline writer and talk show host in frenzy for weeks. It was a bitter fight with a rival at least as tough as he was and resulted in an even more bitter loss. Zanni felt he'd been singled out by the media for ridicule, and looked for someone other than himself to blame for his humiliation. He settled on an easy target: old-line Athens society. Many old-liners barely hid their disdain for what

12

they considered upstart, political opportunist, *nouveaux riches*. Accusing them of relishing his fall was undoubtedly accurate. What he couldn't accept, though, was the obvious fact that old-line society would prefer both men to perish in the press.

His anger simmered for months. Then he decided he'd show them all – all of Athens – his power, by making his name a feared, if not respected, household word in another way: newspaper ownership. And not just any paper, but Greece's oldest and most respected, *The Athenian*. As virtually everyone in Athens knew, *The Athenian* had been in the Linardos family for generations and, though other papers boasted larger circulations, none came close to rivaling its influence among the nation's elite.

'Fuck them,' was Zanni's reaction to a terse message declining his offer to buy the paper at a generous multiple of its economic value and pointedly suggesting that he try going after another soccer team instead; perhaps a second division one in northern Greece up by the border with 'one of those former Soviet countries.'

He did not miss the insult directed at his roots, nor the reminder implicit in the message that there were bounds not to exceed, just as there were clubs not to press for membership; at least not until subsequent generations sufficiently seasoned his family's roots with the right schools and proper marriages to make them palatable. That message had arrived barely more than a month ago. It marked day one of his siege against the Linardos family.

Zanni bought and pursued every Linardos family debt he could acquire, ones creditors dared not press against such a powerful voice; found and financed every libel claim that could be brought or manufactured; dried up much of the paper's advertising base by subsidizing those who agreed to advertise elsewhere; and paid more to those who refused to sell the paper than they could make selling it.

Despite all Zanni's maneuvering, the family didn't budge. The carrot hadn't worked and the stick wasn't hurting enough. He'd decided it was time to strike harder, beat them to death if necessary. He would not be humiliated again. Long hidden secrets of the family began circulating throughout Athens. Affairs of the fathers, addictions of the wives, and proclivities of the children kept finding their way into rival publications. And, now, a particularly indiscreet moment involving a favored granddaughter and two young men, recorded on a cell phone in the men's room of a notorious Gazi nightclub, was a major hit on the Web and the certain ruin of her name.

On each of the four consecutive Fridays following his initial proposal, Zanni sent a renewed offer to the family, each reducing the last proposed price by 25 percent. The family never responded. Two days ago he sent the fifth.

Zanni stopped pacing and stared out the window. He should have heard something by now. He'd ratcheted the pressure up about as high as you could push it. If going after the kid didn't work . . . what the fuck were these people made of?

'Any ideas?'

Kouros kept his eyes on the road. 'Looks like someone's sending a message.'

Andreas nodded. 'You don't go to all the trouble of hiding a body in a place where it's certain to be found, then call

14

the police to make sure that it is, without a very clear purpose in mind.'

'What do you think it is?'

'Not sure yet, but whatever it is, they want the message delivered by us.'

Kouros turned onto Alexandras Street. They were almost back to General Police Headquarters, better known as GADA. It wasn't far from where they found the kid's body, but it sat at the heart of Athens' bustle, next door to a major hospital, down the block from Greece's Supreme Court, and across the street from the stadium of one of Greece's most popular soccer teams, Panathinaikos. GADA was a chore to get to at almost any hour.

Andreas drummed the fingers of his right hand on the top of the dashboard. 'I don't see it as a spontaneous crime of passion or tied to some drug deal gone bad. It certainly wasn't a mugging. This was planned.'

'But why kill a kid . . . can't imagine even our worst, hard-ass, scum-ball mafia types doing that.'

'I know. That's what has me wondering.' *And worried*, Andreas mumbled to himself. 'This can't be the beginning of whatever's going on.'

'Maybe it's the end?'

'Let's hope.' Andreas stopped drumming. 'But I don't think so.'

Noblesse oblige was a French phrase, but for Sarantis Linardos it needed no translation. Not because he was fluent in French as well as German, English, and, of course, his native Greek, but because it described his view of the Linardos family's obligations to Greece so perfectly; most particularly his own responsibilities as family patriarch and publisher of its most sacrosanct asset. Many old-line families in Greece shared the Linardos family's social position, but none its power of the press. A loss of *The Athenian* meant the end to his family's influence over the thinking of its peers and its reign at the pinnacle of Athens society. He could never allow that to happen.

Then again, he wasn't feeling particularly regal at the moment and this battle with that awful Kostopoulos person was taking its toll on his family. He was not concerned with Kostopoulos' economic attacks; the fool had no idea of the reach of his family's resources. One could not have his finger on the pulse of generations of Greece's most powerful without learning their secrets. It was Sarantis' discretion in using what he learned that earned him their confidence and gave him his true influence. There was not a person of position in Greece who did not owe the Linardos family at least a bit of gratitude, measurable in euros. He knew there was far more than enough available to withstand any financial siege.

Still, many of Sarantis' long-time friends had warned him Kostopoulos was not the sort of man who could be trusted to act civilly, and he should take the threat more seriously. Some had offered to intervene to try convincing Kostopoulos to stop. Sarantis refused. He would not speak, much less negotiate, with such rabble, nor allow any of his friends to stoop to doing so on his behalf. He was convinced if he simply ignored Kostopoulos' weekly offers and the half-truths and lies he planted in the tabloids, items of little interest to the public for even their brief time on the newsstands, Kostopoulos would simply give up and go away.

He never saw it coming.

The video of his granddaughter with those two men was a brutal, merciless assassination. It left no doubt as to how far Kostopoulos was prepared to go. The humiliation would haunt her on the Web forever. Her boyfriend no longer spoke to her, no socially prominent girlfriend dared be seen with her, and the tabloid-media harpies now called a racially mixed *ménage à trois* 'doing the Elena.' Whispers and snickers accompanied her everywhere. His favorite grandchild had no choice but to flee Greece in shame. For how long he did not know. Elena might never recover.

And Elena's mother, his daughter, moved into Sarantis' home with her other children until 'you end it with this horrible man, father;' utterly panicked over what else might happen to the children.

Sarantis had lived long enough to understand that people did what they must to survive; but never, not even in war fighting to rid his beloved Greece of Germans and later communists, had he faced an enemy so single-mindedly obsessed with destroying his family as Zanni Kostopoulos.

That's when he knew it was time to turn to his friends. Let them attempt to reason with this butcher. He wanted no further harm to befall his family; certainly no more to the children. He only hoped it wasn't too late.

Andreas' office was on the fourth floor of the building and faced east, away from the heart of Athens. It had two long windows but not much of a view. That was fine with Andreas; he had more than enough to look at on his desk and on the chart of active cases fastened to the wall behind it. He was in his chair, staring at the chart, and wondering where to squeeze in the dumpster case when his secretary came through the door at the far end of his office.

'Here are the photos the lab downloaded from your camera.'

'Thanks, Maggie.' She preferred that to the Greek Margarita.

Andreas placed the half-dozen eight-by-tens on his desk. The crime scene unit had a lot more photographs to study, but he wanted to check for anything that might be helpful in the few he took. He picked up one of the boy's face. Nice-looking kid, he thought. Damn shame.

Maggie was standing on the other side of the desk, staring down at the photos. She'd worked as a police secretary for longer than Andreas had been alive and ages ago forgot her official lowly status in the bureaucratic food chain. 'May I take a look at the one you're holding, Chief?' She reached out and took it without waiting for him to answer.

Andreas couldn't help but smile. He really liked her, and not just because she knew his father from his days as a cop. A lot of people knew his dad, though most wouldn't admit to serving with him during his last years on the force as part of the Junta's secret police. They preferred acting as if they played no part in those seven years of dictatorship. But Maggie was unique. Sure, she had her quirks and told you exactly what was on her mind if you dared to ask, often even if you didn't, but she knew all there was to know about the department and everyone in it. The department was her 24/7 life. She never seemed to leave the building. Pure luck, though some may have described it differently, landed her in his unit. Her long-time boss had announced his retirement a few weeks before Andreas arrived and, when

18

human resources suggested she retire with him, her answer could be heard as far away as Turkey. So, the legendary Maggie Sikestis now reported to Chief Kaldis. Or was it the other way around? Andreas never was quite sure.

'Good-looking boy, Chief.'

'That's what I thought.'

Maggie waved the photograph in her right hand and pursed her lips. 'I've seen this boy before.'

She never ceased to amaze him, but this was too much to believe. 'Maggie, how could you know this kid?' Then he paused. 'He's not a relative or a friend's child, is he?'

'No, nothing like that. I just swear I saw him in one of those tabloids.'

It seemed all of Greece was addicted to *National Enquirer*-like publications. All except Andreas. He was too busy battling with facts to spend time amidst gossip and rumors.

'I think it was in *Espresso*, maybe *Loipon*. Possibly even *Hello*.' Obviously, Maggie saw her job description differently. 'Wait!' She almost shouted the word, then turned and hurried her sturdy, compact five-foot-three-inch frame out the door.

Andreas picked up the phone and pressed an intercom button. 'Yianni, get in here. Maggie thinks she knows our kid from the dumpster.'

Both arrived at the door together. It looked like a mother and son team. Except Maggie had a bit more hair and dyed it close to red. 'Here it is, Chief.'

He took the paper. The headline read, FAMILIES WHACK AWAY AT WAR, WHO'S NEXT? Andreas hated that sort of headline; it reminded him of what cost him his father.

'It's inside.' Maggie pulled the paper out of his hands, turned to the appropriate page and gave it back to him. 'The boy's picture is here.'

Andreas and Kouros looked to where she pointed. There he was, among photographs of members of the two families. One picture of a pretty girl had an 'x' through it. The caption below the photo said 'Whacked' and gave the link to a website.

'What's this?' he asked Maggie.

Kouros answered. 'She's the granddaughter of the publisher of *The Athenian*. She was caught on a cell phone camera doing two guys at the same time in a public toilet at a club in Gazi. That's a link to the video.'

He wanted to ask how Yianni knew so much about it but decided not to ask. He probably was the only one in the room, perhaps all of Athens, who hadn't seen it. Andreas sat quietly for a moment staring at the paper, then let out a deep breath. 'All hell's going to break loose when this gets out. Surprised it hasn't already. Better get media affairs ready.'

'I'll take care of it,' said Maggie.

'Yianni, get a home address on the kid's family. We have to get over there before someone in the coroner's office recognizes the kid and tips off the press.' He didn't bother to mention the number of cops who'd like to pick up the money for such a tip.

Kouros left. Andreas turned in his chair and stared at the chart. He wished he could break the news to the family by phone; that way you didn't have to see their grief, feel it, let it get to you. But this wasn't the sort of thing you could do like that. At least he couldn't. He remembered the day he learned his father had killed himself . . . Andreas tore away from the thought. He waved at the chart. 'Maggie, find a new place for some of this stuff. We have to make room.' A lot of room.

If you lived in Athens' northern suburb of Old Psychiko, people were impressed. At least that's what many of its residents hoped. Just north of Athens and west of Kifissias Avenue, it was a refuge of peace, greenery, and high walls for foreign embassies, exclusive private schools, and the upper echelon of Athenian society. A few nearby neighborhoods and one or two to the south might claim to be as tony, but none would dare argue to be greater.

Psychiko's confusing array of one-way streets, winding every which way about its tree-lined slopes and hills, was designed that way for a reason: to keep out the casual passersby. But it hadn't worked as well on the new money crowd. They flocked to the neighborhood, sending prices through the roof for houses they often tore down to build grander homes than their neighbors'. Among long-time residents, you'd be hard pressed to find anyone happy with the changes to their neighborhood. Until it came time to sell, of course.

Kouros knew how to get to Psychiko; his trouble was finding a way to get to the house. They passed the same kiosk twice trying to find the correct connecting road to the one-way street they were looking for.

'Screw it,' said Andreas. 'Turn up here,' pointing at a DO NOT ENTER sign marking the end of the street they wanted.

About a quarter-mile up the road, an eight-foot-high,

white concrete-stucco wall ran for about one hundred feet along the right side of the street. A ten-foot-high, black wrought iron gate stood midway along the wall. The gate's leaf-and-tendril design was so tightly spaced not even a cat could squeeze through.

They parked outside the gate, and Kouros walked to the intercom on the wall by the left side of the gate. He identified himself and held his police ID up to the camera. They were buzzed in and made their way along a stone path winding around closely planted eucalyptus, lemon, bougainvillea, and oleander shielding the house from the gate. Andreas thought a lot of care must go into this place. A man waited for them outside the front door. He asked to see their identification again. When he asked the purpose for their visit, Andreas told him, 'It's a personal, family matter.'

The man took out his cell phone and called someone.

Andreas' eyes scanned the front of the three-story building. Hard to imagine it was only a house. 'I could live here,' he said to Kouros.

'I'd never find my way home at night.'

'Who said I'd ever leave?'

'Gentlemen, please, come with me.' The man gestured toward the open front door. He showed them into a room most would call a living room but, between the front door and where they stood, they'd passed through so many others Andreas would call a living room that he couldn't guess what this one might be called.

'Please, wait here. Would you like something to drink?'

'No, thank you,' said Andreas. He felt out of place in these surroundings, or maybe it was the purpose of his visit, but whatever the reason he sensed his hand might shake slightly if he held a glass. Adrenaline could do that. He preferred his hands free.

The man left, leaving Andreas and Kouros standing in the middle of the lavishly decorated room, facing a doorway, and looking conspicuously ill at ease. Andreas was still struggling to think of the right words to say. All he could think of was, 'Yianni, you tell them.' Andreas smiled at the thought of the deer-in-the-headlights look that order would get from his taciturn partner.

'Chief Kaldis?' The question came from behind them. He and Yianni turned to face the voice. A couple was standing in another doorway. The man looked much older than the woman.

'Yes, sir, and this is officer Kouros.'

Kouros nodded hello.

'We understand you have a personal matter to discuss with us.'

Andreas drew in a breath. 'Yes, sir, I do.'

'I hope it's not something we should have our lawyer here for.' He was smiling as he said it, but it showed Andreas this man knew his way around police. For if he did need a lawyer, Andreas must tell him now.

'No, sir, absolutely not.'

The man's smile was gone.

'What's wrong? What's happened? Are the children all right?' It was the woman. She was squeezing the man's arm.

Andreas hoped it wouldn't come up this way, so abruptly and directly to the point. But that's how most mothers reacted to police appearing at their homes unexpectedly:

23

had something happened to her children or her husband? And usually in that order.

He must now give these people probably the worst news they'd ever hear. He hoped his voice wouldn't crack. 'Yes, I'm afraid it's about Sotiris.'

'What's happened? Is he all right, did he wreck the car, did he hurt someone, did—' Before she could finish the man cut her off.

'Please, dear, let me handle this.' He looked at Andreas. 'Whatever trouble he's in I'm sure we can work it out. I have a lot of friends.'

Andreas knew how to handle this sort of approach, but not today. No matter how obnoxious or pretentious this guy might be, he would get a free pass on this.

'I'm sure you do, sir, but it's not that sort of situation.'

The man started to say something else, but Andreas put up his hand and said, 'Please.'

Perhaps it was the look of anguish on Andreas' face or a paralyzing, simultaneous chill felt in each one's spine, but each stood perfectly still, quietly waiting for Andreas to speak.

Andreas only paused long enough for them to look directly into his eyes. 'A terrible thing has happened, Sotiris has been killed.' Unconsciously, he crossed himself.

No one moved, not a word was said. It was an eternity. It was three seconds.

'*Noooooooooo . . .*' The word went on forever. The mother kept pitching it higher and higher, twisting her hands about the man's arm, then grabbed her face in her hands. Still struggling to scream, but without the breath for it, she started pounding on the man's chest. He did not move. He did not blink.

Andreas did not know what more to say, and so he said the obvious. 'I'm so very sorry, Mr and Mrs Kostopoulos.'

3

Andreas never got used to delivering such dreadful, un-expected news. He didn't want to; his skin was thick enough. He watched Mrs Kostopoulos go from pounding on her husband's chest to sobbing against it, but he wasn't judging how they chose to mourn. There should be no rules for grieving. Especially for a child.

Ginny Kostopoulos was twenty-four when she met fifty-year-old Zanni. Like so many other Eastern-European beauties migrating to Greece in search of work, she put her natural charms to good use on celebrity-filled island beaches catering to the desires of thirsty sun worshipers. Zanni's were obvious from the start, and Ginny, an unwed mother of a four-year-old son, did not object. They married as quickly as he could divorce wife number two. Zanni adopted the boy, giving him the name Sotiris after Zanni's late father. He had two grown daughters from his previous marriages and, together with Ginny, twin ten-year-old girls. Sotiris was the only son.

Andreas waited patiently; he knew the question would come soon. It always did.

'What happened to our son?' It came from Zanni.

'He was . . .' Andreas swallowed hard. 'He was murdered.' A priest or a social worker might have put it differently, but Andreas was a cop. And cops want reactions. They're more telling than words.

'Murdered? Murdered!' It was Ginny. She dropped her arms from around her husband and turned away from all three men. Her right hand was over her mouth and her eyes fixed on the floor.

'Who did it . . . how did it happen?' Zanni did the asking. Ginny didn't move from her spot.

'We don't know yet, sir. It occurred a few hours after midnight. Your son's body was discovered at dawn and the coroner hasn't completed his examination.' Neither parent responded. Andreas' instinct was to say more. 'But we think it was directed at your family.'

Zanni's expression did not change. His face had turned to stone since Andreas first said his son was dead. Ginny was frozen in place, her breathing increasing rapidly, as if about to hyperventilate.

They were in shock, a normal and expected reaction.

'Thank you, Chief, for your concern.' Zanni sounded as if tipping a waiter.

Andreas thought perhaps he hadn't made his last comment clear enough or they may have missed it in their grief. 'Mr Kostopoulos, did your son or your family receive any threats? Or can you think of anyone who might have done such a horrible thing as a message to your family?'

Zanni stared straight ahead. 'No, sir.'

27

Andreas pressed him harder but got no better an answer than an interviewer trying to force genuine beliefs from a politician. Nor was there a hint of Zanni's legendary temper; no matter how hard Andreas pushed him it was always the same: 'No, sir.'

Zanni eyes stayed focused somewhere in the middle-distance while Ginny stood with hers fixed on the floor, clutching her arms across her chest and swaying from side to side. She said not a word and was no longer crying.

The chief of Athens Special Crimes Division had just asked the parents of a murdered boy if their son's death was a message to their family, and neither asked what the hell he was talking about. Shock or no shock, Andreas knew their silence definitely was not normal.

They were sitting in their car in front of the Kostopoulos home. 'So, what do you think?' It was the second time Andreas asked that question in the three minutes since they'd left the house.

Kouros' first answer to the question was a summary of what the boy's parents and the household staff told them: Sotiris was almost seventeen, into girls not guys, and well-liked. He'd been playing backgammon at home with two male classmates until eleven when all three were picked up by a taxi for some late-night clubbing. He hadn't been expected home until late Sunday afternoon, at the earliest. Those weren't unusual hours for him or for his friends on weekends, and, yes, they were underage for the clubs, but so were a lot of kids from fancy neighborhoods who hung out there. They got in because they could afford it or some

28

family celebrity-status made them attractive customers. Some, like Sotiris, got in for both reasons.

This time Kouros' answer was, 'About what?'

'Mr and Mrs K.'

Kouros shrugged. 'They were pretty much out of it. Especially her. Until that doctor got there with a sedative, I thought she was going to lose it big-time.'

'Me, too.' Andreas stared at the gate. 'Something's not right about this. They couldn't name one person with a possible grudge against their son or them. All they needed to do was open a newspaper, any newspaper, and find Linardos spelled in capital letters. But they didn't even mention the name. It was as if that family didn't exist.'

'He had to be thinking the same thing we were. The most obvious suspect was someone tied into the Linardos family.'

Andreas nodded. 'For sure, but he's never going to tell us. It's not in his DNA. He can't ask for help. Certainly not from cops.'

'The wife seemed pretty close to saying something. I thought she was going to explode.'

'What I'd give to be a fly on their wall when she wakes up and starts tearing into him.' Andreas gestured for Kouros to start the car. 'May as well stop hoping for miracles and get back to police work. Let's find those two friends of the boy. We'll come back here in a day or so, after the funeral, and try to get her to talk. They're not going anywhere.'

Andreas learned early on as a cop that sixteen-year-old boys lived forever. They all knew that rule. It applied to all boys, not just those with doting parents forgiving all trespasses,

29

indulging all whims, and setting no boundaries. It was a hormonal thing, so every cop knew they were at the core of the most dangerous age groups to predict. Children died of war, famine, disease, and other, far too remote causes, to raise even a passing thought of personal mortality in most sixteen-year-old minds. Thankfully, most grew up unscathed in any serious way.

He also knew not all were so lucky. A few died, some survived close calls, and others were left to grieve the fates of their peers. But even the most personal of accidental tragedies, a friend's horrific, deadly motorcycle crash, rarely had but short-term influence on their behavior. In their minds, they were protected from a similar fate by greater skills, better judgment, and the ever-intoxicating bravado of their hormones.

But that rationale would not help Sotiris Kostopoulos' friends deal with his death. Perhaps, if he'd died in a car or boating accident, or they were kids from a violent neighborhood where crime on the streets many times brought death, it would be different for them, but murder was outside the experience of the Athens Academy crowd.

Andreas and Kouros spent hours speaking separately to the boys in the presence of their parents. That was the quickest way of gaining the parents' cooperation. Now, though, it was time to speak to the two boys individually, and away from hovering adults. When the parents objected, Andreas courteously explained their choices: one, accompany their children to police headquarters for a formal interrogation with stenographer, lawyers, and all; or two, allow the police to complete the questioning, informally, in a private home.

Andreas thought that would get him the desired co-operation, but Greeks were notorious negotiators, even with police, and the father of one of the boys would not relent. Andreas was certain the two friends weren't suspects and knew if he pressed it to the point of involving lawyers it might be days, perhaps longer, before he got to speak to them. So, they compromised: no parents, but the boys remained together.

The home they chose was only a few blocks from the Kostopoulos residence, but settled in another world, one far more familiar to Andreas. He sat on a straight-back dining room chair in what he knew could be the home's only living room, facing two boys seated on a plush-cushion bright-red and green floral-pattern couch. The boys looked about to be devoured by the pillows. Kouros sat off to Andreas' right, at the end of the couch, in another straight-back chair.

Theo Angelou and George Lambrou were dark-skinned, dark-haired, dark-eyed, and pimply. Theo, at five-feet five inches tall, was noticeably overweight. George, though the thinner of the two, was only an inch or so taller. No doubt blond, blue-eyed, six-foot Sotiris Kostopoulos had been the face-man of this crew. The two struggled to sit up straight on the couch. It was obvious from their faces what was going through their minds: *there-but-for-the-grace-of-God-go-I*.

Andreas spoke to them as men, not boys, aiming to create camaraderie and attain a hoped for franker discussion of a very important – stunningly attractive – detail they'd been sheepish to talk about in front of their parents.

'A taxi driver you knew, from the car service you always

31

used, picked you up at Sotiris' house and took you straight to the Angel Club off Pireos Street in Gazi?'

Both nodded.

'That's been your hangout for the past four months?'

More nods.

'And every weekend night it's open there's a specific table reserved just for you whether or not you showed up?' Andreas hoped his tone didn't show what he thought of high-school kids with private tables at one of Athens' hottest clubs, and of the parents who paid.

Perhaps he hadn't masked it well enough or, perhaps, the glamour of claiming such privilege was gone, but the boys didn't nod. George looked at Theo, then back at Andreas. 'Yes, sir, that's right, but really it was Sotiris who had the table. Everyone knew they could find him there after midnight.'

'Ever go to any other clubs, like in Kolonaki?' Kolonaki was Athens' most fashionable and expensive downtown neighborhood, and where Andreas expected these kids to gather, rather than in the dicier clubs of Gazi.

'Not really, Angel was our place. We didn't want to hang out in Kolonaki clubs with everyone else from around here. Once in a while, maybe, if there were a special party somewhere else, but most of our friends came to party with us at Angel.'

He looked at Theo.

'Yes, sir, that's right.'

Andreas paused. He almost was up to what he wanted to cover most, but first, a subject he hadn't raised in front of their parents. 'I understand Sotiris didn't have a girl-friend?'

'That's right,' said Theo.

'Was there some special girl in his life? Anyone?'

'Not that I knew of.'

Andreas looked at George. 'Did he ever have a girlfriend?'

'No, sir.'

'Okay, guys.' Andreas leaned forward. 'I've got to ask this question. Was he gay?'

There was genuine surprise, even a flash of anger on Theo's face. Perhaps because of what the question suggested about the three of them.

George spoke. 'No way, he was the best there was with girls. They were all over him. We'd hang around waiting for the ones he tossed back.'

Andreas shook his head. 'You're not convincing me, guys. You tell me he had no girlfriend and yet girls were all over him. Doesn't sound to me that he liked girls.' Andreas knew he was pushing an uncomfortable subject on already traumatized boys and didn't like it, but he had no choice.

George stared at a photograph of his parents on the coffee table next to Andreas. 'I don't know what else to tell you. He didn't have a girlfriend.' The boy paused, as if emphasizing what he was about to say. 'None of us did.' Then he looked at Andreas' eyes. 'But Sotiris wasn't gay. Neither is Theo.' No disclaimer for himself.

Interesting kid, Andreas thought, he's implying he might be gay to establish his murdered buddy was not.

George continued. 'He didn't want to be tied down to any one girl. That's the way a lot of guys are these days. If you have sex with the girl she thinks it's serious, and if you have it with her regularly she thinks you'll marry her.'

This I'm hearing from a high-school kid, thought Andreas. He smiled at how much simpler his own teenage years might have been had he known that little secret then. Even now, it might be useful.

Time to see if his challenge to teenager machismo resulted in an among-us-guys discussion of his real subject of interest. 'Okay, George, so tell me more about this hot girl Sotiris met last night at the Angel.'

'We never saw her before. As I told you, she looked about twenty, light brown hair, green eyes, great figure. Taller than me.'

Andreas smiled. 'So, guys, now tell me *exactly* what you said when you first saw her. Let's start with what Sotiris said. Don't worry, I can handle it.' He leaned over and gave Theo a man-to-man smack on the knee.

'"Look at those tits." Those were Sotiris' first words. "Fantastic ass," were mine. George said, "She must be Olympiakos" – we're big fans of soccer – because she was wearing red.'

George added, 'Not just red, Olympiakos red. The dress, an Armani, drapée mini, and Jimmy Choo stilettos perfectly matched in our favorite team's color.'

Andreas nodded. 'Theo, anything to add?'

As if consciously trying to distance himself from whatever impression George may have been trying to create about his own preferences, Theo said, 'George's parents are in the fashion business; he knows that sort of stuff. Personally, I thought she was the greatest piece of ass ever to walk alone into that place.'

'We all agreed on that, Theo,' said George. 'But Sotiris said she had to be a hooker. "Nothing that beautiful could be in here for free," he said. We thought she was waiting for someone. But she sat alone at the next table just listening to the music. Didn't even try starting a conversation with us.'

'Was that unusual?'

'Well, a lot of people tried breaking into our crowd. They'd do whatever they could to get noticed by us,' said Theo.

He wondered if these kids had any idea how the other half – make that 99.5% – lived. Andreas actually felt a little sorry for them. In a few years they'd be breaking into a new crowd, one the Greek media liked to call 'the 700ers,' kids raised among the clothes, cars, money, boats, and vacations of their (often debt-strapped) parents, thinking life always would be easy for them, until running head-on into the typical Greek university graduate's starting salary of seven hundred euros per month. Hardly enough to pay one night's bar bill at the Angel Club.

'So, how did they hook up?'

'Sotiris leaned over and asked if she wanted to join us. She said, "No." He asked if he could buy her a drink. She said, "No." He asked if he could marry her, and she laughed.'

'That's when he made his move,' said George. 'He slid out of his chair and onto the one next to her.'

'He was the best at picking up girls. A super-*kamaki*,' said Theo.

They were talking more naturally than they had in front of their parents, and it made them sound like bravado-driven sixteen-year-olds; but he couldn't fault them for being so naïve. Most men, make that virtually all, would be the same in pursuit of a woman that hot. And once there's booze involved, every guy thinks he has a shot. It's the Greek man's mentality. They take great pride in what they imagine to be their skills at pursuing women, even describing their 'whatever-it-takes' behavior by the name for the little trident their ancestors once used to hunt octopus: *kamaki*.

'Did anyone else talk to her?'

'Not that I noticed,' said Theo.

Andreas looked at the other boy. George gave a quick upward jerk of his head in the Greek style for 'no.'

'How long was she sitting there before Sotiris said something to her?'

'Maybe ten minutes,' said George.

Andreas shook his head. 'Come on guys, the "greatest piece of ass" ever to walk into one of the biggest *kamaki* joints in all of Athens is sitting alone at the table next to you, and no one but Sotiris talked to her? For ten seconds, maybe. For ten minutes, never. Someone must have. Think harder.' He raised his voice a bit.

Theo shook his head. 'No, I never saw anyone talk to her.'

George shut his eyes. 'I'm trying to remember, but neither of us ever spoke to her, either. And, once Sotiris joined her, the table was off-limits.'

'What do you mean, "off-limits"?'

George opened his eyes. 'We knew he was doing his thing and we didn't want to interfere. So we started talking to other friends and left them alone.'

'And the bouncers kept everyone else away from her table.' It was Theo.

'What bouncers?'

'Two guys in club tee shirts.'

'Was that before or after Sotiris was with her?'

'After.'

George added, 'But I saw them stop a few different guys heading toward her table before Sotiris spoke to her. I remember, because I was trying to guess who she might be waiting for.'

'Why did the bouncers stop them?'

George shook his head. 'Don't know, but our table and hers were in a section of the club set off from the rest of the room by a velvet rope. The club decided who got past the rope and where they could sit. Maybe she told them she wanted to be alone.'

Andreas looked at Kouros, rubbed the heels of his hands into his eyes, then dropped his hands to smack his thighs as he focused back on the boys. 'So, can you describe the two bouncers?'

George answered. 'Probably late twenties, both about six-four, two hundred-forty pounds, shaved heads, close-cropped beards, dark. They looked like every other gorilla-bouncer you expect to see in a club.'

Andreas had the boys run through the rest of what they remembered. Sotiris had left with the girl about forty minutes after they started talking, telling his friends he wouldn't be back that night and if his parents called the next day to ask where he was, they should say he was 'asleep at Theo's house.' It would not be the first time they'd told that story to Sotiris' parents. Andreas made them repeat everything three more times, with Kouros getting in some practice in the bad cop role. He shook them up a bit, but what they said remained essentially unchanged: nothing

37

seemed out of the ordinary to either of them, although George recalled one of the bouncers disappeared shortly before Sotiris and the girl left the club. They never saw their friend again.

4

They took the back streets of Psychiko into Athens. It was evening rush hour and, though at times it seemed they were following roads laid out by pavers chasing wandering goats, this was the fastest way back to headquarters.

'I think we should stop by the Angel Club before it gets busy.' Andreas hadn't said much since getting in the car.

'That won't be until after midnight.'

'I meant before it opens. I doubt the two gorillas with the girl worked there or, if they did, they're still around, but the ever-charming Angel Club staff is our only lead to them.'

Kouros glanced in the direction of their office as he drove across Alexandras Avenue onto a road leading to one that wound around Lykavittos, Athens' majestic sister hill to the Acropolis. This was a long way to get to the club, but potentially quicker in traffic. On the east side of Lykavittos lay Kolonaki, where wealthy Athenians preferring a more citified lifestyle lived among post-World War II apartment buildings and the rare traditional home not yet sacrificed to developers.

Kouros dodged his way through Kolonaki and the bustling back streets of old Athenian neighborhoods aiming for Pireos Street.

'I think we better be ready for trouble,' said Andreas.

'Should we call for backup?'

Andreas shook his head. 'No, then we'd have to behave.' He grinned and shot a light jab at Kouros' arm. 'We're better off if they think we're as nasty as they are. That way they might try to make a deal. If we come in with backup, they'll just call for a lawyer.'

'Someone at that club had to be in on—' Kouros slammed on his brakes as a motorcyclist shot in front of them out of a garage. '*Malaka!* The bastard never looked!'

'Nice language.' Andreas nibbled at his lower lip. 'Yeah, it was a setup from the start. An irresistible girl at the next table, gorillas keeping everyone else away.' Andreas shook his head. 'I just find it hard to believe that someone from a family as prominent as the Linardos family would be behind such a premeditated, cold-blooded killing of an innocent sixteen-year-old boy.'

'To get back at the father for what he did to the Linardos girl?'

'I understand the motive, Yianni. It's just that killing a child as revenge for the sins of the father . . .' he let the words trail off. 'How could anyone be so naïve or arrogant not to realize a Linardos would be our number-one suspect?'

'Maybe the boy wasn't supposed to die; something went wrong?'

'Maybe. But as bizarre as it sounds, the parents' reaction wasn't complete shock at what happened to their boy. It was almost as if they knew something like that *could* happen, and an idea of who did it.'

'Which brings us back to the Linardos family.'

'Like I said, suspect number one.' Andreas stared out the window. 'Assuming a Linardos is behind this, the only way I see of proving it is working our way link-by-link up the chain from the actual killers, most likely the two gorillas with the girl.'

Kouros nodded. 'Should we start interviewing the family members?'

'Can't think of a better way to meet a lot of very connected lawyers. We'd need something concrete before taking on one of the most powerful families in Greece, but what the hell, let's at least take a run at the head of the family. I'll have Maggie set up an appointment for this afternoon with the grandfather, the one who runs the newspaper.'

'Speaking of the papers, have they picked up on the murder?'

'Don't know, I'm sure Maggie will tell us if it's out there.' Andreas tried calling her but it wouldn't go through. 'Damn it, the phone reception here is as bad as on Lykavittos.'

'Nice language, Chief.'

Andreas smiled. 'Never mind, we're almost at the Angel Club, we'll try again when we're finished here.' He pointed to a glitzy black-glass and steel, one-story warehouse-size building on the right. 'Pull over there, and be sure to block the front door. Let's start pissing them off.'

Pissing off the crew at the Angel Club wasn't something most sane people did. At least not those who wanted to keep breathing. Those who ran it, not the owners on the license, came from one of the most ruthless and powerful clans in Greece. Notoriously short-tempered and proud, it took very little to set them off. But they worked hard at reining in their natural propensities for violence in order to profit off the more civilized city-folk they drew into their club. And profit they did, not just from its high cover charges and questionably formulated booze, but from drugs grown and processed back home in their hillside villages.

Middlemen sold their brands at a premium in Amsterdam and other drug-friendly European cities, but in Greece the consumer bought directly at the Angel Club or other hot-spot clubs in their network. Their business was so long-standing and well-organized that police rarely challenged them, and almost never back in their villages, where their power, influence, manpower, and armaments often outnumbered all but the army.

These were the guys Andreas wanted to piss off.

Maggie saw from the incoming calls listed on her computer that the chief was trying to reach her. She called back but there was no answer. She had news for him on the Kostopoulos case. He wouldn't be happy. Preliminary autopsy results were back. The boy was dead by three a.m. from strangulation; the marks about his neck showed no signs of a struggle and were consistent with those on a victim trying to achieve an asphyxiation-high during intercourse; his penis was badly bruised and scraped from yet to be determined causes; and he was sodomized multiple times, by multiple partners, again with no signs of a struggle.

The media will love this. It was all the evidence they

need for endless, 'Rough Sex Night Gone Bad' headlines, and he-got-what-he-deserved slants to every story. Yes, the chief definitely wouldn't be happy.

'Who the fuck do you think you are?'

Andreas looked at Kouros, then back at the pro wrestler-size giant standing in the vestibule of the Angel Club. He was dressed all in black, with a gold 'A' embroidered on the lapel of his jacket. Andreas pointed his left index finger at his own chest and said meekly, 'Us?'

The gaint gestured to a slightly smaller version of himself standing just inside the club to step into the vestibule. 'These two assholes are looking for trouble.' He glared at Andreas.

Andreas smiled and looked at Kouros. 'I guess we should introduce ourselves,' and then fixed his eyes on the giant, all the while keeping his index finger aimed at his chest. 'We're police. Yianni, please show this gentleman your credentials.'

The giant took a step toward Andreas. 'If you're cops, get the hell around the back with the rest of the help. Only paying customers come in the front.'

Andreas didn't move or say a word; just continued to smile and point at himself.

The giant was two steps from Andreas. 'Asshole, if you don't get the fuck out of here, you're gonna get hurt real bad.' The second guy stepped into the vestibule and stood facing Kouros, arms crossed and glaring. Kouros didn't budge.

The giant took another step forward and was halfway into his next when Andreas drove the heel of his left hand full-thrust up, into, and through the giant's jaw. A perfect, never-saw-it-coming knockout.

Before the giant hit the floor Andreas had turned to face the second man, now reaching for something in his jacket pocket. 'Uhh, uh,' said Andreas, waving a finger at him. 'Play nice.'

The guy paused, as if not sure what to do. But Kouros did. He delivered a Champions League-quality soccer shot directly to the man's balls. Two down.

'Nice work,' said Andreas. 'Now, smile to the camera,' pointing to the security camera above the door to the club, 'show your badge,' pulling his own out from beneath his shirt so that it hung free on the cord about his neck, 'and let's make sure they get some good shots of these,' pulling a nine millimeter semiautomatic from the belt of the giant and taking from Kouros the similar one he'd removed from the jacket of the other guy.

Andreas waved the guns in front of the camera and yelled, *'We were in mortal fear for our lives. Now get your ass down here, Giorgio!'*

Everyone knew Giorgio, at least everyone in law enforcement. He ran the place for the clan back in his village. Although Greek, he preferred the Italian version of his name. Probably would have liked to hear 'Don' in front of it too.

Two minutes later a slight, trim, swarthy man dressed all in white appeared in the doorway. His head completely shaved, his three-day-old beard jet black. No way of telling if he was in his thirties or forties. Two more giants were with him. 'Andreas, my friend, come in. Please.'

Andreas nodded and stepped inside. They'd tangled before. Andreas still was holding both pistols. He handed one to

44

Kouros as he passed him and Kouros fell into step right behind him.

All the lights were on at this hour, so that the club's faceless crew of Eastern-European workers could ready the place for the crowds of Greeks to come. In bright light there was no mystery here. The burgundy carpets and matching, bordello-style banquettes were a mash of cigarette burns, spike-heel stiletto tears, and stains from spilled drinks and God knew what else. Long, black Formica-top and metal-leg tables filled the center of the room. They were nearly as badly beaten-up as the mostly matching chairs.

Every bit of wall space was black, except for a huge video screen that dominated the wall behind the block-long bar at the far end. The club ran nonstop ads on that screen for whatever brand of cigarettes or booze was willing to pay, filled with sounds of the hottest new music and images of nearly naked, please-fuck-me-looking young girls.

'Here's fine,' said Andreas. They were about ten feet from the door. No reason to go any further, especially with three more all-in-black gorillas standing about twenty feet further inside.

Giorgio smiled. 'Nice touch, setting up those two like you did.'

'You never did much go for the brains, Georgy.' Andreas knew he hated being called Georgy.

Giorgio stopped smiling. 'Too bad they threatened you on camera.'

'Yeah, modern security cameras are a great boon to law enforcement.'

'So, what the fuck do you want?' The fangs were showing.

'Want to know about a certain lady who was in your place last night.'

Giorgio snickered. 'That narrows things down.'

'She was in probably between midnight and one, sat in your private area and "was the greatest piece of ass ever to walk into your place."'

'As they say, "Beauty's in the eyes of the beholder."' He wasn't cooperating.

'This one was all in red.'

He shrugged. 'Still, don't remember.'

'Two of your gorillas were watching out for her.'

'Still don't know her.'

'Would a picture of her help?'

'No, I doubt it.' He was making clear there'd be no cooperation.

'Well, let's see. Just to be sure. Who knows what you might remember when you have to.'

'I won't.'

'Good, then you won't mind showing me your tapes from last night, say, from between eleven and two?'

'Fuck you.'

Andreas smiled, and kept his eyes locked on Giorgio. 'Yianni, call headquarters and tell them we need someone from the prosecutor's office to get an order shutting down this shit-hole.'

Giorgio smirked this time. 'Try.'

'Tell him two employees of the Angel Club, armed with unlicensed semiautomatic weapons, attacked the chief of the Special Crimes Division and his partner on club premises after the officers identified themselves as police. Be sure to tell him that the entire unprovoked attack was

46

recorded on security cameras and undoubtedly carried out on the orders of club management to interfere with this division's investigation into widespread drug trafficking on the premises.'

Giorgio wasn't quite smiling, but still had a grin.

'And tell whichever son-of-a-bitch prosecutor handles this that if I don't have an order signed and down here in two hours, his sorry ass is my next investigation.' Andreas smiled. 'Just in case you might be thinking you have a buddy or two out there to help you.'

Giorgio clenched and unclenched his fists. The smile was gone.

Shutting down the club for even a couple of nights would lose him a lot of money. Andreas was betting money was more important to Giorgio and the people he answered to than his macho hatred of Andreas.

'Okay, asshole. This way.'

There were eight cameras in all, some in the most un-expected of places. More than a few customers must have found themselves starring in films they never intended to make. Andreas wondered how many of Athens' rich and powerful were in Giorgio's pocket because of their, or more likely their children's, performances.

A small security room, more accurately a closet, stood next to the bar. It was furnished with a table filled with video equipment and two chairs facing a wall of monitors. Andreas stood over Giorgio, watching him copy the tapes. There would be no accidental erasures. Kouros stood outside the room, his back to the door and his eyes on the five giants. It took about a half-hour to make the copies, and not one man said a single unnecessary word the entire time, as if doing so might send the delicate equilibrium they'd achieved into irreversible chaos.

Andreas was anxious to see the tapes, but knew better than to do it here. He'd wait until they were back in friendlier surroundings. For now, he just verified the time-lines to make sure they were getting what he wanted. He didn't want to come back a second time. Giorgio only could be pushed so far, as he made clear in his through-the-teeth-smiling goodbye to Andreas:

'Come back soon. We'll be expecting you.'

Andreas sat behind his desk staring out the window. There was nothing to see, but, then again, he wasn't looking. He wondered how long before Kouros and the lab guys came up with something on the tapes. They'd been at it for over an hour. The preliminary autopsy report confirmed what Andreas suspected. Someone went to a lot of trouble and torture to make it seem like the kid got what he was looking for. And not just to the press; to the police, too. This was made to look like the kind of case cops don't care if they ever close: one that simply fades away as an ignored, unattended file. And that bothered Andreas big time.

How did anyone, even a Linardos, think they could murder the son of one of Greece's richest and most visible men without the police getting a shit load of pressure to solve it? Then again, he hadn't received a single pressuring call from anyone, including the boy's parents. Perhaps they're still in shock and hadn't gotten around to the angry, let's-get-the-bastards stage. He shook his head.

On the other hand, it would take a fool of a cop, or one blithely unconcerned with his future, to press ahead with

48

a case this explosive when no one was pushing him to do a thing. He thought of the boy's father and what must be going through that man's mind. Then he thought of his own father and the question Andreas asked himself over and over since he was eight: how different might my life have been if dad had lived, if he'd stood up to that now-dead bastard who set him up to look corrupt?

Andreas buzzed Maggie on the intercom. 'Have you set up that appointment with Sarantis Linardos?'

'Still waiting to hear back from his secretary. It won't be for today, though. He's in London, and she's not sure when he'd be back in Athens. Said she'd call me as soon as she knows when he's available.'

'Yeah, like she doesn't already know. Keep on her.'

He hung up just as Kouros burst into his office. 'Got her, Chief, and the two guys, too. Perfect shots of all of them.' He put a half-dozen photos on Andreas' desk.

'Any more?'

'It's all we've been able to find so far. Uhh, there is a problem, though.'

'What is it?'

'The camera covering the rear parking lot – its lens was painted over. From the recording timeline, it happened just before Sotiris left the club with the girl. We've got nothing after that on that camera.'

'Not surprised. This was a professional job. It also explains why one of Sotiris' friends recalled one of the bouncers disappearing before Sotiris left the club with the girl. He must have had some painting to do.'

'And it gives Giorgio a convenient alibi for why there's no tape of the assault.'

Andreas picked up one of the photos showing the girl in full frontal form. 'Wow, she *is* hot.'

'Tell me about it, I threatened to break the technician's head if he made an extra copy for himself.'

'I gotta admit, if she hit on me as hard as she did on that kid, I'd probably be the one in the dumpster.'

Kouros grinned. 'Might still be worth the risk.'

Andreas looked at the rest of the pictures, paying particular attention to the two men. 'You recognize them?'

Kouros gestured no with his head. 'I didn't see them at the club today.'

'Me either.' Andreas drummed his fingers on the desk. 'It's a bit sloppy wouldn't you say?'

'What do you mean?'

'All this care at setting the kid up to look like he bought it in a rough sex gone bad deal, but not caring how simple it is for us to get a picture of the girl and the two guys who probably killed him?'

'Maybe they never thought we'd get the pictures from the club, or they didn't know about the cameras?'

Andreas shook his head no. 'And paint over the one in the parking lot? Maybe they just didn't care if we got them? After all, what we have doesn't show them doing anything to anyone. Besides, who knows where the hell they are by now.'

'Do you think the girl's dead?'

'Don't know. Guess we'll have to find out.'

'How?'

'Ask Giorgio.' Andreas smiled. 'I mean, you ask Giorgio.'

Kouros shrugged. 'Okay.'

Just then Maggie buzzed him. 'What is it?'

50

'Uh, sorry, Chief, just wanted to know if you're taking calls.'

'Not unless it's something urgent. I've got to catch up on everything else going on in this office.'

'Thanks. Bye, Chief.'

Andreas stood up and walked around the desk to where Kouros was standing. He patted him on the shoulder. 'Be careful, Yianni. Take along a blue-and-white for backup.' He paused. 'Make that two blue-and-whites.'

'Will do, Chief,' and he left.

Andreas held his breath for a moment, and slowly let it out. There was another potential explanation for why whoever was behind this didn't care who found out about the girl and the two muscle guys: they had friends in high places prepared to protect them. That was not an unheard of scenario in Greece, or elsewhere for that matter. Just the thought of that possibility pissed Andreas off. Really pissed him off.

'Uh, Chief?' It was Maggie's voice over the intercom. It was the first time she'd disturbed him since just before Yianni left his office.

'Yes?'

'It's Yianni.'

'Thanks, put him through.'

She clicked off and the call came through.

'Chief?'

'Yes, what's up?'

'We have an ID on the girl.'

The first good news in a long time, thought Andreas. 'Great, who is she?'

'Name's Anna Panitz, lives over by the university near Filis Street.'

'That's hookerville.'

'Yeah, Giorgio says she's a semi-pro; works a couple of legit jobs and turns tricks when pressed for money.'

Andreas had never understood the concept of a semi-pro prostitute but, what the hell, they had an ID. 'And the two guys with her, the ones wearing Angel Club tee shirts?'

'He didn't know them. Said they didn't work for him and anyone could get a tee shirt. They sold them at the bar for thirty euros.'

That didn't surprise Andreas. He expected as much, or at least that Giorgio would say it. 'Why do you think that prick is suddenly so cooperative?'

There was a very long silence on Kouros' side of the phone.

'Yianni!'

The reply was sharp and quick. 'I guess because of television.'

'What are you talking about?' Andreas asked, though his gut already gave him the answer.

'The story's everywhere. It broke before we got to the club.'

It was pounding headache time.

'Giorgio said he had nothing to do with what happened to the kid and would tell us anything we wanted to know. His exact words were, "I'm not fucking stupid enough to get caught up in the middle of this shit storm. It could ruin the reputation of my place. You ask, you get."'

Great, thought Andreas. 'Did you show the photos to the club's employees?'

'Yeah, to the ones working tonight. Just about everyone recognized the girl, she'd been in before. But no one knew the guys or ever saw them before. Thought they were private security wearing club tee shirts so not to look conspicuous. Happens all the time they said.'

'Anybody else work last night?'

'Yeah, I got their names and addresses. Thought I'd try to run them down now.'

'Okay, let me know.' Andreas hung up.

He waited a minute before buzzing Maggie to come in. She was by his desk in less than five seconds. 'Yes, Chief.'

His voice was calm. 'Maggie, why didn't you tell me the Kostopoulos murder was all over TV?' There was no reason to ask whether she knew. There was no doubt that she did. The department's secretarial gossip network must have gotten word to her within thirty seconds of it hitting the air.

She gave a motherly smile. 'I did, even though you told me not to disturb you with anything but the urgent.'

'You didn't think this was urgent?' His voice was still calm.

She shrugged. 'Not really. There was nothing for you to do but get aggravated. Everything's being handled by media affairs, and they didn't ask to speak to you.'

He looked down at his desk. 'And exactly how did you inform me?'

She leaned over his desk and hit the space bar on his computer keyboard bringing the screen back to life. Centered, within a message box, were the words, 'If you're interested, the Kostopoulos story is all over television.'

He hadn't touched his computer in a while, ignoring

every message ping. Andreas nodded and said, 'Thank you.'
He kept nodding for about ten seconds after she left. '*Damn it!*' he yelled, slamming his hand on the top of his desk and scattering the photos everywhere.

He needed to do something, anything, to get this case moving. He thought of paying a surprise visit on the Linardos household but then thought better of it. He picked up one of the photos and studied it for about a minute. Then put it down, stood up, and walked out of his office. Finding Anna Panitz might work. Assuming she still was alive.

5

The area around Filis Street was not a place you came to by accident. It was north of Omonia, and cops generally avoided it. Sure, there were worse neighborhoods, but this was Athens' most notorious one for hookers and the parasites that fed off them. Here was where you came to find things the Bible forbade. That's probably what gave the neighborhood its 24/7 popularity, and cops the attitude of *hey,* you knew what you were getting into when you came here, so don't call us for help.

Andreas hoped he wouldn't need to make that kind of call. He'd come with no backup, and only Kouros knew where he was. He convinced himself that was the best way of protecting her, assuming he found her. If the bad guys knew cops were looking for her, she probably wouldn't live long. Assuming she wasn't dead already.

He borrowed a cheap, beat-up motorbike from the department's impound garage and wore the old jeans, work boots, and ubiquitous long-sleeve shirt of a laborer out for a good time. He wanted to look like any number of other horny guys trying to get laid.

Her last known address was in a dirty-yellow four-story concrete-slab architectural nightmare. It looked like one of those tenements you expect to see sitting on the outskirts of some third-world slum. Regrettably, they'd taken weed-like root in Athens and indelibly scarred parts of a city once compared in beauty to Paris.

He parked the motorbike across the street and a few doors down from her building. The street was packed with parked cars and motorcycles battered nearly as badly as his own. No one paid him much attention. Strangers frequented these streets. A couple of girls on a third-floor balcony of the building next to where he parked called out to him in broken Greek. He ignored them and walked as if he knew where he was going.

He stepped into the vestibule of the building, under the white light, and started climbing the concrete-slab steps. The address for the woman put the apartment on the top floor. He didn't bother looking for a buzzer. He wanted to surprise her.

Andreas noticed only two apartments per floor. That meant several rooms for each apartment. He wondered if someone else lived with her. That could be a problem. Just one of many things that could go wrong.

Andreas was at her door. Time to decide. He felt his crotch. That's where he hid his gun in an American-designed holster that fit around his hips under his jeans and held the gun flat against his family jewels.

He listened for a sound but heard nothing. He knocked lightly. 'Anna.' He whispered the word.

No answer. He knocked slightly harder and whispered again, 'Anna.'

He heard something move inside. He listened. The sound came toward the door.

'Anna.' He whispered without knocking.

He heard a sleepy, 'Who is it?'

'Andreas.'

'Andreas who?'

'From the other night.'

'I don't know you.' The voice sounded more slurred than sleepy.

'Sure you do. We met at the Angel Club.' He braced for a reaction. None came. 'Anna, open up. You know who I am.'

She practically yelled, 'Leave, or I'll call the police!'

She must be panicked, he thought. That was about the worst possible thing she could have said if the guy at the door was involved in the murder. 'Bingo, my love, you guessed who it is.' He no longer whispered. 'Look through your peephole at my ID.'

He heard her moving away from the door. '*Get back here.*' It was his official, cop voice. 'If you don't cooperate, in five minutes I'll have cops all over this place, and you know what that means.' Andreas held his breath and stepped to the side of the door just in case something other than an eyeball aimed through the peephole. He heard her step forward and fidget with the cover on the inside of the door. There was no lens, just an opening the size of an egg.

'Where are you, I can't see you?' she said.

He leaned in from the side and saw an almond-shape, light-green eye, then stepped in front of the door and held the badge around his neck up for her to see. 'Andreas Kaldis, Special Crimes Division, Athens Police.' No reason to scare her with his title. 'You know why I'm here, open up.'

He heard a chain fumble along a channel, and the click of a dead bolt. The door opened slightly. He thought of going for his pistol, just in case, but didn't.

A dim light flickered inside, and only the eyes and hair of a woman's head showed around the edge of the door. She looked different from her picture, almost vulnerable. Her hair was auburn. He could tell she'd been crying.

'Come in.' She said the words without looking at him.

Andreas immediately looked behind the door, did a quick scan of the room, and opened the only closet in it. There was no one else there, at least in that room. A well-worn gray couch sat against the wall across from the door, just beyond a glass-topped coffee table. Two taverna-style wood and rattan chairs stood on the other side of the table and everything sat on a faded, gray-and-red carpet. Each wall had a picture of a different saint. There were two standing lamps in the room but the only light came from a television flickering at the near end of the couch. The sound was off.

'How many rooms in here?'

'Huh?'

She was out of it. 'How many rooms in this apartment?'

'Uh, this one . . . a bedroom . . . bathroom . . . the kitchen.' She couldn't seem to concentrate.

'Anyone else in here with you?'

'Just Pedro.'

Andreas reached inside the front of his pants and gripped the butt of his gun. 'Pedro, get out here. *Now!*'

'Shhh.' She put a finger to her lips. 'You'll wake him up.'

'Get him out here.' He was in no mood to negotiate.

'He's a baby.' She gestured for him to follow her to the bedroom.

Cautiously, Andreas studied the bedroom from the doorway. Sure enough, there was a baby, probably a six-month old, asleep in the crib. He pointed to the crib. 'Stand next to him and don't move.' He checked the bedroom's two closets and under the bed. Then the other rooms and anywhere else someone could hide.

He learned three things from his search. One, no one else was living in the apartment; two, the apartment was smaller than he expected because it had an outdoor deck off the living room; and three, the place was impeccably clean and tidy. Whatever else she was, Anna Panitz took care of her place.

And, now that he was relaxed, at least a bit, he could tell she took damn good care of herself, too. Even in dim light, she was an extraordinarily beautiful woman. Probably in her early twenties, about five-foot-eight, with a thin but full-breasted, absolutely stunning figure; one he kept seeing more of each time she moved, more like flowed, around the living room. She wore a man's light-blue cotton shirt, buttoned only to her navel. He could see her breasts and that her nipples were pink, for she wore no bra. Then she turned and bent to pick up a rattle and he saw everything else, for she wore no panties. His holster suddenly was quite uncomfortable, almost painful. But he didn't tell her to button up.

He gestured for her to sit on the couch. He sat directly across from her on one of the chairs. He had to regain his focus. She started rocking back and forth, as if trying to hold back tears, opening and closing her legs as she rocked. Andreas moved his chair so that he saw her only from the side. He'd seen a lot of naked women in his life, certainly during his time on Mykonos. Some were as stunning as this one, but there are certain women who, for reasons a man can never figure out, stop your heart with just a look. It wasn't as if she were trying to seduce him. She was dressed this way when he pressured his way into her apartment, and she was crying before he got there.

He was about to ask what was bothering her when she saved him the trouble.

'That poor boy, that poor boy.' She was crying. A photograph of Sotiris Kostopoulos was on the television screen. 'I knew I shouldn't have, I knew it.'

He let her go on. Silence often made people talk more than they should. Besides, the confession was dampening his desire and making his pants a lot more comfortable. She spoke for about thirty minutes, sobbing and, at times, pacing. He stayed focused as best he could during the pacing moments.

Two guys had knocked on her door one day, just as he had. She had no idea who they were, but they were the same two who ended up with her in the club. They said she was recommended by a friend and asked if she wanted to make five hundred euros to get someone out of a club and into a parking lot. She needed the money. It was tough working three jobs without papers, and the baby didn't make it any easier. They never said what they wanted with the mark and she never asked. They weren't the type to answer questions or take kindly to anyone who asked. She figured he probably owed them money and at most they'd rough him up.

She had no idea who the mark was until the two pointed him out in the club. When she saw the target was a boy she said, 'No way.' They told her either she went through with it, or her baby would take his place.

She started to cry, 'What could I do, I had no choice.'

Andreas said nothing.

Once she got the boy out in the parking lot, Sotiris was so busy feeling her up against a car that he never saw them coming. Whatever was on the rag they held against his face knocked him right out. Real professionals. She wanted nothing more to do with them, ever. They didn't have to tell her what would happen if she ever remembered a thing – both to her and her baby. That was the last she saw or heard from them and had no idea how to find them. They always called her and always spoke in Greek, although they weren't Greek. Probably from the Balkans. She guessed someone from one of her day jobs gave them her address. None of her johns knew where she lived.

'I'm strictly an I'll-come-visit-you sort of girl.' She smiled and shrugged.

Andreas nodded. He hadn't said much. Too many emotions were distracting his thoughts. She's a hooker. Involved in a murder. Okay, probably not any more than she said. Men got seriously involved with hookers all the time, but not ones from Filis. They fell for the high-priced

61

call girls, ones who turned tricks for the rich and married. Some even hooked their johns into marriage.

He knew he was trying to justify to his mind what was going on in his pants.

Anna stood up and walked to where he was sitting. She smelled of flowers. 'Would you like something to drink?'

'No, thank you.'

She strode into the kitchen and came back with two glasses and a half-empty bottle of white wine. She waved the glasses. 'Just in case. Let's sit outside.'

He didn't object.

The deck ran the length of the apartment and was about half as wide as the living room. Green plastic sheeting stood at the edge of the roof. It wasn't pretty, but practical. It gave privacy and a sense of being surrounded by nothing but sky, away from the lives being lived below. It was a place of sanctuary in the midst of chaos.

She sat on a cushion and told him to sit on the one next to her. Again, he didn't object. She took a sip from her glass, poured wine into a second glass and handed it to him. Andreas took a sip and thought to be careful how much he drank, then took another. She began telling him the story of her life: surviving war in the Balkans, looking for work, tying up with the wrong guy, fleeing him and her country, et cetera, et cetera, et cetera. It was not a new story. But he listened, his eyes never off of her.

It was an unusually warm night and the bottom of Anna's shirt was well above her hips for most of the first bottle of wine, and all of the second. She left to find a third. When she walked back onto the deck she was completely naked. Andreas tried to think of something, anything, to maintain control. No tattoos anywhere, rare these days, was what came to mind, and that hardly was the sort of thought to help.

Anna plopped down next to him, smiled, and poured both of them more wine. 'I decided what's the use, we both know where this is headed.' She picked up her glass to take a sip with one hand, and with the other patted the inside of his thigh dangerously close to what Andreas had been struggling to keep under control.

'Excuse me, I need to hit the bathroom.'

She looked at him as if she knew that wasn't his reason.

Inside, he stood facing the mirror. Andreas knew he should leave, but . . . He walked back to the doorway and stood staring at her. She seemed to be dozing on the pillows. He turned and left, saying nothing.

He'd respect her wishes on how best to say goodbye.

6

The street was deserted, except for a few mangy-looking characters lurking around a doorway across the street from her building. Must be looking to pick off a quick score, some straggler heading home still in the glow of blissful, oblivious passion. *Take a shot at me assholes*, Andreas thought. I need to vent. He stared at them, daring them to try, but they looked away.

He started to cross to where he left the motorbike, glancing left and right as he did. He took another step then paused again and looked back to his left, away from where he parked. Someone was there who shouldn't be. He stepped back onto the curb and walked over to a beat-up, white Fiat. He studied the dozing driver, then pounded twice on the roof. 'Open up.'

The driver jerked awake and did as he was told.

'Chief.'

Andreas got in. 'Get me out of here.' Screw the bike, he thought, let someone steal it all over again.

Neither looked at the other.

'Drop me at home.' Andreas needed a shower and a few hours' sleep. He stared out the windshield. There was a paper on the dash. It was a police vehicle-impound form. Kouros had shopped for his ride there, too. 'Anything you want to say?' Andreas said it flatly, still looking straight ahead.

'No, sir.'

Andreas looked at him. 'For Christ's sake, Yianni, say something.'

'She was the greatest piece of ass I ever saw, and you're not the first cop to stumble.'

Andreas didn't respond, just turned his head and looked out the side window. What was there to say? That he didn't have sex, just listened to a hooker tell her life story? To a cop that would sound worse, at least dumber, than whatever Kouros was thinking. No one would believe him anyway. He couldn't believe it himself.

'Besides, you're my boss, what the hell do you want me to say? That "every crooked politician, influence peddler and bad guy in Greece would kill for proof of what you just did. You'd be their forever get-of-jail-free card. Or ruined."'

Andreas nodded but kept looking out the window. 'In other words, if I weren't your boss, you'd say I must be out of my mind.'

'No, sir, "out of your fucking mind," sir.'

'Well, thank you for not saying that and—' turning to look at him, 'for watching my back.'

Kouros nodded. 'I spoke to the other Angel Club employees, but they gave me nothing.' A few seconds later he added, 'So, Chief, did you get anything interesting tonight?'

Andreas gave him a sharp look, then a grin. 'Cute, very cute. Yes, as a matter of fact I did. Our likely killers aren't Greek, but probably from one of our Balkan neighbors. I think someone from one of the places she works set her up. She waitresses at coffee shops over by the Polytechnic University.' He pointed out the window.

'Those places where anarchists and communists merrily plot away together at creating their grand new world?'

Andreas nodded. 'Yes, those. Never quite understood how anarchists and communists find common ground. One's dead-set against government, other's all for it.'

'That's easy, Chief, they share the same public tit.'

'Now, now, Yianni, let's not let our personal feelings enter into this.' Andreas was smiling.

'Yeah, you're right, Chief, I should be honored at the opportunity to bust my ass at this job every day so that some asshole who passes a national exam can stay in university forever and the state pays for it, even if the bastard never passes a course or goes to a single class.' He was worked up, but then again, so were a lot of people on both sides of that issue.

'Yianni, whoa. Not all of them are like that.'

'Yeah, but I'm still paying for the ones who are . . . and the ones whose deep fucking thoughts get them thinking up new reasons to riot and throw rocks and Molotov cocktails at us.' He was squeezing the steering wheel. 'Then they run back to their universities to hide, so we can't grab their asses.'

That part bothered Andreas too. A law, enacted as the result of Greece's experience under the dictatorship of 1967 to 1974, provided that police could not enter university grounds, no matter what the reason. Needless to say, a lot of folks, students and others, some literally wearing masks, took advantage of that sanctuary for many varied and at times violent criminal purposes. They'd do their business in cafés and bars bordering universities, then scoot like rabbits back to campus when police showed up. And they got away with it, just like the veteran of the 1973 demonstrations legend had, still living in the basement of the university where it all started, producing Molotov cocktails for new generations of demonstrators.

'Relax, we have to be nice to those guys. They're our only chance of getting anywhere with this.'

Kouros squeezed the steering wheel twice more, then let out a breath. 'So, what about Anna?'

'What do you mean, "What about Anna?"'

'Chief, she's involved in the murder. Shouldn't we bring her in?'

'And achieve what? Keep her locked up so she can't get away? Fine, if we want a quick collar for the newspapers, sure. But what's the charge going to be? I don't see any kind of murder conviction in this for her, do you?'

Kouros gestured no. 'Not on what we have now.'

'Right, we need more. And if we arrest her, she's not going to give us any more than she already has, and everyone tied into this will disappear off the face of the earth. If they haven't already. As long as she's walking around there's a chance someone might show up.' He stared straight ahead. 'But have someone keep an eye on her.

She's our best link so far to the two who probably killed the boy.'

'Who should we use?'

'Check with the office to see who's available.'

'I'm available nights.' Kouros grinned.

Andreas did not return the smile. He wanted the subject to go away.

Kouros stopped in front of Andreas' apartment building.

As Andreas was getting out he said, 'Pick me up tomorrow morning at eight. Don't eat breakfast. We have a lot of coffee shops to visit.'

Kouros nodded. 'Hopefully with ugly waitresses.'

Andreas slammed the door.

Maggie wanted to hide from the phone. It hadn't stopped ringing all morning. Someone tipped off the press that Chief Andreas Kaldis had assumed personal charge of the investigation, and now every journalist in Greece wanted to speak to him, not some anonymous talking head out of media affairs. It had been years since so many suitors were after her favors, and their general approach for getting her to give up her boss was almost the same as that once aimed at her virtue: 'I promise to be gentle.' They had no more success now than then.

She had spoken to Andreas twice this morning, and his instructions were firm: 'All inquiries must be directed to media affairs, no exceptions.' Still, she wondered if she should call him a third time, because now Greece's most watched, vicious, scandal-mongering, and feared television journalist, Marios Tzoli, wanted to speak with him. What concerned Maggie was that he personally placed the call.

Big television egos didn't call for routine interviews. She'd better warn Andreas that Marios must sense blood in the water or sex anywhere.

So far that morning they'd had two breakfasts, but Andreas couldn't tell you what he'd eaten if you asked him while he was chewing it. He and Kouros didn't say much more than 'pass the sugar.' Sort of like an old married couple dining alone with nothing left to say on any subject. The only interruptions were two calls from Maggie.

It was a little before eleven, the heart of morning classes at the university. That meant local coffee shops filled with students who knew better than to corrupt their original thinking with some lecturer's old ideas and historical biases. Whatever they might need to supplement their innate understanding of the world could be found elsewhere, like online. After all, it was life that mattered, not classes. Besides, if teachers really knew what they were talking about, they'd be doing something else.

Andreas and Kouros approached the front door of the third of Anna's places of employment. They'd also stopped at two where she didn't work, to keep anyone from wondering why only her jobs attracted cops. There was no time for an undercover operation, and so they took the opposite approach: two bull-in-a-china-shop cops looking for a quick score off a couple of drug dealers, a regrettably routine pastime for some of their not-so-honest brethren on the force. So far, their performances netted them only blank stares when they flashed the photo of two guys partially blocking the logo of a notorious drug-trafficking nightclub.

It was a nondescript place in a nondescript building filled with young men trying in the most nondescript way to look anything but. A coffee house of the post-World War II beatnik era as envisioned by twenty-first-century youth: pale orange-yellow walls with chair railings – unusual for Athens – wooden floors, unmatched hardback chairs for twenty-four, and scraped and burned two-top wooden tables covered with coffee, cigarettes, and cell phones. After dusk, there was barely enough lighting to see.

Kouros held the door open for Andreas. Every eye in the place fixed on them. They were about as obvious and welcome as tigers at a tea party.

A carefully framed poster of Che hung behind the service counter alongside a six-foot-long by three-foot-tall unframed mirror. The mirror gave the place a look of greater size than it had, the poster an impression of greater meaning. What looked to be the artistic contributions of its customers occupied the other walls, with no discernable curator or standard for what could be posted. The only apparent rule was not to cover over a colleague's contribution, no matter how artistically constructive such an act might be.

It was exactly the sort of place you'd expect to find bordering Exarchia Square, the symbol of Greece's student revolution and epicenter for its current revolutionaries. The media unwittingly had helped make it that way. Greek children grew up watching Greek television showing Greek students wearing Greek masks protesting against Greek authority by throwing Greek rocks (and Molotov cocktails) at Greek police. And virtually always, in one way or another, Exarchia was part of the story. The place had become a romanticized land of Oz for disillusioned and rebellious young. Not many from the old days still were around, though some remained geograph-ically close by, just on the other side of the hill in Kolonaki, but in every other respect far removed from the revolution.

Andreas stood in the doorway. At first, he looked to be staring at the walls, but he quickly fixed his gaze on the faces gathered around the table closest to the door. Then his eyes moved on to those at the next table. He didn't say a word, just studied one face after another, lightly drumming the fingers of his right hand on a manila enve-lope held in his left as he did.

'What do you want?' said the man behind the counter.

Andreas turned to face the man and smiled. 'Good morning, sir. And how are you this fine day?'

The man did not return the smile. 'Like I said, what do you want?'

'Is this your place?'

'Yeah. Who's asking?'

Andreas walked to the counter, leaned over, and motioned with his right index finger for the man to come closer. The man hesitated and Andreas wiggled his finger again. The man took a step forward and leaned in.

Andreas whispered, 'Police. I need your help with some-thing.'

The owner's eyes darted to his left, then just as quickly back. Andreas didn't turn to find where he'd looked, he could see in the mirror behind the counter that it was to a man sitting alone at a table in the rear. He wasn't one in the photo. He looked half their size, probably five-six, 140 pounds at most. His dark hair was long in the student fashion of the day, eyes dark, skin relatively light, with a razor-thin wisp of a beard running from the middle of his lower lip to the base of his chin. He was in jeans and a plain white tee shirt, nondescript except for one thing: his eyes were studying Andreas in the mirror.

'Yeah, what?' The owner didn't whisper.

Andreas kept whispering. 'I need to know if you've ever seen these two men.' Andreas pulled a photograph out of the envelope and placed it on the counter between them.

Andreas looked back at the owner. 'So, do you recognize either of them?'

'No, never saw them before.'

Andreas smiled. 'Yeah, sure.' He patted the bar, and turned around. 'Hi folks, hate to interrupt your morning coffee, but I have a question to ask you. Have any of you ever seen either of these men?' With that he walked from table to table, pressing the photo in front of every face. Most immediately shook their heads no. A few looked more intently at the photos before saying 'no.'

Andreas spoke to the man at the rear table last.

'So, my friend, have you ever seen either of these men?' Andreas handed him the photograph.

He stared at it for a moment as if studying it, then handed it back. 'No, sir, not that I recall.'

'Thank you,' said Andreas courteously smiling as he put the photo back into the envelope.

Andreas turned and said to the owner. 'I guess that's it.' He started toward the door, then paused. 'But, since we're here, we might as well earn our pay. Yianni, check the tables, and I want IDs on everyone.'

By checking the tables he was telling the owner that there better be appropriate receipts for everything in front of every customer. It was a must for any business hoping to avoid

72

stiff penalties from the tax authorities, or off-the-record gratuities to any who caught them.

Andreas heard a muttered 'bastards,' from behind the bar.

Kouros pulled a receipt out of a shot glass. Most places used them to hold receipts. 'It's from yesterday.'

Andreas looked at the owner and waved his finger at him. 'Tsk, tsk, you are in trouble my friend. Our government doesn't like people trying to cheat it. The proper authorities should hear about this.' Andreas made it sound like the shakedown was coming. 'Anybody else work here?'

'No.' The owner was fuming.

'Just you?'

'I'm a poor man, with a lousy business, I can't afford help.'

Andreas walked behind the counter and started opening drawers.

'What are you doing?' shouted the man. 'Who do you think you are?' This time he cursed Andreas aloud.

Andreas ignored him and kept opening drawers until he found what he wanted.

He dropped a pair of women's shoes and a waitress' apron on the counter. 'Let me guess, you wear these when you want to express your feminine side.' Then he dropped a box of tampons and a lipstick beside them. 'Dare I ask what do you do with these?'

The man was clenching and unclenching his fists.

'Now, why would a nice man like you lie about working alone? Could it be that she—' picking up the apron '—is illegal?' He patted the man on the shoulder. 'So, once again you're trying to steal from our government?'

A boy got up and headed toward the door. Kouros gestured for him to sit down.

'But I have a class.'

Kouros repeated the gesture and the boy sat down.

Andreas gave an I-have-your-ass-now look to the owner. 'Unless you want this place shut down and more problems than you can imagine, I want you to get everybody who works for you over here *now*. I want these two bastards' and slapped the envelope with the photograph across the man's chest; then he leaned over and whispered in the man's ear, 'so I can get back to making some real money and you can continue doing whatever the hell it is you do.'

The owner was nervous and blurted out, 'There's only one girl, she works part time.'

Someone cleared a throat. 'Officer.'

Andreas turned and smiled. 'Yes, sir?'

It was the man at the rear table. 'I may know those men after all.'

'Really?' Andreas' sounded sincerely surprised, or at least he hoped he did.

'Yes, all this excitement must have jarred my memory. I seem to remember seeing them before.'

Andreas walked over and sat down at the man's table. 'Sorry, sir, I didn't get your name.'

'Mavrakis. Demosthenes Mavrakis.'

Andreas nodded, as if truly thankful for the man's sudden recollection and utterly oblivious to his undoubted interest in stopping the owner from giving away information that could lead them to Anna. 'So, who are they?'

'I don't know their names, sir, I just saw them around the neighborhood.'

74

'Ever see them in here?'

'No, sir, they're not the coffee shop type, if you know what I mean.' He smiled.

Andreas smiled back. 'Yeah, sure. So, what do you mean by "around the neighborhood"?'

He suddenly looked uneasy, but in a way that made Andreas sense it was because that's how he was expected to look and not because he actually was. 'You know, the kind of places where students go to get *things*.'

'"Things?" What sorts of "things"?' He already knew the answer was drugs but sensed he better keep playing dumb.

Demosthenes rolled his eyes. 'Come on, officer, you know what I'm talking about.'

Andreas smiled as if he suddenly saw the light. 'Yeah, that fits with why we're looking for these guys. So, how come you know so much about the neighborhood?'

'I go to school here.'

'You look a little old for the university.'

He shrugged. 'It is what it is.'

Andreas smiled again. 'Yeah, sure is. So, where can we find these guys?'

'I don't know. I noticed them about a week ago and haven't seen them in a couple of days. They weren't the kind of guys I wanted to get to know.'

Andreas nodded. 'Ever speak to them?'

'No.'

'Know anyone who spoke to them?'

He gestured no.

'So where and when did you first see them?' Before he could answer, Andreas put up his hand to stop him and

75

said to Kouros, 'Yianni, once you get their ID information, let them go.' There was a rush for the door.

'So, where were we?'

'You wanted to know where and when I first saw them.'

Andreas nodded. 'Yeah, that's right. Okay, just tell me everything you remember about them.'

They spent a half-hour together. Andreas never once tried to trip him up or show interest in anything other than the men in the photograph. He pressed him to remember every physical detail about them. Not because he needed that information, he already had it from the club's videos, but he wanted to make sure Demosthenes wasn't just saying he saw them. He described the two perfectly, as if he realized it was a test.

By his questions, Andreas let enough slip out for Demosthenes to piece together that someone in the Angel Club fingered the two as drug dealers. That way, anyone who knew the truth would think that whoever the cops were squeezing for busts at the club got a real break when two strangers turned up masquerading as club employees and spared the snitch the risk of turning in any of the club's real dealers.

In exchange, Demosthenes gave Andreas absolutely nothing of value. The places where he claimed to see them were all very public: a subway station, open park, and fast-food restaurant; each was extremely busy and notorious for drug trafficking. Even if what he said were true, and Andreas didn't believe him, there was little chance of finding them that way. All he'd really given them was a grand, old-time wild-goose chase; but Andreas sensed there was more to this guy than he was letting on, and he didn't want to risk spooking him until he knew what it was.

76

Maybe they'd get lucky and find something after they lifted his prints off the photograph. Demosthenes and Andreas were the only ones who touched it, and Andreas was careful. All Andreas was certain of was that Demosthenes didn't want cops finding Anna, but was that to protect her or the two gorillas? After all, she was illegal. From the way the owner looked at Demosthenes when Andreas said he was a cop, he might be part of the local protection racket paid by places like this to keep from being hassled. But he didn't seem the physical sort. Then, again, he was the first to give them anything on the gorillas. Maybe he's the one who connected them to Anna? What the hell, he'd give Anna a call, just to see what she knew about Demosthenes.

Demosthenes watched the two cops leave. Then looked at the owner still standing behind the counter.

The owner spoke quickly. 'I'm sorry Demon, I didn't mean to involve you in this.'

Demon was what everyone called him. He motioned for the owner to come to his table, and the man hurried over as if summoned by a king from his throne. Perhaps he was, for no matter how busy the place might be, and though Demon rarely was there, no one sat at that table but Demon. Complete control over a single, small table in a twenty-foot by thirty-foot university coffee house might not seem like much to most, but it stood as an ever-present symbol to the Exarchia community of Demon's influence. But he wasn't a king; he was an anarchist. Or was he a communist? No one knew for sure, and Demon liked it that way.

'What did the cop say to you?'

'Nothing. They were crooked, looking for a payoff from drug dealers.'

'I see.' That's what he'd thought and why he sent them chasing after two guys who no longer existed. At least not in Greece.

'And what did he ask about Anna?' He doubted she was smart enough to link him to the two guys, but he couldn't risk the cops finding her. She might say something to get them making the connection.

'She never came up. Honest, Demon, he was only interested in a payoff.'

But could he be sure of that? Things often were not what they seemed. Himself for example. He was far older than he looked, far less educated than he put on, and if what he'd been told countless times were true, far brighter than practically anyone on the planet.

He stared at the owner. Demon had carefully kept to the shadows, quietly amassing power and secretly applying it in whatever measure he deemed necessary. Now this man, this *inept* man, had caused his name to fall into the hands of the police.

The owner bit at his lip and looked down at the floor, but he did not move from the spot where he stood. Demon did not show his anger. He still needed him. For over a decade Demon had been amassing an army of minds and wills from their most fertile source: children recently liberated from their parents, filled with ideals and burning to change a world their parents had so screwed up. His gift was not in knowing such ready converts existed. Politicians knew that for ages. It was in picking those who would do *anything* for a cause they

78

believed in, and remain committed to *him* long after their university days were over.

And this coffee shop was where he found many of them.

Demon smiled. 'It was not your fault, you did the right thing.'

Whatever you wanted or needed to hear Demon told you. He had a knack for that and never worried about the truth. It was far too cumbersome a convention for his goals. Whether or not that made him a clinical sociopath was of no concern to Demon. He did what had to be done.

7

'So, Maggie, what's so important for you to call me four times in the last forty-five minutes?' He sounded nonchalant but, knowing Maggie was not an alarmist, expected hearing that life on earth as he knew it was over.

'You're pretty popular, Chief. Everyone's calling for you, from the prime minister on down.'

Maybe it really was over. 'We're heading back to the office. Be there in fifteen minutes.'

'Better turn around and head the other way. You have an appointment in—' she paused, Andreas assumed to look at her watch, 'ten minutes at the Tholos.'

'At the what? And why did you schedule an appointment without clearing it with me?' His voice was sharper than he intended.

She didn't seem bothered. 'I didn't schedule it for you. The prime minister's office did. Tholos is a virtual reality theater inside a big dome, looks like a planetarium. The show starts with the burning of Athens by the Persians and focuses on life in the Agora during Athens' classical period. Makes you feel like you're living back in the fifth century BC. It's on Pireos Street.'

'What the fuck's going on – sorry, Maggie, I didn't mean that for you.'

She laughed. 'Don't worry. I was wondering the same thing.'

'Can't seem to get out of that neighborhood.' Andreas gestured for Kouros to turn the car around and head in the opposite direction.

'No, Chief, it's in the Tavros section, on the other side of town from Omonia, at 254 Pireos.'

'Who am I meeting?'

'That superbitch from the prime minister's office wouldn't tell me, just said to tell you to "be there," but if I had to guess, I think I know who it is.'

He'd learned to trust her instincts. 'So, tell me already.'

'Marios Tzoli.'

'Shit.'

'Thought you'd like that. He called me twice, insisting he must speak to you—'

'Personally called?'

'Yes, and I told him I couldn't reach you. Then I got a call from the office of the minister of public order telling me you must call Marios immediately. I told them the same thing, I couldn't reach you.'

That minister was his boss. 'Let me guess. Then came the call from the prime minister?'

'Five minutes later.'

'Boy, he really must be owed some favors.'

'Shall I tell you some of them?' said Maggie giggling.

'Not on the telephone, my love.' Andreas smiled.

'Let me know what happens.'

'Will do. And Maggie, have a blue-and-white meet me at that dome-thing. I have fingerprints I want the lab to run STAT.' He hung up. 'Yianni, who do you think actually runs my office?'

'I'd need permission from Maggie to answer that.'

Andreas smiled again, and shook his head. 'Well, what do you think has Greece's number-one scandal-chasing TV personality all hot and bothered?'

Kouros' look turned serious. 'You don't think he somehow found out about, uh—'

'Last night?' Andreas shook his head no. 'Don't think so. Only if it were a set-up from the start would he be so pumped up so quickly. Besides, as important as I seem to you,' he smacked Kouros' shoulder, 'I'm not close to the sort of person his viewers are interested in watching screw up their lives. Certainly not enough to get this kind of personal attention from *the Man* himself.'

'So, what do you think it is?'

Andreas shrugged. 'Whatever it is, he's sure anxious to tell us. Maybe it has to do with where he's picked to meet?'

'Yeah, it seems a bit dramatic, even for him.'

'I think when referring to Marios he prefers that you spell "him" with a capital H.'

Kouros grinned. 'Oh, yes, I forgot he's one of our modern gods.'

'All-knowing, all-powerful, gazing down upon us mere mortals from Mount TV, deciding who shall live, who shall die, and what bullshit gets the best ratings.'

'Wonder who he's after?'

'Well, if it isn't us, let's not give him a reason to change his mind, like by keeping him waiting. Step on it, we're already late.'

They parked where parking was 'strictly forbidden.' Cops always ignored those signs; it made them feel more like civilian Greek drivers in need of a parking space. Though in a hurry, they had to wait for the uniform cop to pick up Demosthenes' fingerprints. They stood by the curb and stared at three connected structures identified by a sign atop the middle one: HELLENIC COSMOS.

The futuristic Tholos, or *dome* in English, stood to the left and was by far the most dramatic architectural element of the 23,000-square-foot complex. It was a virtual-world sphere, created by civic-minded Athenians in the midst an old neighborhood of gas stations and commercial spaces badly in need of aesthetic attention. Here visitors experienced life amidst the commercial, political, cultural, and religious center of ancient Athens – the Agora – while sitting in a 130-seat theater 'losing all sense of time and space.' At least that's what a sign by the entrance read.

Andreas pointed to the sign as they passed it. 'Let's hope that happened to Marios.' They were twenty minutes late for what he expected to be a pissy, *prima donna* performance by the self-styled 'Voice of Greece.'

They entered through the front door closest to the theater. He said to meet him there. They didn't have to look for him. He was standing on the other side of the door looking at his watch. Short silver hair, bright blue eyes, a slim five-foot-six-inch frame, and an age falling somewhere between Greece's past and present generation of leaders, Marios

83

seemed tense. Andreas took that to mean he was about to unload on them for keeping him waiting.

'Chief Kaldis?' It was the voice millions knew. 'I could tell it was you from where you parked.' It sounded like sarcasm, but might be a joke.

Andreas treated it as humor. 'You mean I don't look like my photograph?' Andreas smiled and extended his hand.

Marios did not smile but did shake hands. 'Yes, your minister was kind enough to fax me a photograph of you.'

And probably a copy of his official personnel file. This guy had access to practically everyone and everything he wanted. 'Sir, this is officer Kouros.'

They shook hands.

'I would have preferred meeting elsewhere,' he waved his hands, 'somewhere less public but . . . well . . . you'll see.' Marios pointed to a broad steel and glass staircase leading to a mezzanine lined with floor-to-ceiling windows. 'Let's go up there.'

The actual steps, thirty-five of them plus a landing halfway, seemed the only wood in the place. No question that steel, glass, and light were the principal design elements here and presented a decidedly modern contrast to what Andreas expected. Then again, Andreas didn't know what to expect.

Marios held Andreas' arm as they walked. He gestured toward Kouros with his head. 'What I have to say is very private and off the record.'

'Officer Kouros and I work together. If it's something involving police work he will know anyway.' He looked Marios straight in the eyes. 'If it involves something else, I'm not the person to talk to at the ministry.' If this was about making Andreas one of Marios' 'unofficial official' sources, they may as well have it out right now. It was guys like this who did in his father.

Marios stared back. 'I heard you're a hard-ass.' He let out a breath. 'Okay, have it your way, but if word about what I'm about to tell you gets out, there will be hell to pay for all of us.'

This guy sure knew how to sell. He's about to pump me for information and makes it sound like it's the other way around. 'I understand, sir, there will be no problem.'

Marios nodded. 'Fine, just so you know it.' He made no effort to make Andreas feel comfortable in 'his' presence, such as by saying, 'just call me Marios.'

At the mezzanine they turned left and entered a dark room lined with television monitors along the tops of the left and right walls. Marios said this was where visitors were told what was about to happen inside the dome.

'When do we learn?' asked Andreas.

'Soon.' Again, no smile. Marios led them inside the sphere.

Eight semicircular rows of airplane-style seats descended to the base of the sphere. The screen rose up from the floor in front of the bottom row and seemed to envelope everything but the seats themselves. Marios pointed to two seats, dead center, in the next-to-top row. Each seat arm contained controls allowing the audience to vote during the course of the video on the direction the presentation should take. A bit of democracy in action in the telling of the tale of its birthplace. But the three of them had the theater to themselves and there was no doubt in Andreas' mind that this would be all Marios' show.

85

Marios sat in a seat two rows below and directly in front of them. He turned sideways to face them. 'I want you to watch something, but before it starts you need some background.' He paused for a moment, as if collecting his thoughts. 'Well, we all know about the terrible tragedy that befell the Kostopoulos family.'

No beating around the bush for this guy, thought Andreas. Better be careful; there might be microphones hidden somewhere.

'And I'm sure you think I brought you here to pump you for information about that.'

Andreas was expressionless.

'Of course you would, but I assure you that's not why I brought you here. I don't want to know your thoughts. I want you to hear mine.'

Andreas knew better than to interrupt a rambler. Sooner or later they said something they shouldn't. But, then again, this guy's too experienced to make that sort of mistake. He's a better interrogator than most cops.

'You know about the siege the boy's father, a truly unlikable man, waged on one of Greece's oldest and most respected families for control of their newspaper?'

Andreas nodded.

'When was the last time you spoke to Zanni or Ginny Kostopoulos?'

'Yesterday, we . . .' Andreas caught himself. This guy's smooth, he thought. Almost got me into details of our interview with the family.

Marios didn't miss a beat. 'Of course, when you told them of their son's death.' He paused, as if waiting for Andreas to respond.

Andreas decided not to speak unless asked a specific question and, even then, not to volunteer an unnecessary word.

'Do you know what the family is doing today?'

It was a direct question. 'No.'

'No reason why you should. Would you be surprised if I told you they put up for sale all the real property they own in Greece?'

Andreas gave no response.

'Or that an investment banker was engaged to sell all Kostopoulos family business interests in Greece?'

Still no response.

'And that Mrs Kostopoulos and the children left Greece, first thing this morning?'

Silence.

'Under heavily armed guard?'

Andreas started to fidget in his seat.

'And, my guess is, once the boy's body is released, burial will be outside of Greece. So they need never return.'

Andreas couldn't keep quiet any longer. 'I have no idea why you're telling me this, or if any of it is true.'

Marios shrugged. 'Frankly, I don't want to be here telling you *any* of this. And, on a personal level, I don't give a rat's ass whether you think I'm crazy or not. But when you leave here and check out what I told you, . . .' he allowed his words to drift off. He turned away from them and pressed a button. The lights faded down and images began filling the dome. The journey to Athens of another time had begun.

It was a fascinating experience, with great special effects, but what held Andreas' interest was one simple question:

What the fuck was going on? Kouros kept giving him looks along the same line. They were up to 416 BC, in the time of the Athenian democracy, and thirty-five minutes into the forty-minute presentation.

'This is the part for you to concentrate on.' They were the first words Marios had said since the show began.

The presenter's voice picked up with, '*Ostrakizmos* was a procedure conducted by secret ballot for the protection of Athenian democracy. Once a year, citizens of Athens decided whether to hold a vote ostracizing one of their fellow citizens. If a sufficient number of Athenians wanted to conduct an ostracism, the person banished could be anyone the voters agreed was dangerous to Athens and democracy. Reasons for ostracizing were

1. the citizen had conservative views characteristic of dictatorship ideas;
2. the citizen was dishonest in business dealings;
3. the citizen misled people for personal purposes; or
4. the citizen was rich and bragged.

'Anyone determined to be such a danger was banished from Athens for ten years and required to leave the city within ten days.'

Marios pressed a button, the presentation stopped, and the lights went on. 'So, what do you think?'

Lunatic was the first thing that came to mind. 'Interesting,' was the word Andreas uttered.

'I see, you don't agree. But I'm sure you understand the point and, yes, there could be other explanations for why the family left so quickly.'

Like simple, unmitigated grief, thought Andreas.

'Of course, in those times it was only a ten-year banishment of the individual from Athens, not his entire family from Greece for life.' He waved his hand in the air. 'But, times change, procedures evolve, and everything in life can't be a perfect fit.'

Andreas hoped his loss of patience wasn't showing. 'Sir, you're a smart guy; we all know that. You're also damn good at what you do; we all know that, too. What we don't know is, *where the hell you're headed with this?*'

Marios was unfazed. 'For those who didn't accept the ostracism, the penalty was death.'

Andreas already guessed that. The founders of democracy were notoriously direct in their punishments, even among peers. 'But, with all due respect, sir, it's one hell of a stretch to suggest that this . . . this "ostracism,"' he pointed at the screen, 'was behind the boy's murder.' He knew his frustration was showing.

'What if there were proof linking what you just saw to the death of the Kostopoulos boy?'

Andreas wondered if his minister had any idea how off-the-wall this guy was. 'I don't know what to say, sir. If you have evidence, of course we'll look into it and—'

Marios put up his hand. 'Stop. No need to placate me. I'm not crazy.' His voice was firmer than before, but not strident or angry. 'This involves far more than just the Kostopoulos boy's death. His is not an isolated event. It is perhaps the most dramatic in recent memory, but it is *not* something new. This has been going on in our country for years.'

Crazy or not, Andreas had no choice but to hear him out.

'Okay, so tell me what you know. But I want specifics.' He paused as if wondering if he should say more. 'Based on evidence, not some conspiracy theory woven by a TV producer looking for ratings.'

Kouros' face jerked toward Andreas, and both cops braced for an explosion.

Instead, there was a very long, noticeable silence. Marios kept staring into the row between them. 'Our Greece is a land steeped in history, a country that long ago learned how to survive its people. The question is, in these modern times, does our country require some help, or shall we leave it to the fates to decide its future?' He stopped and looked into the eyes of each man. 'Do you really want to hear this? Because once you do and come to see that what I tell you is true, you will face two choices: accept what you cannot change and live within a system antithetical to your core principles, or endure lifelong, merciless frustration battling against choice number one.'

Andreas smiled. 'You sure know how to set the hook.'

'Millions think so.' Marios forced a smile. It was his last of any sort for more than an hour.

Marios' reputation for telling terrific stories without allowing anything as pesky as the whole truth to interfere with his tales made Andreas wonder how much of what he was saying was true and how much was his form of 'journalistic interpretation' or, as the less sophisticated would call it, *bullshit*.

Marios believed in a world run by bargains and distractions. Bargains by the all-powerful to stay that way; distractions for the masses to keep them that way. It was not a very optimistic view of man. He believed those hungry for power did whatever necessary to achieve it and expended ruthlessly higher quantum levels of effort to keep it.

All of that required distracting the masses from their plight or, where life was not so bad, from the disparity of so much power in the hands of so few. Hate and fear always seemed to work. 'Just find the right scapegoat . . . and run with it.' Different ethnicities – 'find a way to justify to Greeks that it's bad for the Turks and you're home free;' different styles of worship, even within the same faith – 'look a few countries east of here for daily, bloody examples of that;' race – 'name a Western country, make that any racially or tribally mixed place in the world, free of those tensions;' political differences – 'though significant ones are hard to find today among organized parties;' class distinctions – 'my family is better than yours because . . . fill in the blank;' and, in a pinch, fans of a rival sports team – 'no example necessary, GO OLYMPIAKOS OR GO PANATHINAIKOS. The bottom line goal: keep the focus off of us. Whoever *us* may be.'

Andreas had seen Marios perform enough times on TV to know he was building up to his point and that there'd be no hurrying him along.

'Hitler's rise to power in the 1930s should leave no doubt in anyone's mind that even the world's most advanced civilization can, under the right circumstances, allow a mind-boggling many to suffer for the goals of a few . . . and a miserable few at that.

'Since 9/11 much of the world's focus has been on threats of foreign terror, but in the long term what we face from within is likely to be far more menacing and difficult to control, absent a Stalinist-like will.' He paused and looked at Andreas. 'I'm not suggesting a return to the Regime of the Colonels, or anything of the sort. I'm just making my point.'

Andreas took that as Marios' way of saying he knew all about his father's service to the dictatorship and what followed. What Andreas couldn't tell was whether the remark was intended as some sort of threat or just to show that he knew his facts.

'The United States will never forget 9/11 or Pearl Harbor. And it better never forget Oklahoma City – Americans killing Americans for the sake of terror.'

Andreas adjusted his position in his seat.

Marios gave him a quick, sharp look. 'Am I losing my audience?' He paused, no doubt for effect, then continued. 'Okay, here's my point. We all know about 17 November.'

What Greek didn't? It was the name taken by Greece's most notorious homegrown terrorist organization from the final day of the 1973 student uprising at the Athens Polytechnic University credited with launching Greece's return to democracry in 1974.

'Ever wonder how 17 November managed to operate undetected for almost thirty years, assassinating over twenty prominent people in more than one hundred attacks – starting with the assassination of the CIA's section chief in Athens?

'And I'm not just talking about their attacks on US military personnel, Turkish and British diplomats. Their primary targets were prominent members of Greece's establishment. A member of parliament, a publisher, a banker, a businessman, a ship owner, a prosecutor, police.

The list goes on and on. And they got away with it *for almost thirty years.*'

He paused, and spread his arms. 'That is, until June 2002, when a miracle happened and a botched bombing unraveled the entire organization. By December 2003, 17 November's leadership was captured, convicted, and sentenced away. Just in time for Greece's hosting of the 2004 Olympics.'

Greeks see a conspiracy in the number of raisins in a cereal box, Andreas thought.

'I know, you probably heard that before, but that doesn't mean you should dismiss it. As much as we would like to forget our past, in it there is a basis for true concern as to the lengths some might go to retain or *regain* power.'

Another reference to the regime his father served.

'And there are signs of new, at least seemingly new, groups trying to pick up where 17 November left off—' he rolled his left hand out in front of him to finish his sentence without saying the obvious words aloud, *now that the Olympics are over.*

He was right about new groups forming. Isolated bombings with manifestoes were back. Hopefully not for long.

'The trouble with groups on the fringe is you're never quite sure which fringe they're on. You may think you do by their targets and words, but not always. For example, the declared aim of 17 November was to discredit and humiliate the establishment and the US government, not to disrupt Greek society as a whole. At least that's what they said. Yet in the thirty years of 17 November terror, Greece's establishment not only expanded, it thrived. And with every death came a profit of some sort to someone.'

Andreas had enough. 'Okay, I get it, we've got a great

left-wing, or is it right-wing, conspiracy going on out there. Carrying out clandestine acts on behalf of unnamed powers. Assuming there's any truth to all this, what does it have to do with the Kostopoulos kid ending up in a dumpster?' He probably could have been more diplomatic.

'I don't know.'

Is this guy jerking my chain?

Marios continued. 'Over the past several years quite a few foreign-born but Greek families who achieved great wealth in Greece suddenly moved away, selling everything.'

Andreas' patience was nearly at its end. 'So?'

'And none would ever say why they left so suddenly.'

Andreas drummed his fingers on the seat between them.

'But there was a pattern to three of those families, one I admit I never saw until the Kostopoulos boy's death.'

Finally, something relevant. Please.

'In each case a family member died unexpectedly.'

This time Andreas gestured, so?

'And within a day after each death, the rest of the family left Greece. Never to return.'

The thought sat in the air, as if no one dared go after it.

The first thing Andreas could think of to say was, 'Why did you decide to tell me this?'

'I was told to. But I only agreed after I was convinced you're a man to be trusted. And the one man in Greece possibly dumb enough to risk doing something about it.'

He wasn't sure if that was meant as a threat or a compliment. 'Who told you that?'

'A friend.'

'Yours or mine?'

'Does it matter?'

94

Andreas couldn't imagine what sort of friend would drop him into the middle of such a goddamned mess. Then again, he'd already waded in on his own; so possibly it was a warning to watch where he stepped. Or to back off. Either way, he was better off knowing.

'Any suggestions on where to go from here?'

Marios handed him an envelope that was sitting on the seat next to him. 'Inside is all the information I have on the other three families. I also included the name and phone number of a friend who's tied into Athens society. I think she might be able to help you.'

'Does she know about this?'

Marios gestured no. 'But she's smart, so be careful what you say if you don't want her to figure it out.'

They shook hands, exchanged perfunctory smiles, and said goodbye in the theater. Marios didn't walk them out, probably to avoid being seen with Andreas any more than he already had been. Andreas couldn't blame him. He wouldn't want to be seen with himself, knowing what he knew now.

8

'Ever see any of those old-time American Laurel and Hardy movies?'

'You mean the ones with the tall, skinny guy and the short, fat one?'

Andreas nodded yes. They were standing outside Tholos next to their car, engaged in the ubiquitous self-destructive Greek ritual of cigarette smoking. Andreas knew it was bad for him, but he only smoked when stressed. Or so he told himself. 'One always was complaining about the messes the other kept getting them into.'

Kouros smiled and nodded.

Andreas stretched and yawned. 'Marios really was unhappy about talking to us.'

'What do you think it was that had the all-powerful Marios doing something he didn't want to do?'

Andreas shrugged. 'I'm more interested in *who* got him

to do it.' He stared at the ground and thought, *beware of Greeks bearing gifts*. 'How much of what he said do you think is true?'

'No idea. But I'll start checking out those three families as soon as I get back to the office.'

'Have Maggie help you. If anyone knows the gossip or where to find it, she does.' Andreas drew in on his cigarette and exhaled. 'I wonder how long Marios has known what he told us and what his reasons were for not doing something about it sooner?'

'Maybe somebody just told him, someone with enough influence to keep him from breaking the story on TV?'

'More likely someone who pointed out that running it meant his probable immediate and painful demise.'

'Who?'

'Wish I knew.'

'But why come to us now? I mean to you, Chief.'

'Don't know, and until we do, let's assume the worst possible motive. But, my guess is because *we*,' he pointed to Kouros and back at himself, 'already were on to something.' Andreas finished his cigarette and crushed it out on the ground instead of the flick-it-away-burning-live method used by so many others. 'Let's get back to the office. I want to check out this woman Marios wants us to meet before calling her. We already have too many intrigues and big-time players' fingerprints all over this investigation. All I know for sure is we better watch each other's back, assume nothing, and tell *no one* what we learned today.'

Kouros pursed his lips and nodded. His look was serious. 'Can I say it now, Chief?'

'Say what?'

'"*Here's another nice mess you've gotten me into.*"'

Maggie delivered what she had to say to Andreas leaning over his desk and waving her finger. She ended with, 'So, if you're going to leave me to run all the other cases we have in this office while you're off at the movies with big-time celebrities, fine, but at least answer your phone when I'm trying to reach you. I can't make *every* decision. Not at my pay grade.' She had a gift for putting just the right amount of humor into her assaults on her boss.

'I get your point.'

'Thank you.'

'You're welcome. So, what do you have on the Kostopoulos family?'

'Like Marios said, their plane left first thing this morning. The flight plan said Rome. Not sure who was on it, though.'

'Why's that?' Andreas sounded puzzled.

'It was a flight within the European Union, and being a private plane . . .' she shrugged.

Andreas nodded. 'Anyone back at the Kostopoulos' house?'

'I had a cruiser stop by, and they were told the family had left the country. No idea when they're coming back.'

Andreas exhaled. 'Christ.' He looked at Kouros standing next to Maggie. 'Could he be right about all this?'

'About what?' asked Maggie.

'Nothing. Yianni, start going over those files with Maggie, I'm going to see what I can find out about Lila Vardi.'

'*The* Lila Vardi?'

Andreas stared at Maggie, shook his head, and smiled.

'Why doesn't that surprise me? Okay, tell me what you know.'

'She comes from one of the oldest families in Greece. Vardi is her married name. You'll find her maiden name on at least one product on practically every dinner table in Greece.'

He knew the name; everyone who ate did.

'Her husband died in a car crash about three years ago. She kept her husband's name. The papers said as a memorial to him.'

'What does she do?'

'Not much. She has her family money, and her husband was a successful ship owner, not one of the biggies or from one of the old families, but successful.'

Andreas rolled his eyes. 'You mean annual income only in the mega-millions as opposed to multi-mega-millions?'

She smiled. 'Stop with the stereotypes, I'm sure they're just like you and me.'

'Yeah, right.' It was Kouros.

Maggie shook her head. 'Okay, guys, enough with the revolution.'

'What else do you know about her?' asked Andreas.

'She's around thirty, attractive, educated in the US, involved in a lot of charity and museum work, with a reputation as a real lady.'

'Too bad, Chief.' Kouros spoke with a lilt of humor to his voice. Andreas shot him a look that was anything but humorous. The blood drained from Kouros' face; he stared down at the floor.

'What else, Maggie?' Andreas' voice was tight, but if Maggie wondered what was going on, she didn't show it.

'No kids, no steady boyfriend, no scandals, a dog, six cats, and a parrot.'

'Blood type?'

'Probably.' She always was quicker than he.

Andreas smiled. 'Okay, so where can I find her?'

'I'll get it for you.' She turned and left the office.

'Sorry, Chief.' Kouros was looking at Andreas as he spoke.

Andreas stared at him. 'You got the point?'

'Yes, sir.'

'Good.' Andreas paused. 'Do you have someone watching Anna?'

'Yes, a team's been watching her building since first thing this morning.'

Andreas nodded. 'Now, find out what the hell has happened to those three families and where the Kostopoulos family is now. We've got to start talking to people. Maybe we should chase down that Demosthenes guy?'

Kouros shook his head. 'The prints came back. Clean as a whistle. Not even an unpaid parking ticket.'

'Damn, I'd have sworn he was involved in this somehow. Run him by Interpol, just in case.'

'Already did, Chief. Nothing on him.'

Andreas jerked his head to the side as he swore again.

Kouros said, 'Do you think we should start talking to members of the Linardos family? I mean, if all this banishment stuff is true, they'd sure seem likely to be part of it.'

Andreas buzzed Maggie. 'Any word on Sarantis Linardos?'

'His secretary said he's still out of town. She's not sure when he'll be back.'

Andreas looked at Kouros. 'I wish we had something more

100

to go on than a hunch. But until we speak to him,' Andreas pointed at the intercom, 'I don't see us getting anywhere banging away on garbage cans in the middle of every Linardos family member's living room.'

Kouros said nothing.

'Yianni, I made my point before about the . . .' he rolled his hand in the air, 'other thing. That's done and finished, you can return to your normal self.'

'Yes, sir, I understand. No garbage in the living room.'

'Or the bedroom, please.' Andreas grinned.

Maggie knocked before opening the door. 'Here's her home address. She lives next to the Palace at 30 Irodou Attikou.' Perhaps the most exclusive street in Athens; only a few blocks long and filled with money.

'Guess it's time to shine my shoes.'

Beauty is in the eye of the beholder. For many it's blond hair, sparkling (capped) teeth, an overworked gym membership, and of course, big tits. On the other side, it often seems to be his gold Rolex, endless ego, and full-term-pregnant size belly – with the relevance of all else measured inversely against the depth of his financial statement.

Lila Vardi fit no one's mold. Practically every big-time Lothario, *kamaki*, social climber, and fortune-hunter in Athens, plus a few visiting players, took a shot at her. She had heard the same lines so many times she feared her eyes bore a permanent glaze. As if that weren't bad enough, only respect for her mother's incessant good intentions kept Lila from cutting her veins rather than enduring another tortured moment in the presence of one of her mother's 'finds' for her.

101

Lila kept her jet-black hair short, her almond-shaped brown eyes bright, her well-toned skin tanned, her figure trim, and her lovely-to-look-at breasts unhampered by a bra. When she felt like it, nothing stood between her body and what the rest of the world saw her wear. She liked it that way. A little sensual secret she kept to herself, for no man had been with her since her husband died. She liked that, too. His memory was the only man she wanted in her life. She was thirty-five and satisfied herself in other ways.

Her current passion was volunteer public relations on behalf of the Museum of Hellenic Art. Virtually single-handedly, she kept its world-renowned collection in the public eye. Through her society friends and media connections, rarely a week passed without some story, or at least a few photographs, appearing in one of Greece's most popular celebrity magazines or tabloids. It wasn't an ego trip; it was what kept the museum alive. There might be smiles on their faces and dignity in their voices, but among most museum boards fundraising was a relentless battle against fickle giving habits and opportunistic competitors. In keeping with the fundraising truism that 'donors like being part of something important, visible, and sexy,' Lila was as priceless to the museum as anything in its collection. And since the museum paid only her expenses, she truly was priceless.

She planned to meet friends for lunch at Egli in the park across from her apartment, but Marios asked her to meet some pushy policeman who insisted on seeing her immediately. She couldn't refuse Marios; he was far too influential, but she scheduled the meeting for her home. She was certain her place would make the policeman uncomfortable enough to leave quickly. She was used to keeping the who-do-they-think-they-are at bay, especially men.

Andreas wasn't looking forward to this meeting. He'd called the Vardi home, said Mrs Vardi was expecting his call and that he would like to meet with her this afternoon. He was put on hold for five minutes before being told, 'Mrs Vardi is busy this afternoon. Perhaps you could call back tomorrow?'

When he asked if she would be available to meet tomorrow the response was, 'She will let you know then.'

It took a typically Greek, high-decibel-level call from Andreas to Marios to arrange a meeting for that afternoon. How Marios ever thought this woman would be helpful was beyond him. She wouldn't even agree to meet until squeezed. Andreas decided to have a quick, courteous meeting and be done with her. What a waste of time.

Mrs Vardi's apartment building was at the old Olympic Stadium end of the street, facing the park. The lobby showed impeccable old-world taste, and the doormen behaved as expected in such a place: courteous to the point of obsequious while they determined where you fit into the pecking order of things. With cops, doormen could go either way, depending on how many favors they might need. Andreas gave just his name, not title, and waited while he was announced.

'Mrs Vardi's maid said you will have to wait until she's finished with her trainer.'

Andreas smiled. The doorman shrugged and pointed him toward an equivalently elegant sitting room. Andreas walked

in, sat down, crossed his legs and gazed nowhere in particular. If anyone were watching, he looked as much at ease
with the world as a tourist in a deckchair on a Mediterranean
cruise.

Was this woman as self-absorbed as she appeared or just
playing games? This was an old interviewing ploy: keep
someone waiting to put them under stress and establish who
was in charge. Andreas wondered if the camera inconspicu-
ously mounted in the far corner of the room was connected
to monitors in the apartments.

Ten minutes passed before the doorman came in and
said, 'You may go up to Mrs Vardi's apartment now.'

Andreas smiled and walked toward the elevator as if all
were perfect with the world. *It's going to be tough being nice
to this bitch.*

Lila's apartment was on the sixth floor, about as high as
any old residential building was built in earthquake-conscious
Athens. In fact, it was the entire sixth floor with a view of
both the Acropolis and Lykavittos.

The elevator opened directly into a large, welcoming entry
foyer, decorated in the French neoclassical style of Louis
XVI. But the openness, of course, was an illusion, because
these days no one in their right mind left an apartment acces-
sible to the outside world, with or without the most cautious
of elevator operators and doormen.

Andreas stepped into the foyer, and the elevator operator
pointed to a pair of French doors at the far end. 'There's a
bell to the right.'

Andreas pressed the bell. He noticed that the curtains
hanging on each door did not cover windows, but painted
images of windows. And the doors weren't made of wood,

but of high security steel finished in the same style. More illusion.

The doors opened and a woman dressed in a black maid's uniform – starched white lace apron and all – told him to follow her. She led him through room after room filled with antiques and paintings, none of which he recognized nor expected to. It wasn't his thing, even if he could afford them. Strange, he thought, with all the dead bodies he'd seen in his life, he still wasn't used to them; but his brief time in the Kostopoulos home made this seem just another rich person's house.

She led him into a room with a breathtaking view of the Acropolis and told him to make himself comfortable. He expected another let's-make-him-wait experience. He didn't mind, the view kept him occupied. He stood by the windows, looked out at the city, and wondered whether those who had such glorious views took them for granted.

'Mr Kaldis? Or is there a title I should be using?'

He turned away from the window to face the woman standing in the doorway, smiled, and said, 'Whatever makes you comfortable, Mrs Vardi.'

'Then, what exactly *is* your title?' She did not move. Her arms were crossed and her voice coldly professional.

'Chief inspector, Special Crimes Division, GADA.'

'Sounds impressive.'

'I think that's why they gave it to me.' He smiled.

She didn't. 'So, what can I do for you?' She looked at her watch.

He smiled again. 'May I sit down?' He wasn't going to let her rush him out of here simply by looking at her watch. That was too old a ruse. She'll have to be directly rude,

105

something he doubted she'd dare with Marios behind the meeting.

She forced a smile. 'Certainly,' and pointed him to a couch perpendicular to the windows. She sat in a chair across from him separated by a small table.

'I sincerely appreciate your taking the time out of your busy day to see me.' He tried sounding sincere.

She simply nodded. Now both her arms and legs were crossed. She wore a black sweat suit, white sneakers, and no makeup. He noticed the sneakers were a brand even he could afford. Maybe there really was a trainer.

'I don't know what Marios told you—'

She cut him off. 'Absolutely nothing.'

He nodded for a moment. She said nothing more, just sat arms- and legs-crossed in the chair. 'Why do you think that would be?' he asked.

'Why *what* would be?'

He'd play; besides, it was her time she was wasting. He leaned forward and stared directly at her. 'Why would Greece's most famous television journalist insist that the chief inspector, Special Crimes Division, GADA, immediately drop everything he was doing to speak to you about a murder getting 24/7 media attention all over Greece and not mention a single word to you about why or how he thought you could help the investigation?' That gave nothing away and might just be the kick in the ass she needed to start taking this meeting seriously.

She looked away from his stare, leaned forward a bit, then uncrossed and recrossed her legs in the opposite direction, all without uncrossing her arms. 'I assume you mean Sotiris Kostopoulos?'

106

'Yes.'

'I really don't know his family that well, but my family and his do have summer homes on Mykonos.'

Mykonos, I can't seem to get away from that island, he thought. 'I don't think that's the reason he suggested I speak to you. I think it's more because of what you know of their ties into Athens society.'

She laughed. 'Ties into Athens society? Chief, the closest ties that family had to Athens society were the black ones Zanni Kostopoulos wore to formal, opening night affairs. I remember when he practically had to underwrite any he wanted to attend and, even then, most of old-line society wouldn't be there. They'd wait for the third night, after what they jokingly called the "*nouveaux* rush" was over.'

Andreas smiled. 'Like I said, because of what you know of their ties into Athens society.'

She dropped her arms to her lap. 'Well, if that's of help to you, please, ask away. I think it's terrible what happened to that boy. Any idea who did it?'

'Not yet, but we're working on it.'

'In other words, you can't tell me.'

He smiled. 'Did they have any enemies?'

'Who'd kill a child?'

He shrugged. 'I'm not accusing anyone. I'm just asking.'

'But I thought it was a murder that happened because he was in the wrong place at the wrong time.'

'We have to check out every possibility, and that includes determining if the family or the boy had enemies capable of doing such an act.'

'That seems quite unlikely among the people I know.' She didn't sound offended, just factual.

'Which I assume includes the Linardos family.'

'Of course.'

'I understand, but the problem I have is that the reaction of the Kostopoulos family to all this was . . . uh . . . unusual.' He paused but she said nothing. 'They've left Athens and put their property up for sale.'

'Really?' She seemed genuinely surprised. 'And before the funeral.' It seemed more an observation than a question, so he didn't answer. She turned her head and looked out the window. 'You know, this happened before.'

He felt a chill. 'What do you mean?'

'Perhaps that is why Marios suggested we meet. A year or so ago, another family experienced the unexpected death of a child and just as suddenly left Athens, selling everything. I know, because I was in the midst of arranging a very large gift from the family for the museum when it happened. Their reaction seemed very strange to me at the time, but I attributed it to grief.' She paused, still gazing out the window.

'I suffered a similar loss shortly before.' She drew in a quick breath and brought her eyes back into the room, but not to Andreas. 'They simply disappeared in the midst of completing the museum's paperwork and no one knew what to do. Through mutual family friends, I learned they were in Zurich and, when they wouldn't take my phone calls, I flew there and went to their home.' She looked at Andreas. 'I know, it wasn't very lady-like but, after all, it was a big donation.' She shrugged and smiled.

'Anyway, you'd think I was trying to storm Parliament from the way they treated me when I arrived at their flat. Their doormen, more like hoodlums if you ask me, refused to let me in. Only when the wife heard the ruckus and saw it was I did they let me pass. But she certainly wasn't happy to see me. I'm not even sure why she did, except to vent. It was three minutes of "*You Greeks* this" and "*You Greeks* that."

'I know how provincial, at times, we Greeks who never left can seem to Greeks returning from other countries – I think that family had lived in Serbia – and how hard it is for anyone new to break into the "establishment,"' she emphasized the word with finger-quotes in the air, 'but what I couldn't understand was her unvarnished hate for all things Greek. I mean, this was a woman I knew for years, and although we weren't that close, I never saw even a hint of that side to her.'

Andreas tried to stay expressionless. 'Do you recall anything she said to you?'

Lila bit at her lower lip. 'You mean aside from her curses that took up half the time, and the part about the only money the museum will ever see from her family is that which they use to obliterate it and everything else Greek off the face of the earth?'

'Ouch.'

'Yes, it was quite a pleasant afternoon. Everyone on our museum board was as shocked as I when I told them what happened. Come to think of it, that's probably why Marios knew to tell you to speak to me. I'm certain one of them must have told him. They're all such gossips.' She touched her right index finger to her temple. 'There was one thing I distinctly remember. Perhaps because it ended with her throwing something at me.'

Andreas looked surprised.

'It hurt, too.' She pointed at her left arm. 'It was at the end of a diatribe about child-murderers, and how the small-minded and jealous of modern Greece were destroying the country in much the same way as the same sort did in the past. That's when she yelled, "Soon all of Greece will have banished itself," and threw the thing at me. She'd been clutching it in her hand the entire time she talked, as if it were a rosary or something.'

Andreas wondered if she'd noticed his flinch at 'banished.' 'What did she throw?'

'It was a piece of broken pottery or something like that. If it hadn't struck my arm I'm sure it would have shattered into a thousand pieces.'

'Did you get a look at it?'

'Not really, I picked it up but as soon as I did she started running toward me. I thought she was going to hit me. But all she did was grab it out of my hand. I assumed she was on the verge of a breakdown and just let her be. She was crying and shaking her head when I left. It was a terrible scene.'

He nodded. 'Anything more you can tell me about that piece of pottery.'

'It was an ochre color, not that big, about the size of a pack of cigarettes. I'd guess it was something from her husband's family, a potsherd probably.'

'Why do you say that?'

'Because when I picked it up I noticed his family name written on it.'

Andreas jerked back on the couch as if touched by a live wire. He struggled to remember what he'd heard at the Tholos: 'Ostracize is from the Greek word ostrakizein, meaning "to banish by voting with ostrakon." Each vote was cast by writing the name of the one who should be banished on an ostrakon – a piece of earthenware, a potsherd.'

9

Lila's demeanor had changed; she seemed almost perky. 'Chief . . . Kaldos, would you like some coffee?'

He nodded. 'Thank you, it's Kaldis.'

She smiled. 'Sorry.'

'No problem, it's probably easier to call me Andreas, anyway.'

Why did I say that? he thought. He knew better than to make the relationship informal. You always keep an interview with uninvolved, responsible citizens on a formal, professional basis. That's the best way of getting them to talk. They want to help the justice system, not the cop wasting their time asking questions.

She paused, then picked up a tiny silver bell and shook it. The same maid appeared. 'Maria, would you please bring Chief Kaldis a coffee. Do you prefer American or Greek?' Her voice was back to professional.

Well, I guess that put me in my place. 'American, please.'

The maid turned to leave but Lila gestured for her to pause. 'And a frappé for me.' She turned back to Andreas. 'I prefer coffee chilled in the afternoon.'

What a gracious way to thaw an awkward moment, he thought.

'I know you didn't want to tell me before why you reacted as you did to my mention of the potsherd, but I'm sure you understand my curiosity. After all, it's a fatal flaw of my gender.' She was smiling again.

He grinned. 'And cops.' Andreas wondered how much he should tell her. Probably nothing. But she could be a real help. He's not likely to get anywhere with this case without knowing a hell of a lot more about Athens society. He needed someone with a real grasp of it, an insider's view. Not Maggie's sort of tabloid expertise.

The question that bothered him was, *can I trust her to keep her mouth shut?*

'What do you know about potsherds?' he asked.

'Yesterday's mayonnaise jar is today's artifact.'

He laughed.

'I know, I probably shouldn't be saying that, especially since I work for a museum actively involved in trying to recover genuine ancient treasures plundered from our country, but it's true. Generally, potsherds are simply bits and pieces of the most common sort of earthenware cookery and jars from a past civilization.'

'Why would someone write on one?'

'I don't know why one would today, but in ancient times paper was prohibitively expensive, broken pottery was everywhere, and the literate used them as scrap paper. Sort of like our Post-it notes.' She smiled again.

113

She seemed to like to smile. He liked it when she did. 'Can you think of any reason why that woman threw the potsherd at you?'

'Because it was in her hand.'

'Yes, but why was it in her hand, and why would she throw it at you? Had it been a rosary, do you think she'd have thrown it?'

She brushed some hair back over her right ear. Lila was a pretty woman. Not his type, of course, but pretty.

'I think you're right about that. I wouldn't throw something that was comforting me over such deep grief as the loss of a child. Perhaps I'd throw something I was dwelling on, something that represented what I was mourning.' She looked him straight in the eyes. 'So, where are you trying to take me with all this, Andreas?'

Wow, Marios was right; she really is smart. And knows just when to change the pace.

He smiled. 'I really can't tell you.'

'Don't trust me, huh?' She turned toward the door and raised her voice slightly, 'Maria dear, where's the coffee?' She looked back at him. 'See, I don't always need a bell to be heard.'

He shook his head and grinned. 'That's for sure.'

The maid came with the coffee, served it, and left. Neither spoke. They sat quietly sipping their coffees, sharing the space.

Lila broke the silence. 'Well, if you won't tell me, I guess I'm not going to be of much more help to you.'

Andreas' heart dropped. But she was right. He put down his coffee. 'I'm sorry, but you have been very helpful.' He stood up, not wanting to leave, but there was no reason to stay. He reached into his pocket, took out a card, and handed it to her. 'In case you think of anything else, please call me.'

She took the card and looked at it as if about to say something, or so he imagined. 'Thank you, Chief, I mean Andreas. Let me walk you to the elevator.'

He prayed the elevator wouldn't come. But it did. She was standing in front of the elevator doors as they closed, smiling.

Maggie spared Andreas the misery of hours squinting over a computer screen by leaving him a pile of Internet print-outs. It contained every news story she and Kouros could find on the three families. The printouts sat on top of an even larger pile of official reports on the families and the events surrounding their sudden departures from Greece. Andreas told Maggie and Kouros to go home. He wanted to read everything himself. Perhaps it wasn't the most efficient way, but a word here, an instinct there, might pull it all together for him. Besides, he was the only one who suffered doing it his way: sitting at a desk half the night reading.

Nothing seemed out of the ordinary. No reports of foul play, just terrible tragedies. Each family was well off, though none as spectacularly so as the Kostopoulos family, and all had three things in common besides wealth: the head of each family had emigrated to Greece from somewhere else; each had achieved a significant level of professional, business, or social prominence in the press; and beyond a brief story on each family's separate 'tragedy' and 'decision' to leave Greece, not a single, additional word ever appeared again on any of them in the Greek media. It was a perfect example of orchestrating press coverage to deliver an unmistakable message: *Leave – or this will happen to you.*

The deaths took place over a period of four years, and appeared random in time. The first was a particularly grisly accident involving two young children of the same family; the second, two years later, was the death of a wife at the hands of a never-found hit-and-run driver; and in another two years came the drowning of a teenage daughter in a boating accident. That was the one Lila knew about. All were gruesome, painful ways to go, but none likely to generate more than routine police attention.

Andreas rubbed at his eyes, leaned back, and let his elbows drop to the arms of his chair. So, why this time did they do the Kostopoulos kid in a way guaranteed to get police attention? It didn't fit the pattern. And why was it always a wife or a child, never the father? He wondered how many other families receiving a potsherd simply packed up and left. Perhaps Lila would know.

He resisted thinking of her. One personal involvement per investigation was one too many. Besides, she wasn't his type. That was the second time he'd thought that. Perhaps because he was certain he wasn't *her* type, or maybe just because he'd never known a woman like her before. Whatever, time to get some sleep.

It was after three in the morning and Lila hadn't been able to sleep. Something was bothering her. She was sure it wasn't the man. How could it be? She didn't know him at all. And he was a policeman. No, she was sure it had to do with what he was telling her – or rather not telling her.

She turned onto her side and held a pillow over her head. 'Sleep, please, sleep,' she murmured to herself, squeezing her eyes shut.

It wasn't working. She kept thinking of that moment when she thought Andreas might be hitting on her. It bothered her. Why are all men like that? WHY? She drew in a deep breath and repeated the only answer she'd ever come up with: it's our culture, accept it or move. The phrase repeated in her mind, *accept it or move.*

Lila wasn't sure whether the pillow or she hit the floor first. All she knew was that when the thought hit her, she bolted straight up yelling, 'My god that's it!' and tumbled off the bed. It was one of those esoteric little bits of ancient history tucked away unused since grade-school days in the back of her brain. The family's sudden departure from Greece, the mother using the word 'banished,' Andreas' reaction to the family's name written on the potsherd, all pointed to the ancient Athenian practice of ostracism. Accept it *and* move!

She couldn't wait to tell Andreas that she knew what was behind his questions. She reached for the phone on her nightstand and, sitting cross-legged on the floor, called his office. She didn't expect him to be there but let it ring until a machine picked up and his voice said, 'Please leave a message.'

'Hi, Andreas, it's Lila Vardi. I figured out what you didn't want to tell me. And I think I can help you. Why don't you call me in the morning?' She paused. 'Or just stop by my home anytime between ten and one. I'll be here. Thanks, goodnight.'

She hung up the phone and crawled back into bed. Why

did I have to add the last part? She tossed the thought around in her mind until drifting off to sleep, finally.

Andreas checked his messages before leaving his office. He played Lila's back three times, each time looking at his watch and wondering if it was too late to call her. He decided five either was too late or too early. He headed for the door mumbling, 'Damn, why didn't I check my messages sooner,' and wondering what was on her mind.

10

The alarm went off twenty minutes before, but all Andreas could manage, so far, was drag himself out of bed long enough to hit *start* on the coffee maker and plop face-first onto the sheets. His father always had a morning coffee the old-fashioned way: his wife made it for him. But Andreas preferred appliances. Some day he'd get married, raise a family, and make his mother thoroughly happy. For now, there was no time, not even enough to court a new woman into bed for a night. He did his laundry and shopping on a catch-as-catch-can basis and cleaned his apartment in hurry-up style just before the occasional 'stop by' from an old girlfriend.

Of course, his mother did visit once a week to cook for her 'boy' and 'tidy up a bit.' Once, Andreas told her it wasn't necessary, and she asked why he didn't love her any more. So, Thursday afternoons the apartment was his mother's. He tried getting home at least in time to say hello, but many times couldn't. She didn't seem to mind; said she just liked knowing she still could help her boy. She always cooked and left him far more than he could eat, something for which his next-door neighbors were eternally grateful.

The apartment didn't have much of a view, but not many did in this neighborhood. At least not any a cop could afford. But he liked it here, even when the elevator wasn't working. The four flights helped keep him in shape, and his commute was only 25 minutes in traffic or a brisk walk and two stops on the metro.

Pangrati was a neighborhood by Pangratiou Park filled with old five-story apartment buildings 'south of the Hilton,' as the locals would say. These days, new locals likely were students and other young people preferring the more spacious feeling of Pangrati to other better-priced but 'more populated than Tokyo' areas at the heart of Athens. There also was the charm of its trolleys, electrified yellow-orange buses running into Athens; and a walk to Kolonaki, with its fancy bars and shops, or to Syndagma, Athens' central square and the home of Greece's Parliament, took only fifteen minutes. The home of Lila Vardi, and a completely different world, was even closer.

Andreas rolled onto his back and thought of Anna. Not of wanting her but of how stupid he'd been. He meant to call her about Demosthenes but decided he'd better stay away. Any further contact with Anna meant certain suicide for his career and rapacious 'like-father-like-son' headlines shaming his family, especially his mother. *Never again.* He'd get Kouros to talk to her; couldn't risk sending anyone else. God knows what she might say. He was angry with himself.

He knew better: compromise integrity once and cover-up compromises never end. He spun off onto the floor and into his wakeup-workout routine: sit-ups, push-ups, pull-ups, and flexing.

Andreas finished and jumped into the shower. That was where he did some of his best thinking.

There really wasn't all that much to do in a late-night club early in the morning. Of course, there's the booze, the drugs, the noise, and the (lingering) hope of getting laid by someone of your preferred sexual orientation, but if you actually wanted to talk to someone, forget about it. Sure, you had the ramblers, philosophers, stoics, Hamlets, and expletive-stringers – yougottabefuckingshittingmemother-fuckermalakia – all willing to share their predawn wisdom, but when you reached the bottom line, the whole scene got old and boring pretty quickly. And when you had to be there every night making nice to everyone . . .

That was Giorgio's life. Every night he'd be at his expected position by the front door nodding to his regulars, coddling visiting celebrities, embracing politicians, stroking those who despised other guests; all the while smiling. He ruled every aspect of the madness of the place with the pinpoint red-dot of a silver laser pen never out of his left hand. It demanded and received immediate attention from whomever it summoned. That was how Giorgio kept his sanity: by staying in control and sober. Everybody knew that.

Which was exactly why Andreas was yelling at himself in the shower. 'Just how stupid are you? How could you think for a minute that a hooker could walk into his club with two gorillas, take over a table in the VIP section, and

Giorgio wouldn't know exactly what was going on? What are you, Kaldis, a goddamned rookie?'

Andreas finished with a string of more expletives directed at himself and a decision to get the investigation back on track. Enough with this grand conspiracy bullshit. It was a distraction. The murder trail was getting cold. He wondered if that was intentional; the boy's death simply revenge for the Linardos girl's humiliation and Marios' performance a debt owed to the Linardos family repaid by an elegant ruse. Nothing was outside the realm of possibility. He turned off the shower. Back to rule number one: *trust no one.*

Everyone in the office knew the Chief was in a foul mood. Even his pencils could tell. He'd already snapped and thrown three against the wall.

'So, what do you think, Yianni, did the bastard set me up? Does Giorgio have video of me with that girl?'

Kouros didn't say a word. It was the sort of question not looking for an answer.

Snap, BAM. Another pencil casualty ricocheted off the wall. 'Fuck him if he does. It's not going to change a damn thing. If I find that bastard's involved in that kid's murder . . .' his voice trailed off.

'We do have Sotiris and Anna disappearing through that emergency exit into the parking lot, the one with the painted over security camera.'

Andreas had been ranting uninterrupted for so long he was surprised at hearing another voice. 'No way Giorgio didn't know they went out that door. Opening it must have set off all sorts of alarms.'

122

'And security running to make sure no one was sneaking in,' added Kouros.

'Yeah, or running out on a check. Bastard.' Andreas drummed his fingers on his desk. 'We've got to figure out why Giorgio's involved in all this.'

'Money?'

'Yeah, but whose money? Linardos'? That puts us back where we were before: no proof of anything. And we'd get nowhere going toe-to-toe with Giorgio over this on what we have. Damn, we've got to find the link between Giorgio and whoever's paying. That's where we *squeeze*.' He clenched his fist.

'Just tell me who, and I'll start squeezing.'

'Wish I knew.' Andreas drummed his fingers some more. 'Any luck with that gay bar?'

Kouros gestured no. 'Just like you said, there was nothing in the dumpster when they emptied the garbage, and no one in the bar saw anyone resembling the victim or the two gorillas.'

'So, we have the kid dead in the dumpster, last seen alive in the Angel Club.' He flashed the palms of both hands toward the floor in the Greek manner of cursing the party named. 'And, if we believe the girl, they grabbed him in the club's parking lot. Which explains why the camera was out, so that there's no direct evidence linking the gorillas to a crime. Just her word.'

'The word of a hooker.'

Andreas didn't look at him. 'Yeah, the word of a hooker.'

'Wonder where they took him between the parking lot and the dumpster?'

Andreas shrugged. 'No idea. And unless we catch them,

doubt we ever will. All they needed was some private place to—' he didn't want to think about what they'd done to the boy— 'finish him.'

'Could have been anywhere.'

Andreas nodded. 'But I doubt it was some random place on the side of a road. This was too well planned. They knew exactly where they were going and what they were doing. Wherever it was, it was worked out ahead of time.'

'Right down to the specific dumpster and time to use it.'

Andreas nodded. 'For sure.'

'Yeah, but how could they be sure someone wouldn't walk out of the bar while they were in the middle of dumping the body?'

'The bar was closed.' Andreas shrugged.

'Yeah, but how could they be sure some customers weren't still hanging around hoping to get lucky with a late-night quickie out behind the dumpster?'

Andreas shook his head. 'Yianni, they'd already dumped the garbage, the place was shut down.'

'Bars always dump garbage while customers still are inside. They get everything ready to close and lock up the moment the last one leaves. Happens all the time. Especially with good payers you don't want to upset.'

Andreas picked up a pencil and began tapping its eraser end on his desk. 'If you're right, that means someone must have checked to see if there was anyone inside who might come out while they were dumping the body.'

'And since the owner didn't recognize the two gorillas—'

'Someone else did the checking.' Andreas nodded as he finished Kouros' sentence. 'It's a long shot, Yianni, but the only one we have. What time does the bar open?'

'Around seven.'

'Great. It's a date.' Andreas smiled.

Maggie stuck her head in the door. 'It's Lila Vardi on the phone for you.'

Andreas looked at his watch. It was almost noon. 'Okay, I'll take it.'

Kouros shot a look toward Maggie at the door. 'Uh, Maggie, let me speak to you for a moment. Outside.' He pushed up from his chair and was out the door in three quick steps, closing the door behind him.

Andreas smiled. Guess he thought I wanted privacy. The phone buzzed, signaling he should pick up the call. Maybe I do.

Lila's first words were, 'Did you receive my message?' Andreas replied that he had, but was tied up with work all morning. When he heard, 'Even too busy to return my call?' he knew where this was headed. Too many women had said those words to him before, though in a decidedly different context. And, as with the rest of them, she was right. He tried 'Sorry,' but that didn't work. It never did, nor did, 'You're right, I was wrong,' or the old standby, 'Honest, there is nothing more important to me than what you have to say, but can we talk about this at another time?'

So, he wasn't surprised when thirty minutes later he was sitting in her apartment doing penance.

'. . . and that's how I figured it out. They were banished and the boy was murdered because the family didn't listen!' She sounded as excited as a schoolgirl coming home with straight A's.

'That's a great theory but—'

125

'I know, I know, in ancient Athens they didn't banish the entire family and certainly would never kill a family member if the banished one didn't listen, but there were other forms of banishment for actual crimes, ones where the entire family was banished, even the bones of dead family members were dug-up and sent away and—'

Andreas put up his hand to stop her. 'No, that's not what I was going to say. I congratulate you for figuring it out, I really do, but that's not the direction this investigation is headed.'

She glared at him. 'I wondered why you went from being so aggressive to not caring enough even to call. Someone told you to stop.'

Andreas' temper flared, but he kept his tone in check. 'No, I'm just more interested in catching a killer than playing some rich folks' parlor game of cops and conspirators.'

She looked down at her hands. 'I guess I deserved that.'

He said nothing.

She looked back up at him. 'No quarter, huh?'

He still said nothing.

'Fine, you'll just have to settle for coffee.'

He wondered if he should say what he was thinking.

'Would you like a toast?'

'Mrs Vardi, I really must leave.'

'Please, I said call me Lila, and you can't leave now, it's just not proper to come to someone's home without even having a coffee.' She smiled.

He'd had enough. 'Mrs Vardi, I have work to do.' He knew he should keep his mouth shut and just leave.

'I insist you stay. At least for coffee.' Her tone was formal.

He stared straight at her. 'First you insulted me by suggesting

126

I'm part of some cover-up, and when that didn't get the reaction you wanted you lectured me on manners. Don't know how you were raised, but my parents would call that very bad manners.' His temper was showing, but he no longer cared. 'Come to think of it, you probably were raised differently. I guess more along the lines of ancient Athenian traditions, where courtesy was due just to equals, and the servant-class indulged only when absolutely necessary. Perhaps with some simple benevolent gesture, like a coffee and toast with the master.' He stood up. 'No need to show me out.'

She locked eyes with him. Slowly, she raised her right hand up toward his face. It was clenched in a fist. He expected her to flash an open palm, the Greek gesture for something a lot worse than 'asshole.' Instead, she held her fist in the air, brought the tips of her forefinger and thumb together, then slightly separated them.

'Don't you think you've overreacted just a teeny-tiny bit?' She flicked her fingers rapidly open and shut.

He watched her fingers for a moment, and dropped back down onto the couch across from her.

'Let's start over again,' she said. 'I apologize. I wasn't suggesting you're dishonest. I was more angry at the thought that someone had ordered you to stop doing what you knew in your heart was right.'

He swallowed. 'I'm sorry too. I get that way when I think people are talking down to me. It comes from a bad experience my father had.' He'd opened up the subject; he might as well finish it. 'A minister level member of government from the supposed "upper-class" set up my father – the trusting cop – to take the fall for bribes that went to the minister.'

127

'I can't believe he got away with it.'

Andreas shrugged. 'My father died soon after the accusations hit the newspapers. The story died with him.'

'Oh. Sorry.'

He appreciated that she didn't ask for more details, like the tire blowout a year later that sent that minister's car plunging off a mountain road and him to a nasty, officially ruled accidental death. 'Anyway, about this banishment theory, yes, I agree it's interesting.'

'So, why aren't you doing something about it?'

He smiled. 'Something tells me you're this way with everyone, and so I shouldn't take offense.'

She blushed. 'Yes, I guess I am.'

'That's okay, it's refreshing.' *Why did I say that?* 'But to answer your question, I simply don't have the time right now to pursue it. Perhaps later.'

She shook her head. 'You'll never have time. There always will be something else.'

He nodded. 'You might be right, but even if I had the time, I have no leads to follow. All the families with a member who might have been murdered won't talk to police and live outside of Greece. And even if I knew any of the other families that supposedly left after receiving a warning, they're also outside of Greece. I don't even know where the Kostopoulos family is. Besides, I have no jurisdiction over any of them and no way to get them to cooperate.'

She smiled. 'But I do.'

He looked surprised. 'What are you talking about?'

'The world is very small at the top. Everyone up there knows everyone else, or someone who does.'

Andreas stared at her.

'What are you thinking?' she asked.

'Why are you offering to help? That's what I'm thinking. Don't misunderstand me, I appreciate the offer, but why would you, someone with all this,' he waved his hands at things around the room, 'and part of the "small world at the top," want to get involved?'

She stared back. 'You mean why should I want to bring down my own kind?'

He paused. 'Yes.'

She nodded. 'Fair question. Because the kind you're talking about is not "my kind." Sure, I have,' she waved her hands, 'all this, but the fact I was born and raised rich and probably do things you think silly and spoiled doesn't mean I'm a bad person.' She smiled. 'Any more than your being a cop means you're corrupt.'

He laughed.

She stared at a photograph of her husband. 'My family was socially prominent well before the 1900s. My husband's family never was part of that crowd and, in fact, never achieved any sort of prominence, financial or otherwise, until the 1980s. According to *some* in Athenian society, like the ones I'm sure you're looking for, it was a mortal sin for us to have married. How *dare* I elevate one of *them* to *our* level.' She stared straight at Andreas. 'They do not represent my way of thinking, or my Athens.'

Andreas nodded. He understood why she'd kept his name. In her own way, Lila Vardi was one in-your-face tough cookie.

Lila waved a finger at him. 'If you promise not to give me any more of that "you're an elitist," she paused as if deciding on the right word, '*bullshit*, I'll try to find out what I can.'

He smiled. 'Nice language.'

'I wanted to use a word you'd understand.'

He laughed again. 'May I have that coffee now, please.' He studied her hands as she picked up a white porcelain pitcher and poured the coffee into a matching cup. 'But these . . . let's call them banished . . . people aren't part of your "top of the world crowd." So, what makes you think you can get them to cooperate, assuming you can find them?'

She handed him the coffee. 'Well, first of all, I don't consider myself part of that crowd, but I am friends with some, and know many others who are. The banished people, as you say, certainly are not part of that crowd, but from what I know of the families who did move away, they were very socially conscious.'

'Meaning?'

'They knew who the important people were in society and loved to be even a tangential part of that crowd.'

'Don't you think their experiences here soured any interest in further social climbing?'

'To some extent sure, but I tend to think not completely. From what I understand, these people kept their wealth, at least part of it, and had children to educate. They weren't likely to simply go off and hibernate in some cave until the day they all died.'

He took a sip of coffee. 'You might be right. One family is in Paris, and the two others we know of are in Switzerland. Plus, wherever the Kostopoulos family ends up.'

'A lot more than three families have left suddenly. I have

130

no way of knowing if any of them were banished but, if they were, I'd bet their children are in the finest, and most secure, private schools. Where some of their classmates, maybe even friends, are likely part of families—'

'At the top of the world.'

She smiled. 'Exactly.'

He took another sip of coffee, then put the cup down on the table between them. 'You know this could be dangerous?'

'It will come up as just fishing for idle gossip. Everyone does it all the time in Athens.'

'Now you're beginning to worry me. If people are being banished, the ones most likely behind it are from the very pond you're about to fish in. If they find out you're snooping around . . . do I have to tell you what's likely to happen?'

She drew in and let out a breath. 'No, you don't. I guess I'm being naïve.'

'What you're being is very helpful. I just don't want you doing something that might get you hurt.'

She blushed. Perhaps she sensed he wanted to add something more.

'Just promise me you won't do anything without clearing it with me first.'

'Do you promise to return my calls?'

'Promise.' He smiled.

She looked at her watch. 'Oh, my god, I was supposed to be at the museum fifteen minutes ago.'

'Come on, I'll give you a ride. Even use the siren and the lights.'

'As long as you don't make me sit in the back. I can

imagine the field day the paparazzi would have with that picture.'

Andreas imagined a headline: Socialite Held by Police.

On the way to the museum they talked about nothing important . . . to the case. She talked about her husband, how they met while she was at college in Boston, and how his death affected her. Andreas talked about how tough it was losing his father when he was eight, and growing up watching his mother endure all the rumors. Lila spoke of how difficult it was being a single woman in Athens 'even at my level.' He spoke about his sister's children, Nikos, Mihalis, and Anna, as if they were his kids and how his life made it unlikely he'd be having a family of his own anytime soon. She said her own job kept her 'safe from that sort of thing, too.'

He wished the ride had taken longer. He liked hearing her voice. He liked talking to her.

But for now, he was left to talking to Kouros about the four names he just wrote on the marker board on the wall behind his desk. Andreas stared at the names. 'Okay, Giorgio, you're the muscle, but what's your connection to the Kostopoulos family, and Athens society?'

'Maybe it's the drugs?' said Kouros.

'Yeah, there's certainly drugs in that crowd, and if you're looking to find someone to do a murder he's the one to talk to.' Andreas hesitated. 'But suppose, just suppose, that there really is a lot more going on here than an isolated murder. I don't see bringing a notorious drug dealer onboard as a confidant in something so big-time and serious unless you're willing to be blackmailed for the rest of your life. Whoever's running this is too smart to take such a risk.'

'Maybe there's a middleman,' Kouros pointed to Marios' name, 'and he's the link to Giorgio?'

'Or it's the one who forced Marios to talk to us. Marios certainly is connected to both worlds. Everyone likes the press. Especially a press that can be discreet.'

'For a price.'

Andreas nodded. 'Linardos. What are you doing up there on my board? You've got a big name, big power, big money, and a big likely hate for Kostopoulos. But you also have an impeccable reputation.' He fluttered his lips as he let out a breath.

'And then there's Anna,' said Kouros.

'I can't imagine she's anymore than what she seems, but why was she chosen? Who picked her out of all the possible—' he was about to say hookers '—choices available?'

'It's a strange mix.'

Andreas got up, walked around his desk, and stared out the window. 'If this really is something bigger, where's the money coming from? This kind of muscle doesn't come cheap. And who's the son-of-a-bitch tying everything together? The money, the muscle, the messages. He might not be at the top of the pyramid, but he's sure as hell making it all happen for whoever is.'

'Which of our four do you think it is?' Kouros pointed at the board.

Andreas turned from the window, walked back to the wall, and picked up a marker. Touching a spot in front of Giorgio's name he said, 'This one,' then drew a huge question mark embracing all four names. 'Someone who links all of them together. And I don't think we've found him yet.'

'Or her.'

'Yes, or her.' Andreas looked at his watch. 'Let's take a ride over to Linardos' office, just drop in unannounced.' Andreas smiled. 'Who knows, maybe he forgot to tell his secretary he's back in town.'

'And, if he is, maybe we can ask him to join us for a drink at the Ramrod.'

'At the what?' asked Andreas.

'That gay bar. I guess it gets its name from the long, stiff rod used to pack gunpowder, wads, and balls into the end of an old musket.'

Andreas stared at him. 'You really could use some sensitivity training.'

Kouros shrugged.

Great, thought Andreas. Three ramrods to deal with: a ramrod bar, a ramrod-minded cop, and a ramrod-stiff Athenian patrician. This was going to be some afternoon.

11

'Mr Linardos, there are two gentlemen here to see you, sir.'
It was his secretary calling through on the intercom.

'Do they have an appointment?'

'No, sir, and I told them you just arrived from London
and are very busy, but they said it's very important.'

'Who are they?'

'Chief inspector Kaldis and officer Kouros of GADA.'

It was a full thirty seconds before he answered. 'Okay,
I'll see them in five minutes.'

Andreas smiled at the woman. 'Thank you for being so
helpful.' She had little choice. Before she knew who they
were, she'd kept them waiting by her desk while she
finished some tirade with a restaurant over how it 'dared'
to deliver such a 'horrible lunch' to '*the* Sarantis Linardos.'
Andreas never would forget the look on her face when
they identified themselves. Kouros actually had to cough
to cover up a laugh.

Andreas guessed Linardos was using the five minutes to call his lawyers. But how could he explain to them why he was afraid even to find out what the police wanted? Besides, he always could cut off the interview at any time. There was nothing Andreas could do about that.

This guy's life was right out of one of Maggie's magazines. He was isolated from the day-to-day demands made of virtually everyone else on earth: valets to choose and lay out his clothes, cooks to prepare his meals, personal shoppers to obtain whatever product or service he desired, maids to launder and clean up after him, chauffeurs, private pilots, and sea-captains to whisk him door-to-door to anywhere he wanted, and assistants anxious to arrange it all. Andreas wondered if he had any idea of the efficient, ruthless nature of the oh-so-many predators lurking about in the real world. Or maybe he was one of them.

Andreas looked at his watch; four minutes had passed. He smiled at the secretary.

'Let me show you into Mr Linardos' office.' Obviously, she wanted nothing more to do with them.

Andreas always was amazed at how elegant an office could be. Then again, most cops were from the gypsy school of interior decorating: whatever worked and was portable was fine. From the paintings, sculptures, antique French furniture, inlaid woods, and Oriental carpets in this one, it looked nothing like a working office. More like a five-hundred-square-foot throne room for holding court.

When they entered the office, the king was not on his throne, at least not any they could see.

'Please, sit here.' The secretary pointed to a pair of matching, tapestry-covered chairs in front of an ornately carved, gold-trimmed desk. 'I'm sure Mr Linardos will be right with you.'

There was the sound of a flushing toilet. The secretary looked uncomfortable. 'That's okay, we'll wait for him here,' said Andreas facing the desk from the rear of the room.

The desk was in front of a bank of windows, with more windows running along the length of the wall to Andreas' right. Bookshelves lined the wall facing the desk. On the wall to Andreas' left, between the door through which they'd entered and another door on the same wall closer to the desk, were three paintings Andreas knew he should recognize. Conspicuously absent were photographs of the rich and famous. Then again, Linardos had no reason to impress a visitor with whom he knew. He knew everyone who mattered, and anyone coming here already knew that. The only photographs were of his family, and they stood in silver frames on a small table between his desk and the second door.

No one moved. They just waited for that second door to open. Two more minutes passed before it did.

'Sorry, gentlemen.' Sarantis Linardos nodded to his secretary who immediately turned and left, then he shook hands with both men, pointed for them to sit where his secretary had suggested, and went to sit across from them behind his desk.

'So, what can I do for you?' He was smiling and pleasant.

Andreas used his most official-sounding, courteous voice. 'Mr Linardos, I can't thank you enough for agreeing to see us unannounced. I apologize for such an intrusion, but we're hoping you might be able to help us with a rather delicate matter.'

'If I can, certainly.'

'Thank you.'

'I'm certain you're aware of the Kostopoulos murder.'

He nodded. 'Yes, I am. Terrible, terrible tragedy.'

'I know that you and the father were involved in business dispute—'

Linardos cut him off. 'Yes, we were.' He was still smiling.

'I was wondering if, in the course of your dealings, you heard of anyone who might harbor such anger toward him to do such a thing?'

'I'm sorry, "do such a thing?" I thought this was a gay-bashing murder or lovers' quarrel or something like that.'

'That's the delicate part, sir. It looks to have been a pre-meditated murder made to look like what you described.'

'That's horrible.' He blinked rapidly three times. 'How can you be sure?'

'Forensics.'

'But why would anyone do that sort of thing to an innocent child?'

'Don't know. That's why we're here. We were hoping you might have some idea who would. After all, the father was aggressive in his business tactics. I'm sure I don't have to tell you that.' Andreas paused, but Linardos said nothing. 'So, I was wondering if, possibly, in defending against what he was doing to you, you might have come across information on other victims.'

'Victims?' Linardos' voice almost cracked.

'Of Kostopoulos' business tactics. Someone so upset with what he'd done to them, or tried to do, that they might be willing to kill his child for revenge.'

His smile was gone. 'I'm sorry, but I'm afraid I cannot help you. Those are not types of people I would know.'

'No, I don't mean the ones who actually did the murder, I mean someone so angry with the father that he would resort to murder.' He wondered if he should say more. 'Perhaps, to send a message?'

Linardos paused. Andreas wasn't sure if it was to think or explode.

'No, sir, I'm afraid, I know of no such persons. I wish I could help but I can't. If you think my lawyers might have come across that sort of information, I'll be more than happy to arrange for you to speak with them.' Linardos stood up, a clear signal the audience was over.

'Thank you, sir, that would be very helpful.' Andreas and Kouros rose.

Linardos leaned across the desk to shake hands and say goodbye. He did not show them out. Andreas opened the door leading out of the office and allowed Kouros to pass through it first. Just as Andreas was closing it, he heard the bathroom door open. He doubted the problem was Linardos' prostate.

'He didn't even ask to see an ID!' Kouros almost was shouting. 'I mean, we could have been anyone.'

Andreas smiled. 'I guess he figured from the way we looked we couldn't be anything but cops.'

Kouros turned his head and stared at Andreas.

'Hey, Yianni, watch where you're driving.'

'You know he's hiding something.' He looked back at the road.

'Yeah, no doubt about it.' Andreas scratched the top of

139

his head with his right hand. 'I got more than I expected. I pushed him to where I expected to hear "Who do you think you're talking to?" but he let it all pass.'

'We spent more time listening to him piss than talk.'

Andreas grinned. 'That told us a lot more about him than anything he said. The guy was nervous.'

'A lot of people get nervous around us.'

Andreas shook his head. 'Yeah, but not Linardos. He knows our boss. He knows everyone's boss.'

'So, what's he hiding?'

'Don't know yet. But he's definitely involved somehow. I can't believe that if Marios knew about the banishment thing Greece's most influential newspaper owner wouldn't know about it, too, or at least have heard the rumor. And as far as not knowing anyone who might want to harm Kostopoulos . . .' Andreas waved his left hand in the air in little circles, 'that would make him just about the only person in Greece who couldn't name at least one.'

'Maybe he's behind the whole thing?'

'Anything is possible, but I'd think whoever is would handle it better. Be cool. After all, getting nervous in front of cops attracts attention, no matter what the reason, and I don't see the guys running this as nervous types. They've been at it too long and too successfully.'

Andreas drummed the fingers of his left hand on the dashboard. 'I think he's more worried about them than us. If they think he's turned on them, he knows they're capable of killing not just him, but his children. That could explain why he wouldn't point a finger at even a publicly declared enemy of Kostopoulos. He's afraid to be seen as cooperating with us one bit.'

'Can't blame him.'

Andreas looked at Kouros. 'What are you saying?'

'He has to protect his family.'

'From us?' Andreas' voice was rising. 'I'm not used to hearing that sort of don't-trust-the-government Greek bullshit from a cop.'

'Come on, Chief, if this is a big-time conspiracy, don't you think Linardos believes whatever he says to us will get back to the bad guys?'

Andreas' temper was rising. 'Yianni—'

Kouros cut him off but his tone was apologetic. 'Chief, you know I'm not saying we're like that, but how does he know to trust us? Virtually everyone in this country thinks everyone in government is corrupt. We know that's not true but, let's be honest, even we're careful about what information we let out of our unit. If he knows how dangerous these guys are, can you really blame him for wanting nothing to do with us?'

This was not a conversation that the chief of a police unit wanted to have with a subordinate, no matter how valid the point might be. 'Let's head on over to the bar.' Andreas said the words without emotion. He wondered if this was how Don Quixote might have felt had he ever accepted that Sancho Panza might be right about the windmill.

12

*

They arrived at the bar and parked up the street to wait for the place to open. Andreas wanted the undivided attention of the owner, unencumbered by the demands of a busy late-night crowd.

From outside, the place wasn't large as bars go; no more than twelve feet wide at most, with just two small windows, one on each side of a single glossy black door that opened directly onto the street. The windows were done in an opaque, black and silver handcuff motif, leaving no doubt to the casual observer just what sort of place this was; even though no one could tell from the outside what actually was going on within THE RAMROD. That name was announced in all white letters on both windows.

A man dressed in a business suit walked up to the door and went inside.

'Well, I guess it's open for business. Time to move.' Andreas opened his car door.

Kouros was quiet as they walked toward the bar. He hadn't spoken for quite a while.

When they got to the front door, Andreas put his hand on Kouros' arm to stop him. 'One thing, Yianni, I want you to keep whatever feelings you have about this sort of place in check. Do you understand?'

No answer.

'I said, "Do you understand?"'

Kouros exhaled. 'Yes, Chief.'

'Good, let's go in.'

Andreas went through the door first. There was no one inside, and it was not what he expected. A light-colored, well-worn wooden bar with a brass footrail ran for about twenty feet along the left wall. It stood in front of an even longer mirror reflecting three ascending rows of liquor bottles. Four faintly glowing casino-style lights in amber-colored glass hung equidistant over the bar. A dozen matching wooden stools lined the bar. The floor was dark, likely old marble, and there were no tables to be seen. This was where customers mingled. For sitting and other nonvertical activities they had to find someplace else.

At the back of the room were two doors. The one to the right was marked WC, the other unmarked, but if it led to the outside it should be marked with an exit sign. Just beyond the far end of the bar on the left was an open doorway leading to what looked to be a hallway. Andreas walked over and stared through the doorway. This place was bigger than it appeared from outside. There was a closed, unmarked door directly across from where he stood. The hallway ran for about thirty feet straight back to another door, this one marked EXIT. On the wall to the right was

143

another unmarked door. From its location Andreas guessed it led to the same place as the unmarked door in the back of the bar room. Separate entrances for patrons trying to hook up discreetly with each other, perhaps. As for what went on once inside those doors—

'Excuse me, can I help you?' It was the voice of a man coming through the unmarked doorway next to the toilet.

Andreas turned and smiled. 'I certainly hope so.'

Andreas could tell the man was checking them out. Only natural. Andreas was doing the same thing. Hard not to: the man's appearance demanded attention. He was about fifty years old, five-foot-ten, stocky, but not fat, with a gleaming, bald head and jet-black handlebar mustache. He wore a silver velveteen shirt, embroidered in a white floral pattern set off by pearl buttons. A thick silver German cross on an even thicker silver chain hung around his neck. His pants were black leather, his shoes black Pumas with silver laces. This was a man in his element, and certainly not the man in the business suit, wherever he might be at the moment.

'Are you the owner?' Andreas asked.

'Who's asking?' The guy knew how to be belligerent.

Andreas didn't answer, just pulled his ID out from beneath his shirt and showed it to him. Kouros did the same.

'Okay, yeah, this is my place. Name's Pericles. What can I do for you?' His tone hadn't changed. Maybe that's just the way he was.

'We're here about the body in the dumpster.'

'I already told the cops everything I know.'

'Well, we just have a few more questions. Mind if we sit down?' Andreas gestured toward the bar.

Pericles grunted, 'Go ahead.' Andreas hoped he might

be more comfortable talking to them across a bar, something, from the looks of the place, he'd been doing for
decades. The man walked behind the bar and stood in front
of them. 'Want something?'

'Just water would be fine, thanks,' said Andreas.

'And you?' He was looking at Kouros.

No answer.

He reached under the bar and handed Andreas a bottle
of water. 'A glass?'

'No, thanks, this is fine.'

He looked back at Kouros. 'You want a glass to share
your buddy's water?'

Again Kouros said nothing, but his facial expression
tightened. The man didn't seem to notice, or maybe just
didn't care.

'So, like I said, what can I do for you?'

'I was wondering if you noticed anything strange or out
of the ordinary that night.' No need to tell him which night.
The guy knew what this was about.

He smiled. 'Strange and out of the ordinary happen here
every night.'

Andreas laughed. 'Okay, but you know what I mean.'

'No, it was just a typical Saturday night. No rowdies, no
problems.'

'Any strangers?'

'Sure, it's the nature of the place.'

'What about when you were closing up? Anything
different? Anybody come in, look around, and leave?'

'That happens all the time, too. I don't even notice anymore,
except when they yell something. It's mostly kids who do that,
just before they run out. Usually on some dare that if they

hassle gays it proves their manhood. You know the type.' He looked at Kouros.

Andreas looked down at the bottle of water and drummed his fingers on the bar thinking, this guy's picked up on Kouros' vibe and is into busting his balls. Better get out of here. He's got nothing to tell us anyway. He turned to Kouros. 'Anything to add?'

Kouros was tight-lipped and gestured no.

Andreas stood up and pulled a card out of his pocket. 'Well, thanks for your time, sir, and if you think of anything, please give me a call.'

'No problem.' He stared at the card. 'Hey, you know, come to think of it, there was one guy. But he didn't just come in and leave. He sat here for about two hours.'

'Was that unusual?' asked Andreas.

'Not really, he just sat quietly on that stool,' he pointed to the one closest to the front door, 'sipping a Coke and not talking to anybody. Once in a while he'd make a phone call on his mobile.'

'Then why him?'

'Well, it was late and I wanted to close up, but I had two regulars at the bar and this guy.' He pointed again to the bar stool by the door. 'They wouldn't leave.'

'What about back there?' Andreas pointed to the unmarked door next to the one for the toilet.

Pericles hesitated. 'No one was in there. Besides,' he grinned, 'all we have to do to empty out that place is slowly turn up its lights. Anyway, my guy took out the garbage, mopped the floors, and I started turning out the lights in here. Finally, the two regulars got up to leave.'

Andreas interrupted him. 'What about the other guy?'

146

'That's the strange part. He hadn't talked to anyone all night, but when the two headed toward the back door he ran after them and dragged them back in from the hallway as if they were old friends, saying "Let's have another drink on me." I was pissed. I wanted to close, but he gave me a hundred euro tip, so I stayed open another half-hour. He seemed an okay guy. Interesting, too.'

'What did he talk about?'

'That's what made him interesting, he had a real knack for getting everyone to talk about themselves without giving away a thing about himself. I overheard everything they said. I had nothing left to do but listen, and all I heard were stories my regulars had repeated a hundred times before. But that guy made them think it was the very first time they told them, and that he genuinely was interested in every single word.'

'Sounds like a guy trying to get laid.' It was Kouros.

'My god, you can speak.' Pericles smiled. 'Yes, I suppose it does, but if you ask me, this wasn't a guy looking for that. At least not in here, anyway.'

'He was straight?' Andreas didn't sound surprised.

'In my professional opinion, yes.' He smiled.

'How can you be sure?'

'Ahh, he speaks a second time.' Pericles smiled at Kouros.

Andreas touched Kouros' elbow to remind him to keep his cool.

Pericles looked at Andreas. 'I have great *gaydar*. I can tell who is straight and—' he shifted his look to Kouros, 'who's in the closet.'

Kouros didn't budge. He just stared at Pericles, blew him a kiss and said, 'In your wettest, wildest dreams, old man.'

147

The two glared at each other.

'Cool it, both of you. Yianni, this is Pericles' place, show some respect, and Pericles, stay serious, this is a murder investigation.' The glaring didn't stop.

Andreas figured it was only a matter of seconds before World War III broke out.

'Yianni, wait in the car.' His voice was sharp.

Kouros looked at Andreas.

'I said, *wait in the car.*' It was in the unmistakable tone of an order.

Kouros gave a hard look at Pericles, slid off the stool, and left.

Andreas decided not to ask any more questions until things cooled down a bit. After a few minutes, Pericles began wiping the top of the bar.

'Ever see the guy any other time?'

'No.'

'Happen to get a name?'

He exhaled and put the rag under the bar. 'It was Niko or something, but I'm sure it wasn't real. Most don't use real ones in here.'

'Do you remember what he looked like?'

Pericles shut his eyes. 'He was about five and a half feet tall, slim. Dark hair, dark eyes, and light skin. He was in his thirties, I'd say, but tried to look younger. Don't we all.' He opened his eyes.

'What do you mean "tried to look younger"?'

'He wore jeans and a tee shirt like kids do, and his hair was long, like a college student's.'

'Anything else?'

Pericles shut his eyes for a few seconds and opened them.

148

'Yes. He had a beard. Well, not really a beard, I think it's called a chin strip.'

'A what?'

'One of those thin little things that run from here to here.' He pinched his fingers together just below the center of his lower lip and drew them down to the bottom of his chin. 'You might say it was a very gay-looking beard.' He smiled.

Andreas smiled back. 'Anything else?'

'No. As soon as he got a phone call he was out of here.'

'That's it?'

'That's it.'

'Thanks,' said Andreas.

Pericles smiled. 'I want to say thanks, too.' He put his right hand across the bar.

Andreas nodded, shook the man's hand, and left – to deal with Kouros.

The car was rocking from Andreas' anger. He was shouting, shaking his fists, and pounding on the dash. The bottom line: no matter how much Andreas liked him and respected his abilities, if Kouros couldn't control himself and keep his personal feelings in check, he couldn't work for Andreas. It made him too easy to manipulate. Andreas couldn't have made it clearer had he tattooed his words inside Kouros' eyelids, undoubtedly a far more pleasant experience than the one Kouros was enduring at the moment.

'This is your last chance! *Do you understand me?*'

Kouros' chin hadn't left his chest since Andreas slammed the car door and started in on him. 'Yes, sir.' It was said in about as meek a voice as Andreas could imagine coming from someone Kouros' size.

'Good, then let's never talk about this subject again.'

Andreas drew in a deep breath, exhaled and told Kouros to drive to headquarters.

Kouros didn't say a word. The silence was uncomfortable. Andreas tried breaking the tension by filling him in on what Pericles had said after Kouros left the bar.

'Chief.' His voice was tentative.

'Yes.'

'That guy at the bar, the one who, uhh, didn't belong.'

'Yes.' Andreas wondered where this was headed.

'Doesn't he sound familiar?'

'Not particularly.'

'At the coffee shop, where Anna worked, the guy at that back table who said he saw the two who killed the boy. You asked me before to speak to her about him, and I planned on doing that first thing tomorrow. The description of the guy in the bar sounds just like him.'

But for their recent conversation, Andreas would have kissed him. 'Damn it, Yianni, you're right!' He'd been so angry at Kouros, he'd missed it.

'Want to head over to that coffee shop and try to find him?'

Andreas shook his head no. 'Not yet. I want to find out who we're dealing with first.'

'I have the information from his ID and prints back in the office.'

'Good, because if he was in that bar . . .'

'He was the lookout.'

'Explains the phone calls and why he stopped those two from going out the back door. The gorillas must have been in the middle of dumping the body.'

'That last phone call had to be the all-clear, telling him to leave! I'll get someone to pull his phone records. Maybe we'll get lucky and come up with something.'

Andreas was happy to hear excitement back in Kouros' voice. He turned his head slightly toward him. 'Good thinking, Yianni.'

'Thanks, Chief.'

Andreas noticed a bit of a smile.

13

Andreas looked at his watch. It was after midnight and, from what they'd pieced together so far, the story of Demosthenes Mavrakis could have been written by Charles Dickens. At least the part about his early years.

He was an only child. His mother and her brother were the only children of a wealthy, old-line Greek ship-owning family. Demosthenes' father died when he was ten and his mother never remarried. Instead, when her own mother died a year later, Demosthenes and his mother moved in with her father to one of Athens' wealthy northern suburbs. That was when Demosthenes began attending Athens Academy and adopted his grandfather's surname, Mavrakis. His school records showed that he flourished there, but never finished. He withdrew two years before graduation. No reason was given for his sudden departure, and he finished his studies in Athens public schools.

Based on his subsequent extraordinary performance on

Greece's nationwide university entrance examinations, Demosthenes was admitted to his first choice of universities. That was almost a dozen years ago, and still he'd not graduated, but certainly not because of any lack of brainpower. His IQ tested in the genius range.

'The guy doesn't want to be part of the real world' was Kouros' take on him.

'Don't be so quick to lump him in with all those student-types you can't stand who don't want to graduate. It clouds your judgment.' *Prejudices can do that* was a phrase Andreas thought to add, but didn't.

'But why hang out with kids if you're not insecure about facing the real world?'

'Like I said, let's not dismiss him so easily as "just like everyone else." It gives him an edge.'

Kouros paused. 'He could be using it for cover, blend into that life and never be noticed.'

Andreas nodded. 'So, let's assume his reason is unique and there's a lot more to this guy than we know. Like, why his sudden withdrawal from Athens Academy and the move with his mother away from his grandfather's mansion in the suburbs to a rented apartment in central Athens?'

'Lack of money?'

'Sounds like it. But why?'

Kouros shuffled through some papers on his lap. He picked one up. 'It says here that the grandfather died in January of the same year he left school and moved out with his mother.'

'Yeah, but her father was loaded, and there had to be an inheritance.'

Kouros shrugged.

Andreas drummed his fingers on his desk. He looked at his watch. 'Do you think it's too late to call her?'

'Who?'

'Lila Vardi.'

'Why call her?'

'She's the only one I know who might know something.' He picked up the phone and called.

'Hello.' The voice was stiff and formal.

'Lila?'

'Yes.' Her voice sounded a bit more tentative.

'Hi, it's Andreas Kaldis. I hope it's not too late to call.'

Her voice came alive. 'No, not at all. Like I said, feel free to call any time. What's up?'

'Uh, I'm here in my office with officer Kouros and we thought there's something you might be able to help us with.'

'Is it about our case?'

He avoided answering her question directly. 'I have no reason to think so yet, just checking out every possible lead. We're hoping you can tell us about the Mavrakis family. Let me put you on the speaker.'

'Which one?' Her voice came across on the loudspeaker even perkier than before.

'Thanassis. We were wondering what happened to his family after he died.'

She laughed. 'Boy, you sure come up with the juicy ones. You're talking mega-society gossip here.'

'But there was nothing in the papers.'

'Wouldn't be, most truly private *high society* family scandals don't get press coverage unless a family member, or lawyer, wants to make it public.' She'd mocked the words she emphasized.

154

'So, what happened?'

'I don't know the family that well. Thanassis and his wife were friends of my parents, and their children were much older than I. In fact, I think the daughter had a son a few years younger than I am.'

Andreas looked at Kouros. 'What's his name?'

'Demosthenes, I think. Don't know him, not sure I ever met him. Terrible what happened to him and his mother, though.'

Andreas didn't say anything, just waited for her to continue.

'Thanassis was a very successful ship owner, and like many old timers hid what he owned behind a lot of companies. Probably didn't even have his name on the stock certificates showing who ultimately owned the assets. That was common among that crowd.'

'So no one could find someone to blame if anything went wrong?' asked Andreas.

'Or find to pay taxes. Especially inheritance taxes.' She paused. 'I'm trying to remember the gossip. It was so long ago. I know the son worked with his father and that the daughter and her mother did not get along. The brother was the mother's favorite. When the mother died, I believe the father asked his daughter and her son to move in with him. They lived near my grandmother's summer home in Ekali. That's when the brother had a huge fight with his father, accused him of betraying his mother's memory. The father gave the son an ultimatum. Accept his responsibilities to his sister or leave the business.

'The brother became a new man overnight. Doted on his sister and her son, even started calling him his "other son."

155

I think he had two younger ones of his own. Everything seemed perfect. But the moment the father died, the brother reverted to his old self. As I heard the story, after Thanassis threatened to put him out of the business, his son spent virtually every waking moment showing his father what a wonderful son and brother he was. Ultimately, he convinced his father that the best way to save taxes for the family was to transfer ownership of everything to him on his promise to "take care of his sister and nephew."'

'I think I see what's coming. And the father believed him?'

'Well, the father didn't have all his wits about him in his final years, but that sort of arrangement was something many Greek families with hidden assets followed. What happened here was the exception to the rule. Regrettably, not that rare an exception but, still, an exception.

'The difference here was the intensity of the brother's ruthlessness, as if he didn't care what anyone else in the world thought of him. This wasn't only about stealing his sister's inheritance, he wanted her to suffer and did all he could to inflict punishment. Literally forced her and her son out of their father's home just as fast as his lawyers could get it done.'

'Why didn't she go to court?' It was Kouros.

'I don't know. Some said it was her nature. She was a very timid, depressed woman. Death or betrayal had cost her everyone in her life who mattered.'

'Except for her son.' It was Andreas.

'Yes, I don't know what happened to him.'

'What happened to her?'

'Friends of her parents were appalled at the brother's

156

behavior. They paid her rent on a small apartment in some modest building in downtown Athens and found her a job in a government ministry. She worked there until the tragedy to her brother.'

'What tragedy?' Andreas' voice seemed to jump an octave.

'The explosion that blinded him. I thought you knew, and that's why you were calling.'

'No, I didn't.'

'But I don't think it's related. He comes from a very old Greek family. Not like the others. Though he did move away. But you can't blame him.'

Andreas didn't want to show his impatience. 'Uh, Lila, could you tell us what you're talking about?'

She giggled. 'Whoops, it's late and I had a glass of wine. Sorry for rambling. No, as a matter of fact the story had a happy ending.'

Andreas rolled his right hand at the phone in a hurry-up-already gesture. Kouros smiled.

'I guess it shows how a near-death experience can show you the value of family. After the brother was released from the hospital he moved to Geneva and brought his sister to live with him. As far as I know, they're still living in Switzerland.'

'When did all this happen?'

'A bit after the capture of the 17 November terrorists.'

'Huh?' It was Kouros again.

'Don't you remember when a group claiming to carry on the "revolutionary mission of our 17 November brothers" bombed a small, private family church in Ekali? No one could stop talking about it. I still cringe when I think about it. It was his family's church. It was his mother's name day,

157

and he went alone into the church behind his father's house, actually his house then, to light a candle and say a prayer. The bomb went off when he leaned over and kissed the icon next to his mother's wall crypt. It was a miracle he was only blinded.

'I can't image what sort of human could commit such an outrageous sacrilege.'

Andreas looked at Kouros. 'Someone very bitter and angry.'

'But still, in a church, planting a bomb behind an icon?'

Andreas rubbed his eyes. 'Ever hear anything more about the family?'

'No, that's all I remember. Did it help?'

'Sure did. I'm really sorry I bothered you so late, but you helped a lot. Thanks.' His voice sounded burdened with other thoughts.

'Andreas—' she paused.

'What?'

'Oh, nothing. Just call me tomorrow. If you have the chance.'

Kouros gestured if he should leave. Andreas gestured no.

'Absolutely. Promise. Good night. And thanks again, Lila.'

'Good night. Kisses. And good night, officer Kouros.'

'Good night, Mrs Vardi.' The line went dead. 'Sounds like a nice lady.' Kouros actually sounded sincere.

'She is; very nice.' He let out a deep breath. 'What the hell do we have going on here? I feel like mice being run through a labyrinth.'

'At least there's no Minotaur chasing us.'

'But wait, there's still time.' Andreas fluttered his lips. 'That guy was blinded intentionally. If they'd wanted to kill him in such a confined space it would have been easy. The tricky part was just blinding him. These people knew what they were doing.'

'You think it's the same ones who killed the Kostopoulos kid?'

'Not sure, but I'd bet my left nut Demosthenes was behind that church bombing. Revenge on a betraying surrogate father for all the harm done to his mother. Can't say I don't see why the kid might have wanted to kill the bastard, if the uncle's anything like he sounds, but this is . . . is—'

'Sick?'

Andreas nodded. 'Yeah, as in sicko-genius. Instead of just killing his uncle and watching all that money pass on to his cousins, our guy figured out a way to torture the man for life and still get him to take care of the sister he despised.'

'Think he's behind the whole thing?'

'Seems too young to me for that, but who knows. One thing's for sure, he has the right connections and is our only link to them, whoever *they* are. I want 24/7 surveillance on this guy ASAP. But nothing that might let him know we're on to him. He's too smart and runs with too dangerous a crowd.'

'I'll get it up and running first thing tomorrow.'

'And be careful, I don't want him recognizing you from that coffee shop, even though he was studying me, not you.'

'Don't worry. I'll get Maggie to lend me her invisibility cloak, the one she uses to find out everything going on in this building.'

Andreas leaned forward and pointed a finger at Kouros. 'You know, that would explain a lot.'

Kouros smiled and stretched. 'Looks like we finally have something to grab onto, Chief.'

Andreas leaned back in his chair and yawned. 'Yeah, let's just hope it's not that Minotaur's balls.'

His routine was simple: he had none. He lived by that rule. Never could tell where he'd be. Certainly never when he said, unless he was ordered and then always early. How early depended on what he felt the situation required. Routine to him was a weakness, the Achilles' heel of the strong. The only time he was precisely where he was supposed to be was when the habits of a target required split-second timing, and that exception proved his rule: targets died because of their routines.

Demon was a very angry young man those first few years at university. Bitter at the world in general and at his uncle in particular, he didn't realize just how easily one could be manipulated: ponderous thoughts subtly argued out to logical extremes by gifted talkers, patiently reinforcing each point with references to classic literature, ancient history, and modern events were exactly what young, rebellious minds found important when trying to validate their new independence from family and home. That was what made them so vulnerable to those seeking to focus their outrage at the world in general on 'Greece's class system' in particular, and channel undirected anger into violence. For most, their seductions required not much more than that, carried out amid drinks, drugs, supportive friends, and willing lovers applauding their every argument and thesis.

160

But for Demon it was different. Yes, he enjoyed and participated in the Exarchia revolutionary scene, but his reach was far greater than the bounds of any single group or philosophy. He was a creature born of the unique us-against-the-Man rapprochement achieved in that community among the ideologues of revolution and the city's unholy criminal underbelly, and he moved effortlessly through those different worlds.

In that environment, it felt natural for him to talk among his like-minded comrades of how revenge might be had on his capitalist pig of an uncle; but never did he expect things to go so far that his words would become actions. He wasn't even there when it happened; but they told him how his description of the house, the church, and his uncle's routine gave them what they needed, and his words the inspiration to come together to make his plan work. He threw up for days, agonizing over how he'd possibly become part of this, made it all happen. Then he was told his moment was here: there was a message only he could deliver. To his uncle, in person, and at once.

In a heavily guarded hospital room, in the presence of his aunt and cousins, a dutiful, concerned nephew calmly whispered into his uncle's ear, 'Take care of my mother or your children and wife are next,' then kissed him on the forehead and smiled. Not a word was returned, not a gesture made; only a nurse moved, looking for what triggered the heart monitor alarm.

Demon stayed in the room for another five minutes; quietly off to the side feeling no stress, no anxiety, no fear, no remorse. He was perfectly calm and at peace with himself as his eyes drifted over each member of the family, his family, that he'd just threatened to cripple or kill. None of this bothered him at all, and at that moment he realized he had a great gift: he was free of conscience. Never again did he question any method that might achieve a goal. Unless it failed.

But in the years that followed, failure rarely occurred when Demon was involved. No one seemed able to resist his charms and, for the same reason, he served the Exarchia shadow world as its primary liaison to the other world. Not to the planet at large, just to those parts of it necessary for achieving one group or another's seemingly far-fetched goal. He possessed an uncanny instinct for finding the perfect flattery, bribe, appeasement, or threat required, and an equivalently eerie facility at maneuvering past the maniacal egos, outrageous demands, and polar opposite political views of those he sought to persuade.

His skills grew almost as much as his view of himself, and he hungered for greater influence than the banner-painters, bomb-tossers, and political outsiders he served could ever hope to achieve. When a chance meeting with old-line acquaintances of his grandfather led to musings on the fate of their country, Demon saw an opportunity to broker violence for those with real power and jumped at it. But that was years ago, and he believed by now he'd more than proven his value to them – certainly with his Kostopoulos masterpiece.

Demon never wanted to play a visible part in the Kostopoulos operation, but there was no one else he could trust to do it. He'd brokered the arrangements privately, as he always did, among disparate groups who would never work together openly. Only he knew each one's role, and

162

he dared not chance involving another in coordinating the operation. That was how he ended up in the Ramrod.

'Demon, please, be careful how you hold him.' He was holding the baby out in front of him, under his arms, as if looking for a place to dump him.

He'd thought of tidying up the only loose end linking him to the murder, but the death of the mother of his child might bring him more attention than letting her live. Besides, Anna had no idea he was the one who set her up, even if the cops should find her. Still . . .

He smiled. 'Sorry, I'm not used to babies.'

Anna was glaring at him. 'So, why this surprise visit at three in the morning?'

Why is she so angry? 'I felt badly, I haven't seen you or the baby in days.'

She took the baby from him. 'Weeks, and he has a name. If you remember it.'

Ahh, that explains it, he thought, no attention. 'I'm sorry. It's all my fault.' He leaned over to kiss her.

She pulled back. 'I know.'

'Can you use some money?'

She hesitated.

His face didn't show what he was thinking: same old Anna, when money comes up, bye-bye principles. He found that reassuring. It's what kept him interested, her predictability.

'Sure, we could use it.' The fire was gone from her voice.

'Good, put the baby down and come over here. I've missed you.' He put two hundred euros on the table and gestured toward the couch.

Anna hugged the baby as she carried him to the crib, then

163

kissed him, carefully tucked him in, and walked over to the couch. Her face was blank. He touched her breasts, then squeezed them and slid his hand under her nightgown. 'That's my girl.' She just stood there, letting him do as he chose. He pushed her down onto the couch, and within a minute was on her, burying his face in her neck. 'That's my girl, that's my girl.'

He never saw the tears running down her cheek. He was too busy proving to himself how much she still needed him.

14

Lila couldn't sleep. She had an idea how to find where the Kostopoulos family might be. It came to her several hours ago. She kept peeking at her bedside clock hoping for the hands to move to where she'd feel comfortable making her call.

'Hello, Christos?'

'Huh, who's this?' The voice was not a happy one.

'It's Lila. Lila Vardi.' She tried sounding perky.

'Lila . . . it's five fucking o'clock in the morning.' No apology was offered for the language.

'Sorry, hon, but it's really important.'

'Great. You'll have to wait another minute. Since you woke me up, now I have to pee.'

He was the frankest man she'd ever known, perhaps because he was gay. She stared at the drapes beyond the foot of her bed. They masked the steel gates that rolled down every night, over virtually every window, in virtually every home, in every wealthy Athenian neighborhood.

'So, what's so important, kukla?' He called all of his customers by the Greek word for doll.

She started off saying what everyone in Athens but Christos knew wasn't true. 'I know you can keep a secret—'

'Of course, absolutely.' His tone suggested indignation that the statement even had to be made.

'Hon, I have a slight indiscretion to share with you.' She knew that would have him holding his breath for a juicy bit of gossip. 'I don't know who else to turn to for help.' She held back from sobbing. No need to gild the lily.

'Kukla, kukla, your Christos is always here for you. How can I help?'

She let out a long breath. 'Someone asked if I could arrange for them to borrow a rare piece from the museum. They were putting on a very private, ambassador-level dinner party and wanted to use it as the centerpiece. I knew the museum would never agree, but they promised a huge contribution and, well . . . being who they were . . . it wasn't as if they were going to run off with it.'

'Of course not.' His voice sounded thoroughly supportive.

'So, I made some *private* arrangements.' Her emphasis was meant to mean she took the piece without asking permission.

'Yes, yes, I understand. Of course you did. What choice did you have?'

Now she sobbed. 'I don't know what to do. I'm in such trouble.'

'What happened? What can I do to help my kukla?'

She sniffled. 'Ahh, such a mess, and I really can't even

166

blame the people. They have so much going on in their lives right now that I'm sure they've completely forgotten about returning it.'

'Of course, I'm sure. Such people would never betray your trust.'

She could tell he was dying to hear the name.

'I know, but I can't find them.'

'What?'

'I can't find them, they're gone. They moved away in the middle of the night!'

'I can't believe it. But there must be someone you can speak to. A maid or a lawyer, someone?'

'Yes, of course, but how can I ever tell any of them of my . . . uhh . . . indiscretion. *How?*'

He paused. 'I see. But how can I help you find them?'

'Darling, you underestimate yourself. You are a legend.'

His voice showed that he agreed. 'Well, thank you, kukla, but still, how can I help?'

'You are the finest hair colorist in Athens. There is no woman alive who would leave her colorist without at least trying to get her formula to take with her.'

'Many have tried.'

She guessed he was smirking. 'So, I'm praying that the wife is your client, or you know who she sees and somehow can find her for me.'

Silence.

'Christos, is something wrong?'

'No, not at all. I'm just waiting for you to tell me her name.'

She laughed. 'You can tell how distraught I am. How silly, it's Ginny Kostopoulos.'

'Ouch.'

'Why "ouch"?'

'She's not my client. And she uses the biggest dickhead in Athens. We don't speak.'

Lila knew whom he meant. Christos was right; he'd never cooperate with her either. 'Oh.' Her voice was down.

'But don't worry, kukla. All's not lost.'

'What do you mean?'

'There's still Zanni. He's been my client for years.'

She perked back up again. 'No wonder he looks so good.'

'I wouldn't go that far, except of course for his hair.' They both laughed.

'Do you think you could find out where his family is?' She held her breath.

'I don't know. He doesn't seem in the mood to talk about his family and I certainly didn't ask.'

'You spoke to him? I mean since his son's death?'

'Kukla, I'm his hairstylist. Of course we talk; I call him all the time. He says I'm the only one who still makes him laugh.'

Lila laughed. 'I can imagine.'

'Where are they?' She held her breath.

'I don't know where *they* are, just Zanni. He's alone in his summerhouse. On Mykonos. I'll be more than happy to call him about the piece.'

She was about to say *what piece* when she realized her cover story had come home to roost. 'Oh, god, no. Please don't do that. There's already enough trouble in that family. I really should speak just to Ginny. I don't think her husband knows of our arrangement and I don't want to start another problem. If you could find out where she is that would be the best way to approach it.' She spoke so quickly she wasn't sure he heard it all.

He didn't seem surprised. 'Okay, if that's how you want it. As long as I was able to help my kukla. Anything else, or may I go back to sleep now?' He sounded amused, not angry.

As flighty as he might seem to some, Christos was as skilled as any high-society psychiatrist at feigning concern over the most trivial, insignificant matters that his clients chose to elevate to levels of earth-shattering import. She hoped he'd lump this call into that category and not regard it as worthy of repeating.

They said good night, she hung up the phone, and fell back on her pillow. She turned and looked at the clock. Too early to call Andreas. She stared at the ceiling. What the hell is Zanni Kostopoulos doing alone in Mykonos?

Andreas found a pile of new gossip magazines on his desk. The cover note read, 'Just in case you're interested. Maggie.' She'd earmarked specific pages and each had one thing in common: a photograph of Lila Vardi. From what he could tell, there wasn't a significant social event in Athens she missed. He stared at the photographs.

The phone rang. 'Andreas Kaldis here.'

'Hi, it's Lila.'

'My god, I was just looking at your photograph in *Hello*.' He wished he hadn't said that.

'*Flock*, touch red.'

He hadn't heard that superstitious playground phrase since childhood. 'Yes, *flock*.' He smiled and touched a red miniature soccer ball on his desk.

'I hoped you were in early. I've been up for hours dying to tell you what I found out.'

Andreas looked through the magazines at pictures of Lila as she explained how she came up with the idea of calling Christos, and started through them again when she began her word-for-word recounting of their conversation. There she was, sounding like an excited schoolgirl, once more. But she didn't look much like a schoolgirl in the photographs. He stopped looking and interrupted her when she got to the part about where to find Zanni Kostopoulos.

'Where is he?'

'Mykonos.'

'Mykonos?' He couldn't believe it. It made no sense. Why flee Athens to Mykonos? There's no place to hide there. Well, almost none. 'Why would he go there?'

'I've been asking myself the same question all night. As soon as the press gets a whiff of his presence, it will be all over the news. Guaranteed. Christos says he's hiding out in his house, but if Christos knows . . . Kostopoulos can't be planning on keeping it quiet for very long.'

Andreas drummed his fingers on the table. 'Maybe he intends to bury the boy there?'

'Without the mother? I don't think so.' She paused. 'Maybe he had a fight with his wife and wants to be alone?'

He shook his head at the phone. 'If we're right about the banishment thing, Greece is the last place in the world for him to come to nurse his wounds. A lot can happen if the wrong people learn where he is.'

'What are you saying?'

'People could get killed. I think I'll fly over and pay him a visit. Surprise him. Nothing to lose.'

170

'Good, when do we leave?'

His heart skipped a beat. 'What do you mean "we"?'

'Andreas, I'm the reason you know where he is, and if he does agree to see you and starts talking about Athens society, you won't know who he's talking about. But I will. Consider me your interpreter.'

That wasn't a very good argument. But . . . he looked at one of her photographs. 'How's tomorrow? We can fly over in the morning and be back by late afternoon.'

'Perfect, just let me know when and where to meet you.'

'Will do. And Lila . . . thanks. You did some great work.'

The schoolgirl excitement was back. 'I'm so happy you feel that way!'

'But do me a favor. Please don't try chasing down any other families until after we speak to Kostopoulos.' He didn't want her curiosity getting back to the bad guys.

'Okay. This time I'll listen to you. Bye. Can't wait until tomorrow.'

He couldn't either.

The old man sat at his desk toying with an elaborate silver letter opener. Every so often his gold and lapis cufflinks clicked against the desktop. Kostopoulos was soft, a poseur who'd lost his stomach for real blood and fought now only through lawyers and publicists. At least that's what the old man had thought, what they'd all relied upon. Where did he find this Spartan heart?

No matter, the killing was necessary. Kostopoulos had brought it on himself. He chose to ignore the judgment of banishment and continued to wage war upon a family that had turned to the old man for help. Such arrogance left no choice; it was a harsh lesson, but one the old man had been certain must be taught. To Kostopoulos and any others who might think to question their authority.

Yet he persists. He must be taught a new lesson, a more meaningful one. Let us hope that this time Thanassis Mavrakis' grandson is a better teacher.

Demon was back in his favorite apartment. Only he knew it was his favorite. He had three. It was part of his no-routine routine. He'd slept a bit on Anna's couch, left just after sun-up, and passed a few more hours sleeping here. He never set an alarm. Didn't have to, he had an internal clock that did it for him. That's what made the chimes by his ear so unexpected. It was a cell phone, one of a half-dozen he kept around. But this one he only answered, never dialed, and rarely did it ring.

'Hello?' He was lying on his side.

'Do you know who this is?'

'Yes.' Demon's voice was flat, as usual.

'We have a problem.'

Demon sat up. 'What is it?'

'The message wasn't delivered.'

'I don't understand.'

'The message wasn't delivered.'

Now he understood. 'Is there a new address?'

'Mykonos.'

'Where on Mykonos?'

'I'm sure you'll find it.' The phone went dead.

Son of a bitch. The bastard didn't listen. He's still here. Something must be done, and quickly. The attitude of the caller didn't bother him. He had a right to be pissed. There was a lot at stake. For everyone.

'The bastard didn't listen.' This time he said it aloud. He stood up and walked over to the window. The view wasn't great, just one apartment building window after another, but he liked the way the sunlight hit his room in the morning.

He knew the Kostopoulos house on Mykonos – he knew everything about him. At least he thought he did. Now, to make that bastard regret the day he was born.

Kouros knocked on the door to Andreas' office a millisecond before opening it. 'Chief, we found Demosthenes!'

Andreas could tell no response was required to keep him talking.

'I got an address for him off his ID. It was a long shot, but we got into an apartment across the street and did a laser-microphone set-up to pick up sounds off his windows.'

'No phone tap?'

'We never found any phone records for him. He must use prepaid phone cards, and there was no time to get into the apartment to set something up. Besides, going in might tip him off, and you said don't take the chance.'

Andreas nodded.

'We didn't get set up until seven. Someone matching Demosthenes' description paid a three a.m. visit on Anna last night, but there was no way of telling if he'd left. Too many back doors to her building for our guys to cover. So, we weren't sure if he was in his place or not. There was dead silence for about a half-hour, then a phone rang and our boys picked it up. We've got photos of him standing at the window.'

173

'Anything good?'

'Not sure, but he was upset. He left the apartment five minutes after the call, and we followed him as far as the university. Couldn't go in.' Andreas expected Kouros to start in on the law that forbid police from entering the campus, but he didn't. 'On the way over he tore apart a cell phone, dropping pieces of it into garbage cans and sewer grates.'

Kouros placed a plastic bag full of phone parts on Andreas' desk. 'Maybe we can nail him for littering?'

Andreas smiled.

'Even found the SIM card. At the bottom of a sewer.'

'Get all of it to the lab. We might get lucky. Any idea what the call was about?'

'Only heard his side of it.' Kouros pulled a mini-recorder out of his pocket. 'Here's what we picked up.' He pressed the play button and the sound of chimes was followed by a series of phrases, separated by pauses, spoken in the same voice:

'Hello?'

'Yes.'

'What is it?'

'I don't understand.'

'Is there a new address?'

'Where on Mykonos?'

Long pause.

'The bastard didn't listen.'

Andreas shut his eyes and leaned back in his chair. He took two deep breaths, and opened his eyes. 'Yianni, we have a very big problem. He's talking about Kostopoulos.'

'Zanni Kostopoulos? On Mykonos?'

Andreas nodded and leaned forward. 'I only learned

174

where he was a little after six this morning and this guy hears about it an hour and a half later.' He ran his hands through his hair.

'Do you think they found out from the same source?'

Andreas shut his eyes and opened them again. 'I sure as hell hope not. But I can't say for sure.' He patted, then smacked, the top of his desk. 'I'm off to Mykonos.'

'When?'

'The next flight out.'

'I'll go with you.'

'No, stay here and keep an eye on Demosthenes. My guess is he's gearing up to go after Kostopoulos again, and it's going to happen soon. Do whatever it takes, but find out what he's up to—' Andreas pointed his index finger directly between Kouros' eyes, 'but tell *no one* what's going on. Understand?'

'Maggie?'

'Trust *no one*.' Andreas drew in and let out another breath. 'Except for Maggie. And tell her to have our phones swept for bugs, just in case.'

Kouros left the office and Andreas looked at his watch. There was less than an hour until the next plane to Mykonos. He thought to call Lila and tell her his plans had changed but decided against it. The coincidence was too great: she tells him and the next thing he knows someone tells Demosthenes. He couldn't believe she was one of the bad guys but, whatever the explanation, he came out in the same place: trust no one.

Demon had phone calls and arrangements to make. He used, but never trusted, cell phones, certainly not for this

175

sort of thing with these contacts. He always found some anonymous university landline to use but still worried about the other end of the conversation. These people only used cell phones.

They assured him not to worry, that in their country everything was under control. They even bragged they were responsible for their country's first cell phone system, a network that didn't accomplish much more than better co-ordinate their smuggling operations. He wasn't sure whether to believe their bragging, but he needed them, and so far, at least, no problems. Still, at his insistence, every two weeks he received a letter addressed to one of his many post office boxes listing new cell phone numbers for him to call.

He waited for someone to pick up.

'Hello.'

The language wasn't Greek but Demon spoke it. 'We need to make some additional arrangements.'

'What sort of arrangements?'

'Our recent message was ignored.'

'I see.'

'We must meet at once.'

'Where?'

'Location three at one-seventeen.' The man would know that meant five this afternoon in the Omonia metro station, a place where Greek was the minority tongue.

'Okay.'

He ended the call. These people were very good at what they did. But they needed direction. He'd make sure that this time that bastard Kostopoulos got the message – *loud and clear*.

15

It was Andreas' first trip to Mykonos since his promotion to Athens and he told no one there he was coming. No reason to. He wanted anonymity, not dinner invitations. Still, sooner or later he'd be recognized; he just hoped it wasn't the moment he got on the plane. Mykonos was one and one half times the size of Manhattan, but when it came to gossip it was a tiny village – of ten thousand citizens and fifty thousand seasonal visitors.

He boarded before the other passengers and sat in the first row, his face pressed against the window. His plan was to get to Kostopoulos right away, then head down to the old harbor for a few hours amidst the bouillabaisse of fishermen, farmers, politicians, and miscellaneous other spicy sorts who made up Mykonos' version of café society. Andreas hoped acting like he was on holiday might keep the island's wagging tongues from speculating too seriously on the reason for his visit, but he knew there were better odds at keeping the sun from setting.

Maybe I should have brought Lila along, he thought. It would be a better cover story. Yeah, for every gossip magazine in Greece: 'Cop and Socialite on Hide-Away Holiday in Mykonos.' He decided not to think about her; it only aggravated him. He'd focus on her involvement in all this back in Athens.

The flight took about twenty-five minutes and Andreas' eyes never moved from the window. He'd spent a lot of time in his life doing far worse things than watching uncluttered Cycladic Aegean islands roll out beneath him with their round-edge mountains of beige-to-brown faintly accented by slashed, hillside dirt roads and random dots of white and green. And all of this surrounded by coves and harbors of emerald to sapphire waters set against an endless lapis-colored sea. Ships of every type and size sat pasted on the blue, with bold wakes feigning movement carefully painted behind each one. He watched as the blue began picking up sharper accents of white. That meant wind-driven waves and Mykonos, the Island of the Winds, was close-by. The plane turned to approach from slightly southeast of the harbor town of Mykonos, passing by the neighboring holy island of Delos and coming in over Paradise Beach. There was a lot of history down there. Memories too.

Andreas was first off the plane, but instead of heading toward the door marked ARRIVALS he walked toward a half-dozen large and larger private jets parked by the far end of the terminal. Amazing how much money so many people had. Andreas always shook his head when that thought ran through his mind. He wondered why he did that.

He saw what he was looking for: the most popular tourist vehicle on Mykonos, a white Suzuki Jimny parked between the jets and the terminal. The key was in it, and a map. God bless Maggie; he always could depend on her. He picked up his cell phone and dialed.

'Hello.'

'Hi, Maggie, it's me.'

'Everything okay?'

'Perfect. Thanks to you. So, what's the story?'

'The bad news is they found nothing useful on the SIM card—'

'Not surprised, but what about Kostopoulos' house?'

'That's the good news. It's on the northern tip of the east side of Panormos Bay. In the Cape Mavros area.'

'That's in the middle of nowhere! How the hell do I find it?'

'Well, you start by taking a left at the first road you come to in Ano Mera, go past the monastery . . .' Ano Mera was the island's other town, located at its rural center, and Andreas could tell Maggie was reading from something that involved a lot of 'at the big tree,' 'by the light green – not dark green – gate,' 'just past the horses,' and the like. Mykonos had few street signs and virtually no working maps, for that matter. The locals didn't need them, and most visitors considered it 'quaint,' at best, but it did offer a bit of privacy from curiosity seekers randomly searching out celebrities.

'How did you get those directions?'

'I called up Zanni and said "My chief would like to drop by for a chat this afternoon."'

He didn't respond, just started the engine.

'It's illegal to drive while talking on a cell phone.'

'I'm not talking, just listening.'

'Cute. What better things do you have to do for the next twenty minutes than listen to me?'

'Maggie . . .'

'Okay, okay. I called a real estate agency on Mykonos, said my boss wanted to rent a villa for a month like his friend's, Zanni Kostopoulos. They said there was nothing like his in the Cape Mavros area but they had a few others elsewhere they could show me. I said my boss wanted to be as close to the Kostopoulos' home as possible and, after some serious pleading and assurances that I wasn't trying to cut them out of their commission, they gave me "general directions" to one.

'Then I called a liquor store in Ano Mera that delivered, told the man who answered I was trying to find the Kostopoulos home but "got lost by the light green gate," and wondered if by chance he might know what turns I should take to get there. He asked why I didn't call the house. I said, "I tried but no one answered." He asked what number I called and I gave him what I knew was the right one. That's when he gave me directions.'

Andreas was shaking his head. 'Amazing what people will tell perfect strangers.'

'It's the voice. You have to sound like you need to be rescued. Men don't understand. They're all so macho. It gives us power.'

He could tell she was grinning. He didn't mind; she'd made him smile too. 'I think I'll hang up now. Thanks again.'

Andreas looked at his watch. If Maggie was right about the time, only fifteen more minutes until show time.

Should be one hell of a performance. He just wished he knew his lines.

The road was narrow, partly dirt, and filled with blind turns and steep drops, but it was the main and only road to Cape Mavros, at the very end of the area locals called Mordergo. The view across the bay to Panormos and Aghios Sostis beaches was spectacular, but Andreas was too busy concentrating on what to expect at the house to notice. He even missed the turnoff 'by the horses,' but caught a glimpse of three in his rearview mirror and backed up to make the turn. This road ran straight up a mountain, was all dirt, narrower and much steeper than the other. So steep, in fact, that at the crest of the hill he was tempted to get out to make sure the road actually ran down the other side, but he took his chances and kept going.

There it was, huge and obvious. More a compound than a house, it sat on a bluff by the bottom of the hill about a hundred yards above a small, private cove. Andreas could make out three buildings, all of natural stone, and two enormous swimming pools. The entire property was circled by two concentric stonewalls, five yards apart. The space between them was filled with green – trees, bushes, and flowers. It looked so inviting, but he'd bet anyone who made it uninvited over the first wasn't likely to make it over the second.

A military-style Zodiac drifted in the cove. Two men sitting on the gunnels scrambled to the wheel when his car came over the top of the hill. He heard the engines start up. They weren't the only ones moving. Two men leaning against a black Hummer halfway down the road reached inside for what Andreas guessed were weapons. A flash of reflected light off the roof of the main building meant he must be in some sharpshooter's sights. Another black Hummer and two more men stood down by the main gate. And those were the ones he could see. Kostopoulos must have an army with him.

Andreas put the Jimny in first gear and let the gearbox brake the SUV down the hill. The whining of the transmission made the car sound out of control. The two men by the first Hummer scrambled to put it between them and the roaring Jimny. Andreas' improvised David and Goliath confrontation of off-road vehicles ended when one of the men put a grenade launcher across the hood of the Hummer and started aiming at the Jimny. Andreas had the answer to his question, *what am I dealing with here?* He slammed on the brakes and the Jimny slid to a stop about thirty feet from the Hummer. Andreas turned off the engine, opened the door and stepped out.

'Halt, don't move.' The words were Greek, the accent wasn't.

'And a good morning to you, too, sir.' But Andreas didn't move.

'What business do you have here?' The same man spoke.

'I've come to see Mr Kostopoulos.'

'He's not here.' The talker seemed the one in charge.

Andreas smiled. 'Didn't your mother ever tell you it's not nice to lie to a policeman?' He pointed to the ID around his neck.

The man waved for Andreas to walk to him. He was about forty, but four inches taller and had thirty pounds more muscle than Andreas. He looked at the ID, keeping an eye on Andreas' hands as he did. 'He's still not here.'

Andreas guessed the accent was from somewhere in the Balkans. 'I admire Mr Kostopoulos' concern for his garden.'

'What are you talking about?'

Andreas gestured toward the house and the boat. 'All this artillery and professional military talent, just to keep the goats away.'

The man didn't speak, just stared at Andreas' eyes.

Andreas smiled. 'Serbia, right?'

'Why don't you leave now, sir?'

The man didn't lose his cool, a real professional. 'Can't do that, major. I'm guessing that was your rank.'

'You'll have to leave, sir. This is private property.'

It wasn't, but this wasn't the place or the guy with which to debate the legal niceties.

Andreas shook his head. 'I'm afraid I'll have to call this in. I think you need more help here. Those goats look pretty mean. They might attack any minute.' He pointed to three scraggly-looking brown-to-black ones nibbling at thyme and savory a hundred yards up the hill. 'Nope, it's my duty to see you have all the help you need. What do you think, are a dozen local cops and a port police boat in that cove sufficient? Trouble is, I'll probably have to use some of them for crowd control, what with all the attention that much police presence out here is going to generate. Hope the media cooperate. Hate how nosey they can get, don't you?'

The major gestured to the other man to keep an eye on Andreas, went over to the Hummer and began speaking on a walkie-talkie, in Serbian.

A minute later he was back. 'Drive down to the gate. The man there will speak to you.'

'Thank you.'

The major nodded. Andreas liked his style.

The man waiting for him was the same one who'd met him at the door of the Kostopoulos home in Athens. The two men from the second Hummer stood behind him.

'My name is Alex. Good afternoon, Chief Kaldis.'

'Good afternoon.'

'I'm afraid Mr Kostopoulos will not see you. He received your message but said to tell you, "Do as you must."' The tone was courteous, but final.

Andreas looked behind Alex until he saw what he wanted. 'Excuse me for a moment.' As he brushed past him, the two men blocked his way. Andreas smiled and pointed to a potted plant ten feet behind them. 'Just going over there.'

The two looked at Alex. He shrugged okay.

'Thanks.' Andreas walked over, picked up the plant, held it up to eye level, and dropped it to the stone floor. The pot shattered into pieces. None of the men moved; they stared at Andreas as if he were crazy. Andreas took out his felt-tip pen, picked up a piece of broken pottery, wrote three words, and handed it back to Alex. 'Give this to him. I'll wait for a reply.'

Three minutes later Alex was back. 'Mr Kostopoulos will see you now.'

It was a beautiful day, and magnificent terraces surrounded the house, but a maid showed Andreas into what he assumed was an office. Every window was closed and covered by heavy drapes; the only light came from electric bulbs, and faint ones at that. Kostopoulos was sitting in an overstuffed paisley-patterned chair, but the light was too dim to make out any color. He pointed for Andreas to sit on one next to his.

'How did you find out?' The voice was flat and cold. It had none of the charm from their last meeting.

'Does it matter?'

'Are you one of them?'

Andreas was surprised at the question, but then realized it was an obvious one. He shook his head and said, 'No.'

Zanni shrugged. 'As you said, "Does it matter?"' He put the piece of pottery from Andreas on the table between them. Andreas hadn't noticed he'd been holding it. 'Ginny, Alexandra, Georgia. Why did you write the names of my wife and daughters?'

'Sorry, but it was the only way to get your attention. And yes, before you ask, their lives are in danger. Yours too.'

He nodded. 'I'm sure. That's why I have very professional help.'

'I noticed. What about your wife and children?'

He let out a breath. 'My wife took the children out of Greece to where she says no one ever will be able to find them. Won't even tell me where she is. Keeps moving around. All I can do is see that they have the same sort of protection I have, and I've done that.'

'Do you think she can keep hiding like that?'

He looked down at his hands. 'It's not what I think that matters.'

'Why haven't you left?'

'I don't know, maybe it's ego. Certainly anger.' He pulled himself out of his chair, walked over to drapes covering a window, and drew them open. Light filled the room. 'Those cowardly bastards killed my son and I'm not going to let them get away with it. Period. End of story.'

He was angry. 'All this bullshit about protecting Greece from the "wrong kind of people" is just that. Bullshit. It's all about one thing, money. Fuck their talk of principles. These altruistic revolutionary bastards want me to give them everything I've built for thirty cents on the dollar.'

Finally, a motive Andreas could understand, and one that explained what held muscle like Giorgio's interest: big money.

Zanni stared out the window. 'I received a piece of pottery with my family name written on it, together with some press clippings and a message telling me to read what happened to other families who didn't leave Greece within ten days. Then I got a call from someone offering to buy all of my assets in Greece. I told him to fuck himself. Every day he called, I wouldn't take the call and he'd leave a message asking if I'd reconsidered his offer. After the tenth day his calls stopped. Then my son . . .' His voice trailed off and the room was silent except for the sound of wind at the window. 'The day after . . . his death . . . the same person called. I took it this time and again he asked if I'd reconsidered. I told him I had, and we've been negotiating ever since.'

'Negotiating?' Andreas was surprised.

'Until I find them. Then they'll get paid. All of them.' His voice had a bitter edge that left no doubt what he had in mind.

Andreas thought to say something like, *don't take the law into your own hands*, but knew it would sound stupid. Instead

186

he said, 'Do me a favor, if you find them let me know. I don't want to waste my time chasing dead bodies.'

Zanni smiled. 'Are you taping this?'

'Yeah, right.' Andreas got up and walked over to him. 'Listen Mr Kostopoulos, I'd probably be doing the same thing if I were in your shoes, but don't underestimate these people. Think about your family.'

'You sound like one of them.' His voice wasn't angry.

'Maybe I do, but not for their reasons. They know you're here, and with their resources—'

'How do they know I'm here? I came here in a small boat, and at night.' Now Zanni sounded surprised.

'Mr Kostopoulos, you're on Mykonos. It's a small island. What did you expect?' No need to tell him more. 'And I'm sure they'll find your wife and kids, too, no matter where they are.'

Zanni shook his head. 'You don't know my wife.'

Andreas wasn't sure what that meant, but it was clear that part of the conversation was going nowhere. 'Any idea of who's involved?'

He paused. 'Not yet, but I expect to soon. I have people working on it.'

Great, thought Andreas, more people running around asking questions. It's turning into a regular three-ring circus of an investigation. Can't wait for the clowns to join in. Probably already have. 'Any chance of telling me what you have so far?'

Zanni just smiled.

'What about the one you're negotiating with?'

'Uses a voice scrambler, and we can't track him. We've tried.'

Andreas nodded. 'Just be careful. Like I said, they know you're here, and I'm certain they'll go after your family.'

Zanni nodded but Andreas doubted he'd said anything to change the man's mind. A few minutes later Andreas was on his way back to town, but he made a point of exchanging goodbye nods with the major. Andreas wanted to stay on that guy's good side.

16

The underground Omonia metro station came into being as part of Greece's show of pride at the 2004 Olympic Games. Omonia's orange-wall underground station for the old electrikos train still operated, but the new metro connected Omonia to the rest of Athens in a way that it hadn't for years, except in the memories of old-timers. Omonia once was Athens' central square and remained the home of thriving, vibrant, daytime markets and well-known hotels, but now it was referred to as Immigrant Square, and most Greeks shied away from the area. Still, the metro made commuting much easier for the mix of peoples who now lived there or had business there.

Demon walked to the station. It was only a few blocks from the university, and he wanted time to think. He had a plan; it just required a bit of ingenuity and he'd supply that. He'd leave the muscle to the guy he was meeting. He bought a ticket at the kiosk in the square by the entrance and followed the rush hour crowd into the station and down onto the platform. It was five minutes to five. His contact should be here any minute. Demon walked to the far end, leaned against a pillar, and waited.

'What's so important?' It was a voice behind him. Demon didn't turn around, just turned his head so that he was looking at the pillar as he spoke.

'He's still in the country.'

'So?'

Demon didn't like the tone, but kept his own in check. 'He was supposed to leave. That was the point of the message.'

'The point of the message was to get him to pay.'

Demon felt his anger rising, but kept it out of his voice. 'Yes, but also to get him to leave.'

'That's not our concern.'

'Of course it is. My people, the ones who select the ones whose assets you get to purchase, don't want him here. You profit when they're happy. And they're not happy.'

The man's tone didn't change. 'We do all the dirty work. That's why we get to buy the assets. If they don't like the arrangements, tell them to find someone else to do their persuading.'

'Is that the message you want me to pass on? Do you really want to start a war with these people?' The man didn't know who they were, just that they were among the most powerful in Greece.

The man hesitated before answering. 'Tell them we're not going to do anything to him now. He's negotiating with us.' The man sounded like he was talking through clenched teeth.

190

Demon's face tightened but his voice didn't show it. 'He must be taught a lesson. Now.'

'We're talking about a lot of money here and a lot of complicated asset transfers. Do I have to remind you why we never killed the one who had to sign the papers? Once he's dead it's in the hands of Greek probate courts, and we get *nothing*. We're not going to blow a once-in-a-lifetime payday because your . . .' he paused, obviously grasping for a noncurse word, '*people* are pissed that this guy's showing some balls. Tell your *people* we'll take care of him in good time. But not now.'

Demon knew this was going nowhere. But he couldn't let the Old Man down. There was too much at stake for him. He must give the Old Man what he wanted; Kostopoulos out of Greece. He needed to find other muscle. That was a very dangerous risk to take. He'd been working with this mob for years; since its early drug-dealing days in Exarchia. If they ever found out he'd gone behind their back . . . He walked away from the pillar without saying another word. It wouldn't have mattered if he had; the other man already had left.

Andreas' drive back to the old harbor covered five miles and five thousand years. The granite-strewn mountainside above the Kostopoulos house probably looked much the same to whatever gods once played there; nothing but nature on that slope. Aside from the Hummer, of course. On the other side, back down along the way he came, were signs of the presence of humanity: stone walls and huts of an agrarian past out of antiquity; a magnificent, seventh-century fortified conical hill, the Palaiokastro, built by invaders trying to protect themselves from a similar fate; the graceful, eighteenth-century Palaiokastro convent nestled on a hillside above Panormos Bay; and the outskirts of the once quaint farming village of Ano Mera, where a two-lane paved road connected to modern Mykonos and all its cruise ships, hotels, mega-million-euro private villas, and legendary nightlife.

But all Andreas wanted was coffee in the old port. When he reached the entrance to the town harbor, a rookie cop sitting next to a guardhouse put up his hand to stop the Jimny. During tourist season, only taxis and authorized vehicles were allowed into town. Unless, of course, you were local or had a good story. Andreas showed his ID and the rookie jumped up and waved him on with a salute. Andreas had planned on making a big entrance, but that was a little much.

He drove along a stone-slab road beside a tiny beach at the northern edge of the crescent-shaped harbor into the taxi square and parked next to a port police SUV. He didn't walk ten steps before locals started yelling, 'Andreas, Andreas.'

For over an hour he bounced from taverna to taverna hearing stories and complaints covering everything from the plight of fishing, undeserved parking tickets, and age-old property disputes to the predicted end of the world as we knew it, caused, of course, by the political party in power. Andreas just kept nodding agreement, expressing concern, and offering regrets that he no longer was in a position to help.

Almost everyone asked why he was there. He said he missed the island and decided to come over for the day.

He wasn't sure they believed him, but everyone said they understood how getting out of Athens to Mykonos, even for a day, made perfect sense.

He kept refusing offers of ouzo, beer, and all sorts of other booze, claiming he needed a clear head if his office called, but his resistance was fading. There was a certain rhythm to this place that did that to you. He was contemplating an ouzo when a hand touched his shoulder and he heard a familiar voice. 'Hi honey, I'm home.'

It was Lila.

The look on Andreas' face fell somewhere between shock and horror.

'Aren't you going to introduce me to your friends?' Lila smiled and, with her hand still on Andreas' shoulder, nodded to the six other men at the table.

He said nothing but several of the men asked her to join them. One got up and took a chair from the next table while the others scrambled to make room for her to sit.

'No thanks, we've got to go.' It was Andreas speaking.

Two men asked, 'What's the hurry?' The others didn't say a word, just exchanged grins and tried sneaking knowing nods and smiles to Andreas. He quickly stood and offered to pay, but didn't insist when they refused. After a fast thank-you, he pushed her out from under the taverna's awning onto the harbor front road in what anyone watching would think a cutesy gesture. Lila probably knew better.

They walked south along the harbor, the sea to their right. He smiled and waved to a mix of people calling out his name, but his voice was angry. 'What the hell are you doing here?'

'Put your arm around me so they get the right idea.' She seemed to be having fun with this.

'Sure, honey.' He reached behind her and gave a long, visible squeeze to her ass. She jumped. 'What do you think you're doing?' Now the anger was hers.

'Just making sure they get the right idea.' He smiled, leaned over, and kissed her on the cheek. Then put his arm around her waist, gripped like a vise, and dragged more than directed her forward. 'Like I said, what are you doing here?'

She practically had to skip to keep up. 'We had a deal, remember?' There was a different anger in her voice.

He mumbled something Lila couldn't hear.

'What?'

'I don't want to talk about this here.' He turned their bodies toward an opening between two jewelry shops. It was one of many twisting paths that opened onto the harbor from the maze known as the old town of Mykonos. Most lanes weren't much wider than six feet, many narrower. Each was paved with island-quarried flagstones outlined in white and ran between two-story, all-white buildings accented by bright blue, green, or red doors, banisters, and window frames.

At a sandwich shop about thirty yards from the harbor, Andreas made an abrupt right onto a smaller path. He still didn't let go. A few turns later the path opened up into a tree-filled square lined on the east by four small churches snuggled together in a row. He stopped, dropped his arm from her waist and pointed to a low wall flanking three steps leading up to the first church. 'Sit there.'

She was wearing a scoop-neck white peasant-style blouse over straight-leg designer jeans, and dark brown Tod's – the shoes with little bumps for soles and heels. Her hair was in a tight bun, and large Chanel sunglasses covered her eyes.

She wore only a hint of makeup, and a dark-blue Longchamp tote bag probably held whatever she thought she might need for the day. Andreas wondered if she considered this her I-can-blend-in look.

Lila sat on the wall as if waiting for him to join her. Instead, Andreas stood a few feet in front of her, staring up at the church. Then he looked at her and told her what he was thinking.

'You're the only person in the world I can trust.' He kissed her.

Anna didn't respond.

'I'd do anything for you and the baby, you know that.'

She didn't answer. Demon didn't care. He'd come to her place for a reason and didn't have time to fuck her. She'd just have to stay moody.

'I need a telephone number for that old friend of yours, the one from Sardinia.'

She flinched. 'Efisio?'

'Do you have it?'

'Why?'

Demon touched her cheek and gently stroked two fingers back and forth along her jaw line. 'Don't worry, my love, it's not about you.'

Efisio was her ex-boyfriend and the first to pimp her out. They'd met in her home country. He fled there to escape the Italian police. A year later she fled to Greece to escape his beatings. In an intimate, misguided moment of after-sex trust Anna confided her story to Demon, and he became the second. He didn't beat her. He had more insidious ways of controlling her.

She shook her head. 'I can't. If he ever finds out where I am . . .' her eyes moved toward the baby's crib, 'where we are . . .'

Demon's fingers kept moving along her face. 'He'll never find out. But I must find him. It is very important. Please, help me.'

She shook her head and said, 'No.'

'Please, I don't want to have to go to Sardinia.'

This time he felt her flinch. 'He's not there, he can't go back.'

'Yes, yes, I know but he has family there, and they must know how to reach him.'

He felt a twitching begin in her cheek.

'What is the name of his village?'

'I don't remember.'

He kept stroking. 'That place in the mountains. In north central Sardinia.'

She said nothing and turned her eyes away from him.

'Ah, yes, Mamoiada.'

She jerked away from his hand.

'My love, please, I don't want to have to go to that village. You know how dangerous those people are. You're the one who told me. They'll start asking why I want to find him, how I know him—'

She locked her eyes on his. 'You miserable bastard.'

'I'm not trying to harm you. But you're leaving me no choice than to bring up your name. Otherwise, they might kill me. But, if you find him for me he'll never hear your name. There will be no reason to tell him.'

She stared at the floor.

'If I wanted to harm you, do you really think I'd need

to call your old boyfriend?' He touched her cheek. 'Besides, you know I'd never harm you. You are my love.'

When she looked at him there were tears in her eyes. 'Please, don't make me do this.'

Demon said nothing, just kept stroking her cheek. The tears now touched his fingers.

'I don't have a number for him.' Her lip was quivering. 'I'll have to find someone who does.'

'That's my girl. But please, try to find it before tomorrow morning. My plane for Italy leaves at noon. I don't want to go if you can get me the number.' He kissed her on the forehead and left.

Demon never heard the tearful string of curses, in several languages, that followed his departure. But Kouros did.

'I can't trust you.' Andreas didn't move.

Lila didn't say a word.

He waited for her to speak but all she did was stare. Or at least he thought she was staring. He took a step forward and lifted her sunglasses onto her forehead. He wished he hadn't, her eyes were filled with tears.

'What's wrong?'

She shook her head, and reached into her bag. 'Nothing.' Out came a handkerchief. She patted at her eyes. 'Absolutely nothing.'

Andreas knew he was losing ground fast. This was not the sort of response he expected. His immediate instinct was to console her, be her rescuing knight. Perhaps she knew that too. He better be careful. There was too much at stake, and too many intrigues.

He wanted to sit next to her but didn't move. 'Let me know when you want to talk.'

'When *I* want to talk? Perhaps I'm missing something here, Chief Kaldis, but you're the one who should be doing the talking. Or are you expecting me to try to convince you to trust me?' She jumped up, grabbed her bag, caught her sunglasses as they fell off her forehead and pointed them at Andreas. '*Fuck you!*' And stormed-off down the narrowest of the four paths out of the square.

Andreas let out a breath and walked over to a foot-high white-concrete wall encircling a large eucalyptus tree at the edge of the square. He lit a cigarette and put his right foot on the top of the wall. He stared down the path she'd taken and looked at his watch. Three minutes had passed since she left.

'So, are you going to come out, or stay in there all night?'

He heard a muffled word that he was pretty sure was 'bastard.'

'Lila, you took one of the only dead end paths in town. Consider it a sign. Come out and let's talk.'

Another minute passed. He first saw the feet. She'd been sitting on the steps of a house about fifteen feet down the path. The rest of her body swung out into the lane and marched straight at him.

She swung her bag into his belly. 'Carry this,' and continued on out of the square down a path to the left.

Andreas followed, carrying the bag. He couldn't help but smile.

The path connected to others leading to Little Venice, perhaps the most popular part of the old town. It was a good choice. More tourists than locals came there. Not likely to run across paparazzi there, either. She stopped at the doorway to a bar with a rainbow painted on the door frame. 'This seems nice.'

He looked in. It looked like an English pub. Two young-looking men, one blond and one dark, were behind the bar talking to a large woman on the other side. 'It is. It's a piano bar. But once the music starts, it gets busy fast and attracts a lot of locals. Athenian society types too. I have a better idea.'

He led her around the corner and up a flight of stairs to the veranda of a bar overlooking the sea, the windmills, and sunset. Many thought it the most romantic view in Mykonos. That wasn't his reason for coming there. He came because it was filled with tourists. He chose a table in the easternmost corner of the place; that way everyone would be looking away from them at the sunset.

'Are you ready yet to tell me why you're here?' He was looking at her eyes; her sunglasses were off.

She looked back. 'I kept calling and leaving messages at your office. I wanted to know our plans for coming here. You never called back, and when I called your secretary, all she said was you were unavailable and she wasn't sure when you'd be free to return my call. I left two more messages on your phone. One, that I'd been captured by terrorists who threatened to cut off my toes if you didn't call back immediately, and another, that I'd meet you at the usual place and please wear black leather.

'You never check your messages, do you?' Anger was in her eyes.

Andreas grumbled something unintelligible.

'I figured you decided to go to Mykonos without me, or

were too busy to be bothered talking to me. Either way, my decision was easy. I caught the Sea Jet from Rafina and, *voilà*, I'm here. If you'd called back, I'd say, "Surprise, I'm here, where are you?" and if you didn't, big deal. I'd spend a day or two on Mykonos. I was sure I'd find someone on this island who wouldn't mind my company.' The anger now was in her voice.

He shrugged. 'What do you want me to say? There are too many coincidences involving you.'

She started to get up. He thought she was going to walk out again. Instead, she sat back down, shut her eyes for a few seconds, and opened them. 'You mean bumping into you in the harbor. I just got off the Sea Jet. Check the schedule.'

'That's one.'

'Okay, what exactly are you talking about?'

'I can't tell you.'

She patted the table with her right hand. She nodded. 'Can't tell me.' She nodded again, drew in and let out a breath. 'Andreas, you owe me. I expect you to tell me why you don't trust me.' Her voice was calm.

He swallowed. 'Okay. One example. Within an hour after you told me that Kostopoulos was on Mykonos, someone told the bad guys the same thing.'

He could tell she was struggling to restrain herself. 'And you think I told them?'

His face tightened. 'That's possible. Though I want to think it's more likely you mentioned it innocently to someone, and that's how it got back to them.'

'I see. I'm a dumb, gossiping bimbo who doesn't realize what she's saying?'

'I didn't say that.'

'Or does just the fact that I'm a woman mean the same thing to you big, strong, all-knowing, macho Greek men?'

Andreas decided not to answer.

Lila reached over and patted Andreas' arm; it wasn't an affectionate gesture – more like an enough-of-your-crap one. 'Andreas, you have a lot of serious "trust issues,"' she flashed quotation marks with her fingers, 'but that's not my problem. I'm not your shrink . . . or your girlfriend.' She paused. 'What upsets me is that you're judging my character based on your hang-ups. I'm trying to help, no more no less. You came to me. *Remember?* And I didn't want to help. *Remember?* Unless you think I'm a magnificent actress playing out a part in this conspiracy, you have absolutely no reason to lump me in among the "not to be trusted."' Lila flashed her fingers on each of her final four words, dropped her hands to her lap, and stared out to sea.

Andreas looked at the ceiling, then back at her. 'So, how did they find out?'

'How should I know? You're the cop.'

He drummed his fingers on the table.

She started talking. 'There are a dozen possible ways. A hundred. I found out by speaking to his hairdresser. Who knows what Christos might have said to someone after our phone call? He chit-chats with practically everyone who is anyone in Athens. But forget about him, what was Kostopoulos doing on Mykonos? Hiding in some cave?'

Andreas paused. 'No, not in a cave. You know he was in his home.'

'Brilliant. Last place anyone would think to look for him. At home. And I bet he's kept a low profile, nothing to attract attention from anyone happening to pass by his place.'

Andreas thought of the Hummers and the major. 'But it's not a place where people just happen by. You don't even see his house until you're on his property.'

'Even from the sea, by a fisherman?'

Andreas shrugged.

'What about gardeners, delivery men?'

Andreas shrugged again.

'And his household staff? I can't imagine him without at least a half-dozen. And all of them talk about their employers. It's part of their DNA. Finding good help these days is virtually impossible, finding help that won't talk *is* impossible. There's a pecking order among domestic help just as competitive and hierarchical as their employers' high-society networks. Maids and cooks trying to impress each other brag as much as Athens' most aggressive social climbers, but instead of exchanging boasts over wealth, it's all in the confidences they have to share about their bosses.

'All it took was for one maid from his house to mention to a domestic working elsewhere that her boss, the famous Zanni Kostopoulos, was on the island, and every domestic would know. And sooner or later they'd all find some way to pass the gossip on to their employers. Just to let their bosses know how plugged-in they are to what's going on in everyone else's home. And how much they should be appreciated for their discretion in safeguarding their own employers' secrets.

'Do I have to tell you how many old-line Greek families have homes and staff here on Mykonos? Any one of them could have been the source of the tip to your "bad guys."' More finger quotes.

'And another thing—'

202

Andreas put up his hand to stop her. 'No need to say more. You've convinced me. I'm sorry.'

She let out a breath. 'But I have so much more to say.'

'I bet.' He smiled.

She smiled.

They ordered a bottle of wine and watched the sunset in silence. Both looked to need the break.

17

Kouros and two cops from his GADA unit followed Demon to the Omonia metro station. They lost him in the crowd on the platform but found him at the far end, next to a pillar. Kouros didn't realize what Demon was doing until he saw an angry look on the face of the guy standing behind him. They'd been talking. Thirty seconds later Demon was standing alone by the pillar and the guy was heading toward a train about to leave the platform.

'Stay with Demosthenes,' Kouros told the two cops and scrambled for the train. Luckily the guy was in the next car and couldn't see Kouros struggling with the closing doors.

Two metro trains and about an hour later, Kouros and the guy were at Athens' Venizelos International Airport. The guy walked past the ticket counter to the boarding pass checkpoint line for domestic and EU departures. Kouros stayed back, watching. After the security guard let the guy through, Kouros hustled to the head of the line and showed his badge to the guard, but the guard wouldn't let him pass. Kouros got the attention of a supervisor when he threatened to use the guard's laminated ID badge to slice off his nuts. By the time the supervisor realized what was going on, and let Kouros through, the guy was gone.

Kouros was about to return to the checkpoint and begin performing the promised surgery when he saw the guy looking at cell phones in a shop across from a coffee bar kiosk. Kouros sat at the bar with his back to him. He kept an eye on the guy by watching his reflection in shop windows on the other side of the kiosk.

Ten minutes passed before the guy left the store. He was headed toward the departure gates. That meant metal detectors. Kouros wasn't about to risk letting another numbnuts security guard start some commotion over all the forbidden pieces of metal he carried. He stopped two soldiers detailed to airport protection, showed his ID, and they let him into the departure gate area through a private access door.

Kouros stood by a window watching the reflections of passengers clearing security. The guy came through without a problem. He paused to look at a monitor, checked his boarding pass, walked to the gate next to where Kouros was standing, and sat down.

Kouros waited. A few minutes later the guy started talking on a cell phone. That's when Kouros walked past him and glanced up at the monitor with flight information on that gate. The flight was to a city about as far north as you could go in Greece. That figured. By staying in Greece and not flying directly to a non-EU country he avoided the more rigorous security screenings for international flights. From northern Greece he could get over the border undetected in any number of ways. No doubt this guy was from the Balkans.

Kouros bought a bottle of water from a kiosk directly across from where the guy was sitting. With one hand he took a sip and with the other reached for his cell phone, perhaps the most common gesture in Greece, and held it up to his ear. Then he turned sideways to the guy and took a few photos. It was a YouTuber technique mastered by many cops.

Kouros found an open seat at the next gate among a crowd waiting for a delayed flight to Rhodes. He sent the photos to Maggie by MMS, along with the flight information and specific, bold face instructions: HAVE UNKNOWN SUBJECT FOLLOWED MOMENT PLANE LANDS. DO NOT INTERCEPT. MUST BE PREPARED TO CROSS BORDER. CONSIDER EXTREMELY DANGEROUS.

Kouros hung around until the guy boarded a bus taking him from the gate to the plane. Then he checked his missed calls. He hadn't taken one since jumping on the train in Omonia. There were three from the cops following Demon.

He stood up and walked toward the exit, dialing as he did. 'Angelo, what's up?'

'Where are you?'

'At the airport.'

'We have something you'll want to hear. The guy went straight from the metro to that girl's apartment. Damn good idea you had putting surveillance on her place. How'd you know about her?'

That was not a question Kouros was about to answer.

It was bad enough he set it up without telling Andreas. He just hoped there was nothing on the tape he'd regret. 'Angelo, just play the tape.'

'Okay, here's where the good stuff starts.'

The first voice Kouros heard was Demon's.

'I need a telephone number for that old friend of yours, the one from Sardinia.'

On the word *Sardinia* Kouros reacted like a cop, not a tourist. His first thoughts weren't of that Italian island's modern-day reputation as paradise for tourists in love with its beauty and pace, but of a sordid and notorious decades-ago past filled with tough guys and big-time kidnapping, at ten to fifteen million euros per snatch, with victims rarely turning up alive.

'I can't. If he ever finds out where I am ... where we are ...'

She's scared of that Sardinian guy.

'But I must find him. It is very important.'

What's important enough to get him running around Sardinian mountains looking for people dangerous enough to kill him just for asking the wrong question?

'I don't have a number for him. I'll have to find someone who does.'

He knows how to work her.

The next sound Kouros heard was a door opening, then closing, followed by a string of curses.

'That's it, Yianni. Nothing else of interest, and she hasn't called anyone since he left. But we're on it if she does.'

'Good. Anything else on Demosthenes?'

'He went to some apartment we didn't know about. We're trying to get listening over there, but doubt it will be up for awhile.'

207

'Okay, text me his new address. I'll get there as soon as I find a ride back to Athens.' He paused. 'And Angelo, get a copy of the tape to Maggie. Ask her to find out what she can about the places they're talking about and everything there might be on that Efisio character.'

'Will do. Ciao.'

'Yeah, ciao.'

Kouros wasn't sure what was happening, but he was damn sure it wasn't something good. He pressed a speed dial key. Time to bother the Chief.

Through most of the sunset Andreas thought of his father and how trust cost him his life. If his dad hadn't trusted that government minister, he wouldn't have been accused of taking bribes or have felt the need to save his family shame. Yes, he thought, I definitely have trust issues.

Lila was staring at a bright orange and deep blue horizon. The sun had just set. He let his mind – and eyes – wander to other things, like cleavage.

She turned to him and smiled. 'Drachma for your thoughts.'

He choked. 'Ahh, I was thinking of my father.'

'I bet he was a great man.'

'The best.'

'Is your mother still alive?'

'Yes.'

'Bet she misses him.'

'Every day.'

'I can understand.' She turned back to the sky.

'What was he like?' He didn't have to say more.

'The nicest, sweetest man I ever knew.' She talked for

208

quite a while about her husband, not of his money or accomplishments but of simple things that mattered and defined character. Lila showed such open passion in her memories of her husband that Andreas felt a tinge of jealousy. He wondered if his feelings were out of desire for the woman or envy at the man for finding a woman who loved him so unconditionally.

Suddenly, he jerked forward in his chair.

'What's wrong?' She sounded alarmed.

He reached into his pants pocket. 'Just my phone. It's on vibrate.'

She giggled.

'Hello, Yianni? What's up?' That was all Andreas said for five minutes, though every so often he looked over at Lila. She smiled when he did.

Kouros finished his report with, 'I'm on my way to his apartment.'

Andreas checked to see if anyone could overhear. 'Looks like there's a lot going on.' Eavesdropping was a Greek national pastime. He had to be careful, even though most tables seemed filled with foreign tourists. 'Our boy here is in negotiations with the bad guys. My guess is the guy from the metro is with the muscle talent up north of the border. It fits with what D said setting up the metro meeting.'

Kouros added, 'The guy on the platform seemed really pissed at him.'

'And the next thing we know D's off to the girl's apartment, pressing hard to find fresh talent. What do you think?'

Kouros paused. 'He must be pretty desperate if he's shopping this sort of shit around to strangers.'

'My guess is there's trouble in . . .' he caught himself just

209

before saying *terrorist*, 'paradise. Let's see what we can come up with to make it worse. Press Maggie for anything she can find on the girl's ex. Make sure we don't let D out of our sight. And try to pick up whatever he says.' Andreas paused. 'By the way, good thinking on covering A's place. Thanks.' He felt relieved, no matter what the tapes picked up.

'I knew that's what you'd want done. When will you be back?'

Andreas looked at his watch, then at Lila. 'First plane in the morning. It leaves at seven. See you then.'

Andreas put the phone on the table and looked at Lila. 'Get the picture?'

'Yes.' She played with her glass. 'So what do we do until then?'

'Until when?'

'Seven.'

'I have some ideas.' He grinned.

She smiled and flirted back. 'And what would they be?'

He pointed to a restaurant over by the windmills. 'How about dinner over there?' If this were a game of chicken, Andreas just blinked.

Lila didn't turn to look. 'Nope; it's filled with Athenians dancing on tables all night and having a wonderful time. Not in the mood.'

'Okay, how about a place across from where I parked?'

'Nope.'

'I'm out of ideas.'

'Let's find a place out of town, on a beach.'

He felt a new tingle, not from his phone, from her words. 'Sure, any preference?'

210

'No, you pick the place. I want to see what you think I might like.'

They walked back to the car along mostly deserted lanes. Lila wanted to avoid the paparazzi perched on Mykonos' main streets, and Andreas needed time to think, not shake more hands and resist more invitations. He was as anxious as a schoolboy on a first date with the prom queen. Where can I take her? He weeded out the obvious choices: extra-ordinarily expensive beach tavernas favored by many who simply wanted to show they could afford them whether or not they could, and cozier places too far out of town for what must be an early night.

He settled on a lovely taverna that sat on the beach closest to town, Megali Ammos. But as Andreas slowed down to park he recognized a group of locals walking toward the place. He preferred avoiding them and, so, kept driving. Five minutes later they were at Ornos Beach. It looked out on one of the island's prettiest coves – and its most romantic one at night.

Andreas turned left at the beach and took the first right into a parking lot. He drove to the far right corner and parked alongside a tall bamboo windbreak. Five feet in front of the Jimny, pots of green plants and brightly colored flowers lined a two-and-a-half-foot-high by four-foot-deep concrete ledge running the length of the solid white wall behind it. Everything disappeared when he turned off the headlights. It was an almost moonless night.

Andreas took her hand and led her around the windbreak to the beachfront entrance for the restaurant. He waved to the owner. He was talking to a customer and motioned for them to wait a moment. Lila turned and faced a mirror framed in an intricate mosaic pattern. His eyes fixed on her image.

'Stunning, absolutely beautiful.' Lila's eyes met his.

'I couldn't agree more.' He smiled.

She laughed. 'Not me, the mirror. Don't you love it?'

The owner came over and pointed to the mirror. 'My wife did that. The food's great too.' He was right, but Andreas and Lila weren't likely to remember what they ate.

Several complimentary drinks and two bottles of wine later, they were walking barefoot along the beach, shoes in hand. She reached out and took his free hand. They stopped between parallel rows of virtually invisible beach lounges and umbrellas. A couple was cuddling in the darkness several chairs away, and they didn't want to disturb them. Although from the looks of things they were oblivious to everything but each other.

'Let's sit over there.' Lila pointed to a lounge chair two rows back from the sea and far away from the couple.

Andreas walked to where she pointed and sat sideways on the chair. She poked him around until he looked as if he actually were lounging. Then she positioned herself between his legs, her back to his belly, using him as if he were her chair.

'Comfy?' was all Andreas could think of to say.

Lila took his hands and put them across her belly. 'Very.'

They sat staring out at the sea. He didn't speak. He figured there wasn't much left for him to say. Lila should be able to tell what was on his mind from what was pressing up against her backside.

'I like this.' She stroked the back of his hands with her fingers.

212

'Me, too.'

The only light came from villas dotting the western edge of the cove, and that faded into darkness long before reaching their part of the beach. And, of course, from lights on the riggings and masts of ships anchored in the cove, but they offered no more than the dim glow of candles and Christmas lights.

She pressed her butt against him ever so slightly, and her nails now ran along the back of his hands. He kissed the back of her neck. She turned her head toward his, and he kissed her lightly. She twisted onto her side and pressed her nose against his. 'Would you please kiss me like you mean it?'

He laughed. 'Like this?' Andreas drew his hand up under the back of her blouse and pulled her toward him. As he kissed her, he moved his hand along her back. He liked the feel of her bare skin. Andreas felt her lips relax and lightly danced his tongue between them. They parted slightly and he pressed into her mouth; he pulled her closer and ran his fingertips along her spine – bare all the way.

Suddenly, he stopped. 'So, how was that?' He thought it was a funny thing to do.

She was breathing too rapidly to answer, but from her expression he realized this was not a time for humor.

He kissed her again, and her mouth opened immediately. He slid his hand under the front of her blouse. She wore no bra. He pressed his hand back and forth across her chest, touching and squeezing as he did; she pushed to meet his touch. He fluttered the tips of his fingers around her nipples. Her breathing changed, her tongue pressed deeper into his mouth, and her hand groped for his groin.

He gripped a nipple between his thumb and index finger, then firmly rubbed and squeezed. First one, then the other. She began to moan and he lost track of time.

Her sounds, her touch, her taste, her hand driving at his crotch had him quietly battling orgasm but when she slid her hand into his pants and grabbed him bare, Andreas whispered, 'Don't, I'll come.'

She jerked her hand away, twisted onto her back and started undoing her jeans. He grabbed her hands.

'No, not here. Someone will see us.' He'd forgotten all about that until now.

'Then take me somewhere where they won't.'

'I'll get a room.'

They made it as far as the car. She stopped him there, put a 'be quiet' finger to her lips, and pointed to the ledge in front of the car.

'Are you crazy?' he whispered. Those were his words, not his thoughts.

Lila walked to the wall, pushed a few plants aside, and sat on the ledge. She pulled her blouse above her breasts and up to her neck so that it hung down her back. She leaned back and undid the front of her jeans, then slid off one pant leg. She allowed the other leg to slip down so that he could see there was nothing that separated him from her. She leaned back, separated her legs, and smiled.

Not a word came to Andreas' mind, not a thought of a car or person passing by, every thought was directed to that ledge and to her. He stepped to between her legs, pulled open his shirt and dropped his pants and briefs. He was naked to his ankles. He leaned over and touched her breasts, then put an arm around her waist. She wrapped her arms

214

around his back. He felt her breasts against his chest, her bare leg straddling his. He braced his knees against the wall, one hand on the ledge beneath her, the other now on her naked ass pulling her toward him. They moved in separate ways trying to find each other and when they did, each paused.

Andreas moved first. Lila flinched but didn't refuse. Slowly, he found the way and they found a rhythm. But it did not last for long. The warmth and touch of her bare skin against his, her stuttered bursts of breath at his every thrust, and that erotic edge that came with the risk of being caught at any moment had him on the brink of orgasm the moment he entered her.

He tried holding back, but when she moaned and started shaking he was gone. He came so hard and intensely he thought he hurt her. He caught his breath, and when he heard her crying he was certain he had.

He didn't know what to say.

She was sitting on the ledge, sobbing. He put his arm around her.

'Thank you.' Her face was covered in tears.

Now, for sure, he didn't know what to say. He helped her put on her jeans and straightened out her blouse.

Finally, he thought of something to say. 'I'm sorry.'

She sniffled and stood up. 'Don't be silly. You did nothing wrong.' She drew in and let out three deep breaths, then took his hand. 'It's just . . . just that you're the first man since my husband . . . and . . .' She let go of his hand and threw hers in the air. 'I can't even say it.'

Andreas didn't say anything. Just reached for her hand. She gave it.

'Okay, I know it sounds stupid . . . but it's the truth. Look what we just did.' She pointed back at the wall. 'I mean that was crazy. Admit it.'

He shrugged.

'But I had to do it this way. Down and dirty. I don't think I could have gone through with if if I'd waited until we had a room. I hope you understand. I'm still not sure I do.' She shook her head. 'I guess it's just my hang-up.'

'Come with me.' He tugged at her hand.

'Where are we going?'

He led her across the parking lot to a hotel on the other side, got a room, took her upstairs, and made love to her for the rest of the night. It was the only way he could think of to cure her of her hang-up.

18

Andreas just made his seven a.m. plane. Thank God the night clerk didn't forget the wake-up call, though Andreas forgot he'd asked for one. They fell off to sleep at five and the call came at six. Lila refused to get out of bed. She said she'd be fine, had plenty of friends on the island, and needed 'at least two days to recover.'

Again, he had a first row window seat, but this time he was alone in his row. *Great, I can sleep.* Andreas leaned his head against the window and shut his eyes. He heard the doors close, and the engines start. That's when he felt the bounce of significant weight on the seat next to him. *Shit, someone switched seats.* He didn't bother to look or even open his eyes, and by the time the plane was airborne he was asleep.

His thoughts were of Lila: he dreamed of her next to him . . . stroking him . . . prodding him . . . wanting him to turn to her. He could feel her touch . . . her finger in his side—

Andreas jerked awake and twisted to confront the passenger next him.

'Morning, Andreas.'

Andreas' exhaustion was gone. Adrenaline did that. Now all he had to shake was shock. '*Tassos?*'

'In the flesh.' He smiled and patted his belly. 'A bit more than the last time you saw me.'

That last time was the last time Andreas ever wanted to see him. 'What are you doing here?' Andreas' voice was angry.

Tassos was cheery. 'I think it's fair to say if I tried getting an appointment with you, or even called, you'd never speak to me.'

'And for goddamn good reason.'

'The past is past. Let's talk now as colleagues. You as chief of Special Crimes GADA, me as chief homicide investigator for the Cyclades.'

Andreas looked around for other passengers who might be listening. No one else was in the front row. He looked behind them. No one in the second row. Or the third. He gestured behind with his thumb. 'Your doing?'

Tassos shrugged. 'We needed privacy.'

Tassos was a real old-timer, with more connections than hair, as bushy and dyed brown as it might be. Whatever else Andreas thought of Tassos, he never underestimated his ability to get things done, no matter what the means. Some might say Tassos, not Andreas, was a truer example of the traditional Greek cop. An undoubted point of pride for both men.

'How did you know I was on this plane?'

'You haven't exactly been hiding.'

Andreas looked for a smile. There was none. 'Like I said, how did you know I was on this plane?'

'People saw you and told me you were here. I wanted to talk to you, so I checked with the airlines. They gave me your flight information, and I set this up.' He gestured toward the other seats.

Andreas said nothing, just kept looking for a smile.

'I also set up your wake-up call.' Big smile.

Andreas rubbed his eyes with his left thumb and index finger. He wondered what else Tassos might know about last night. No matter, Tassos would never turn against him on a personal level. Their differences were professional, and they'd still be friends but for that. 'Okay, asshole, why did you want to see me?'

'Ah, glad we're back on a first-name basis.' Tassos paused. 'It's about the Kostopoulos matter.'

Andreas shook his head. 'Let me guess, you're the one "looking into things" for Zanni Kostopoulos.'

Tassos nodded.

'Officially or unofficially?'

Tassos shrugged. 'It's a private retainer arrangement. I decided to catch up on some long overdue vacation time.'

Andreas snickered. 'Doesn't surprise me. So, like I said, what do you want from me?'

'Not sure anything at the moment. It's more what I can do for you.'

'Don't hustle me with your bullshit.' Andreas had trouble keeping his temper with Tassos. It was a trust issue.

Tassos shook his head. 'Don't worry, I'm not. But judge for yourself.'

Andreas shrugged. 'So tell me.'

'Kostopoulos came to me after he got that potsherd. And, yes, before you ask, I've helped him before.'

Again, Andreas wasn't surprised.

Tassos continued. 'I'd heard rumors, more like occasional gossip, of that sort of shit going on. Families being told to move or else, but it wasn't any of my business, so I never looked into it. But, after Zanni called, it didn't take long for me to find that the story was for real, involving seriously lethal people who followed through on their threats.' Tassos turned away from Andreas and rubbed his forehead with one hand. 'His son was a really great kid. I wish the son of a bitch had listened to me.' He didn't have to say he was talking about the father.

'I told him to take precautions, take the battle to them. He wouldn't listen. He's not the sort that does. He said no one would dare go after him. His wife pleaded with him, but he wouldn't listen to her either. Don't know if she'll ever speak to him again.'

'Do you know who the bad guys are?'

'I'm working on it.'

Andreas was not about to offer an exchange of information.

'What I do know, aside from what Marios told you, is—'

'You told Marios to speak to me?'

Tassos smiled. 'He owed me big time, he's the one who filled me in on the potsherd bit, too. I know how Marios comes across, but the bottom line is he's also worried about what's threatening our country. He just feared that getting involved might get him dead, and not just career-wise. I convinced him there were many ways to die.

220

And not telling you would bring on one of the worst he could imagine.'

Andreas rolled his eyes.

'Despite what you think, I like you. Liked your father too. And I didn't want you wandering around in the dark, not knowing what might be out there waiting for you.' He waited for Andreas to respond.

'Go on.'

Tassos shrugged. 'You're welcome. Anyway, when Zanni said you told them about their son, I knew I had to let you know what you were dealing with, even though you won't talk to me. Zanni doesn't know about Marios talking to you, and certainly not about this little meeting, but screw him. Besides, you and I are on the same side in this.'

Andreas wasn't about to take his word on that.

'Here's what I have. I was a rookie cop working in a Junta prison for political prisoners . . .' Andreas knew that part of Tassos' story, and of how he took great care to befriend all the politicians in there as a hedge against Greece's return to democracy. 'That gives me an interesting perspective on our current situation. You see, I have friends some might call outright fascists and others who are definite to-the-core communists. "And never the twain shall meet," or at least you'd think so.'

Tassos liked his little riddles. Andreas hated them; they always led to lectures.

'What the hell are you talking about?'

'Since a year or so before the 2004 Olympics, things have been relatively calm as far as Athens goes. Demonstrations and strikes yes, but certainly not the sort of terrorist violence and assassinations of the prior thirty years. Many have prospered, a lot more haven't. The media sees corruption everywhere, the people accept it as a way of life. Everyone argues over whether government is out of control and politicians out of touch. Most see both as inevitable consequences of power.'

Andreas was getting antsy. 'It's like that most everywhere, not just Greece.'

'True, but we're living here. And that's all I'm concerned about.'

Andreas gave a hurry-up wave.

'Are you going somewhere?' Tassos sounded a touch angry. 'There are people who still believe the best thing for Greece is a return to dictatorship. With them, of course, in charge. They have all the answers for Greece's problems, and there's no need to waste time listening to another point of view. Especially from the "wrong sorts" of people.' Tassos paused. 'Then we have the other fringe, the ones who want to return Greece to a time that never existed . . . except in a university coffee shop.'

Andreas thought Kouros and Tassos would get along nicely.

Tassos shook his head. 'I even heard an Athenian taxi driver complain the other day that "there's no one to keep the politicians in line since they broke up 17 November." Think about that: middle-class Athenians speaking openly to strangers of a twisted sort of admiration for the effect of terror on bettering their government?'

'Where the hell are you headed with this?' Andreas was happy the pilot announced they'd be landing shortly.

'I think there's more than one group involved in this. We've got different ideologies working together.'

'But why?'

'I don't know, but for as long as I can remember, each generation of Athenians has bitched about the *nouveaux riches* coming out of the next, and all the targeted families have one thing in common, new money. The left wouldn't be so selective. And this potsherd stuff . . . it's way too esoteric for revolutionaries. They go for symbolism tied directly to their cause.'

'Sounds to me like it's just your old fascist buddies at play.'

Tassos ignored him. 'But they don't, or rather didn't, have the horses they needed to get their crazy ideas moving. Something's happened. They have some real muscle behind them.'

'I still don't see why you think that means fascists are working with leftists.'

Tassos patted the arm between their seats. 'Because, associates of the guy trying to get money out of my principal used to blow up people for nuts on the left.'

The plane touched down on the runway.

'Kostopoulos said you didn't know the negotiator.'

Tassos grinned. 'You believed him? Let's put it this way: some of his playmates were on watch lists in the days of 17 November.'

'What's his name?'

'Not a chance, at least not until Zanni says it's okay.'

Andreas wasn't surprised. 'So, why are they working for the right?'

'Probably for the same reason they worked for the left. Money. They're not ideologues, just muscle working for a payday. Not uncommon. But something, or someone, has brought them together. And I think the link is from the left.' He paused and let out a breath. 'Like I said, "who would have thought?"'

The plane was taxiing toward the arrivals area.

Andreas thought whoever could bring right and left Greek extremists together in common cause must be one hell of a statesman. Greek leftists were demonstrating against the government with ever-increasing ferocity, and the right was clamoring for the government to crack down much harder on those responsible for the violence. The country was polarizing at the extremes. If there were someone who could bring those two groups together, that guy would get Andreas' vote for sure, unless he was some general roaring in on a tank. Or responsible for the murder of Sotiris Kostopoulos.

The plane stopped, and people started pulling things out of the overhead bins.

'So, what do we have?'

Andreas shrugged. 'Don't know. You tell me. You're the only one who seems to know the players.'

'Am I?' Tassos studied Andreas' face, then stood and stepped out to block the aisle. He gestured for Andreas to step in front of him.

'Aren't you getting off?' Andreas asked.

'No, the plane is going back to Mykonos.'

'Rather not be seen with me?' Andreas grinned and stepped in front of him.

Tassos smiled. 'Stay in touch.'

The door opened and Andreas headed for it.

'And say hello to Maggie for me.'

★　★　★

She hadn't slept. She no longer slept at night. She barely slept at all. The beautiful, always coiffed and bejeweled Ginny Kostopoulos no longer cared. She hadn't showered in a day, or touched a brush to her hair in two. She just sat with her children while they played, while they ate, while they slept. Never letting them out of her sight. She sat through each night watching them dream, checking their breathing, and whispering memories of her childhood, her first loves, and the birth of her son. She stopped at that point and rewound the loop. Not a word about her husband or her horrid present. She wanted her daughters to hear only happy thoughts.

Ginny looked at the porthole on the other side of their beds. It was sunrise. The children would be up soon. She must speak to the captain about the course. She trusted only herself to set it.

She stared, looking for the horizon. Her husband had promised to protect them; to keep them safe from harm. She believed him, trusted him with her children's lives.

She looked at her sleeping babies. She'd never trust another with their lives. *Never.*

Maggie rarely got to work on time, and Andreas usually didn't care. Today he looked at his watch for the fifth time in ten minutes.

A quick knock and immediately opening door meant Maggie was here.

'Hi, Chief, understand you're looking for me.'

'You're late.'

'Hmm, something must be bothering you.'

He stared at her. 'I have regards for you.'

'From whom?'

'Tassos Stamatos.'

Her face lit up like a three hundred watt bulb. 'Really! What did he say? Tell me everything.'

Andreas was flustered, she seemed to be missing the point. 'Maggie, I have to know if you're talking to him.'

'I wish. It's been years.' She seemed to be swooning. 'Ahh, Tassos. He was the last man I—'

Andreas thrust up a hand. 'Stop, I don't want to know any more.' He was certain Tassos was laughing himself silly imagining this moment. He mumbled, 'Son of a bitch set me up.'

'What?'

'Nothing. Tell Yianni to join us.'

Maggie opened the door and shouted down the hall, '*Kouros, get in here.*'

Andreas put his right hand against the side of his face, rubbed it a few times and shook his head. 'What am I going to do with you?'

'Did he say anything else? Please, tell me.'

'Honest, not a word more.' Andreas paused. 'But it was the very last thing he said to me. I'm sure you were on his mind from the beginning.' Andreas said it sincerely; no reason not to make her happy.

'Morning, Chief.'

Andreas nodded hello. 'So, Maggie, did you find anything on the Sardinian connection?'

'The town he mentioned is in central Sardinia among some of the wildest mountains on the island. Its tourist website says 2,700 people live there and that it's known for wines and cheeses. The place goes back to ancient times and has lots of history to it. It's also the source of one of Sardinia's symbols, the mask of Mamuthones. Damn scary looking thing if you ask me. But I think Demosthenes was interested in something a lot scarier about Mamoiada. It's in the area that was home to a ruthless kidnapping industry. Italy had to change its banking laws to limit cash withdrawals and send in the army to stop it. That was in the mid-1990s.'

'Guess that sent a lot of locals back to minding cows,' said Kouros.

Andreas shook his head. 'Not all of them, I'm afraid. Has Demosthenes contacted the Sardinian boyfriend . . . what's his name?'

'Efisio. Not sure,' said Kouros. 'Don't think so, but he may have a telephone number for him. He went to Anna's apartment about three this morning and asked if she had anything for him. She said "yes," but yes could have meant something else.'

'Like what?' asked Maggie.

'Like would you . . . sleep with me, because two minutes after he asked all we heard was . . .' he looked first at Maggie, then at Andreas, rolling his hand as if trying to mime the word.

'Fucking?' Maggie suggested with a smile.

Andreas ignored them. He saw this as the sort of banter cops needed to stay sane. 'So, Maggie, what do you have for us on Efisio?'

'It's a common first name. Interpol and the Italian police show six from that area wanted on big time kidnapping and murder charges, and not a current possible location for any of them.'

'Wonderful.' Andreas tapped his pencil on the desk. 'What's

with this Demosthenes character? What's he up to?' He kept tapping. 'It's pretty clear it's tied in to what our old friend and colleague Tassos Stamatos told me this morning . . . which reminds me, neither of you is to speak to him about *anything*.'

He watched Maggie's face drop. 'Concerning this investigation.'

She smiled again.

He waved his finger at her. 'But you better be damn careful.'

'Am I missing something?' It was Kouros.

Andreas waved off the question. 'Okay, Maggie, see if you can find anything else on Efisio. Try going backward from anything we have on his ex-girlfriend, Anna.'

'Will do.'

Maggie left, and Andreas filled in Kouros on his conversations with Kostopoulos and Tassos.

'Seems pretty clear Demosthenes is the link.'

Andreas shrugged. 'If you believe everything Tassos says.'

'You really don't trust the guy.'

'You're one of the few who knows why.'

'Yeah, but he wasn't trying to set you up. You just don't like his ethics.'

Andreas pointed a finger at Kouros' heart. 'Once you make the first compromise, it's so much easier to make a second, and bigger one, and by the third . . .' he rolled his finger over into circles in the air. 'Bottom line, don't do that first deal with the devil for what you think is just a tiny bit of your soul unless you're prepared to lose the whole thing somewhere down the line.'

It was tough keeping cops straight. Most made less than

a thousand a month. All Andreas could do was keep making his point and hope some, like Kouros, got it. He hoped he didn't sound hypocritical, considering the other night.

'Anyway, if Tassos is correct, we have an ultraconservative group looking to keep Athenian society pure involved somehow with revolutionaries hot to bring down the rich. From what we know, that makes Demosthenes our most likely candidate for making both sides happy.'

Kouros nodded. 'He feeds the leftists the rich meat they want.'

'And protects the wacko rich from the revolutionaries by letting the wackos pick who gets slaughtered.'

'How's the paid muscle fit in?'

Andreas shook his head. 'Not sure yet, but from what Kostopoulos told me about getting press clippings along with a message telling him this was what happened to families who didn't leave, my guess is most fled because of psychological strong-arming, not muscle.'

'Quite a monster.'

'Better believe it. Fascists for a head and revolutionaries with retractable, professional killer claws to capture and destroy the prey.'

'What part is Demosthenes?'

'Central nervous system, bringing it all together.'

'More like the asshole if you ask me.'

Andreas grinned. 'So, where do you suggest we go from here?'

'Why don't we bring him in?'

'For what? Being inside a gay bar the night the kid was murdered? He has a room full of alibis. And all we have on tape is Demosthenes asking for an address on Mykonos and the telephone number of some guy from Sardinia. Big deal. Bringing him in only sends the whole operation spinning out of control and underground. We're better off letting him run loose, on a tight leash. He's our only chance of finding whoever's at the head of whatever this is – and cutting the damn thing off.'

'We've got 24/7 coverage on him and the girl. It's up to Demosthenes to make the next move.'

Andreas leaned back and stretched. He yawned, too. He'd forgotten how tired he was. 'Just make sure to be there when he does.'

Kouros left and Andreas buzzed Maggie. 'No interruptions except for Kouros. I've got a lot of work to catch up on.'

'Nitey nite.'

Andreas looked at the phone, then walked over to the couch, pushed some papers onto the floor, and lay down. He kicked off his shoes, and fell asleep to a single thought: Is it just Andreas Kaldis, or is every man transparent to the women who know him?

19

It was tougher than usual finding a phone to use at the university, but Demon did.

'Hello, is this Efisio?' Demon spoke in Italian, using his most conciliatory, solicitous voice.

'Who's this?' In the tone of those two words Demon sensed what Anna feared.

'I have a proposition to discuss with you.'

'How did you get this number?' Menace was the tone.

'Through a mutual acquaintance.'

'Who's that?' Now anger.

'Can't say.'

'Conversation's over.'

Demon panicked. 'Anna, it was Anna.'

Dead silence. Demon thought he hung up. 'Are you there?'

'Where is she?' For an instant Demon wondered if it were the same person; the voice was so unexpectedly calm. As at the eye of a hurricane.

'In time, my friend, in time.' Demon spoke softly.

Efisio exploded. '*She's dead, do you hear me, dead. You, too, asshole, if you don't tell me where she is now!*'

Demon felt back in control. He loved it when adversaries lost their tempers. 'That would be a terrible shame, and a loss of a lot of money for you.'

'*Where is she, where is the miserable—*'

'Now, Efisio, if you don't need forty million euros just tell me, and I'll take my business elsewhere.'

'She's dead.' He did not scream this time.

'Going once . . .'

'What did you say?' The voice was back to flat.

'Going twice . . .'

'About the money.' Efisio's voice showed just the touch of anxiety Demon was hoping for.

'Ah yes, the forty million euros. Are you interested?'

'Are you some sort of wacko?'

'If you're willing to meet, you can decide for yourself. You pick the time and place, as long as it's in Athens and by no later than tomorrow.'

'If you're fucking with me . . .' Efisio was back to threatening, but his tone wasn't.

'I know, don't bother telling me what you'll do to me, but if I'm not, I'm the person who is about to set you up for the rest of your life. That will make me your boss, and I'll expect to be called sir.'

Demon heard a muffled curse, no doubt from Efisio's attempt to cover the phone with his hand, followed by a calmly said 'How do I tell you when and where?'

Demon said a cell phone number and told Efisio to text the details there.

Efisio grunted, 'Okay,' and hung up.

Demon put down the phone and ran his hands through his hair. It was a long time since he'd dealt with someone as out of control as Efisio. The guy probably was a psycho. He must be careful. He knew that ultimately he'd have turn over Anna, and the kid, too, when Efisio found out about him, but not until after he finished the job. Demon shrugged, as if talking to himself. Too bad for them – but shit happens.

'Chief, it's Kouros.' The words came over the intercom. Maggie said them three times.

'Okay, be right with him.' Andreas twisted off the couch, stretched, and looked at his watch. He'd slept for all of forty-five minutes.

He reached across the desk for the phone. 'Yianni?'

'He's made contact.'

Andreas still was a bit fuzzy. 'Who are we talking about?'

'Demosthenes. He spoke to the Sardinian. He went to the university again this morning to make a call. We thought he might, so we set it up to shut down every line but the ones we'd covered.'

'Must have pissed off a lot of people trying to make calls.'

'Imagine if they knew we did it.'

Andreas preferred not to. Cops tapping phones while illegally on university grounds was not a wise career move. 'So, what did they say?'

'They're meeting sometime today or tomorrow in Athens. Efisio is text-messaging the details to Demosthenes. We got the cell number, so we can intercept.' He paused. 'Chief, there's something else.'

'What is it?'

'I think we should pick them up when they meet.'

'Why?'

'This Efisio is a real crazy. My bet is he's wanted by the Italians for serious shit.'

'So what? We've got our own serious shit to worry about here.'

'The guy promised to kill Anna. I mean he screamed what he intended to do to her.'

'Does he know where to find her?'

'Not yet. But I wouldn't bet on Demosthenes keeping it secret much longer.'

Andreas didn't answer immediately. 'I understand where you're coming from, but the only reason I've heard so far for blowing this investigation out of the water is to question, not even arrest, an Italian living outside of Greece who *might* be wanted in another country. And why? Because in an angry rage he told a third party what he wants to do to his ex-girlfriend *if* he ever finds her. I'm not convinced.'

Kouros paused. 'There's the forty million euros he offered Efisio.'

'*Forty million euros!* To do what?'

'Didn't say.'

'Holy Christ, Yianni, we're in the wrong line of work.'

'I was thinking the same thing.'

Andreas rubbed at his eyes with the heel of his left hand. 'How can we do anything but let this play out? Either Demosthenes is a nut-job or into something so big I don't want to think about it. *Forty million euros.*'

Kouros cleared his throat. 'But don't you think we have enough to squeeze Demosthenes into making a deal to give up whoever killed the Kostopoulos kid?'

'And turn us into media heroes?'

'I was thinking more along the lines of catching the killers we're looking for and letting someone else chase after whatever else is out there. Hiding in some cave, with long sharp teeth and claws, breathing fire—'

'Okay, okay, I get your point. I'll think about it. In the meantime, make sure whoever's watching Anna's apartment knows the ex-boyfriend's threatened to kill her, and that they're to protect her, if necessary. Okay?'

'Okay.'

They hung up. No way Andreas could go back to sleep now. Too excited. He leaned back against his desk and stared out the window toward the sky. What Yianni said made sense. The only crime his unit was officially investigating was the Kostopoulos murder. They probably could nail who did it with the right amount of heat on Demosthenes. But there was something so much bigger going on . . .

Curiosity always was one of Andreas' weaker – or stronger – traits, depending on whether curiosity killed the cat. Or, satisfaction brought it back.

'*Forty FUCKING million euros!*' He'd made up his mind.

Demon was feeling the pressure. Kostopoulos was doing things they'd not expected. He had to be stopped. And quickly. It wasn't just the Old Man who was pressing him. There was unhappiness throughout the pack. He had to keep the old lions in line. They were his future. He smiled. Make that a *pride* of lions. Yes, he had to keep the pride of his old lions intact. He enjoyed smiling at the little jokes he made in his mind. They helped keep him calm, too. Which was what he must remain if he hoped to survive being dumb enough to meet alone with a psycho-killer-kidnapper.

He looked at his phone again. The message read, 'Four. Plaza opposite Hadrian's Arch. Wear PAOK hat backwards.' The message came in at three-thirty. Not sure if it meant today or tomorrow. He made it here with only seconds to spare. Finding the Arch wasn't the problem. It's been standing in central Athens for almost two thousand years as the symbolic entrance to the city, and the square across the avenue marked the start of today's main pedestrian walkway into the area of the Acropolis. The problem was finding the hat. PAOK was a team from northern Greece with legendary, insane fans. They regularly started fires inside their basketball stadium to celebrate, and no one seemed to notice or care except those charged with carrying fire extinguishers. Come to think of it, no surprise he picked that team's hat.

Demon stood by the front of the square looking up and down the street. He walked twice around the square's dominating statue of actress Melina Mercouri, one of Greece's more modern symbols, and stared back into the square. Maybe it's tomorrow. The phone beeped once and another message appeared: 'Syndagma to Omonia. NOW. Nice hat.' Demon looked around, but people were everywhere. He could be any of them. Syndagma to Omonia made no sense. Why not say one or the other? Then it hit him. The message was about metro stops.

Demon ran to the metro entrance closest to Parliament and in two stops was in Omonia. As he was coming up to the square from the platform below, he noticed another message on the phone: 'Piraeas.' It was Athens' port city and as far south as you could go from Omonia on the old electrikos train line, with its almost two dozen stops between Kifissia on the north and Piraeas. 'Shit, the mother fucker's playing with me.' But he got on the train.

In Piraeas the message was 'Larisis,' which meant switching to another train and heading for the railroad station northwest of Omonia that linked Athens to the rest of Greece. He was not going to leave Athens, no matter what the next message said. Or so he kept telling himself. He didn't have to decide, because at Larisis the message switched him back to the metro and back to Omonia station, two stops away. In Omonia there was no message waiting for him. He looked around. No one seemed to be paying attention to him.

Demon checked the phone to make sure there was cell service and looked around again. That's when he heard the beep and saw 'Kifissia.' That meant switching for another ride on the electrikos; this time as far north as the line ran. He'd been traveling for hours and now was the height of rush hour; he was pissed, but made it.

One stop later, as people pressed into the car, a little guy who'd been standing nearby bumped into him. The man turned as if to say 'excuse me' but what Demon heard was, 'Drop the hat, follow me,' in a voice unmistakably Efisio's.

Demon froze. He watched the little man walk to the doors and step off the train, never looking back. Demon pulled off the hat and rushed to follow him, pushing and shoving passengers out of his way. He even knocked a woman to the floor also trying to reach the doors. But he made it.

He looked around for Efisio and saw him walking slowly

toward the exit at the center of the platform. This was Victoria Station, and they were headed up to the street. Demon thought, *if you were looking for a neighborhood in which to meet someone you might want to kill, without shaking up the locals, this was a very good choice of metro stop.* Demon didn't smile at that joke.

Once on the streets, Demon stayed twenty yards or so behind Efisio. A few blocks from the station, on Feron Street just past Aristotelous, Efisio stopped beside a parked black Fiat. Two men were in the front seat and the engine was running. He waited until Demon was next to the car before opening the back door. 'Get in.'

Demon didn't see a choice. One way or the other, this was the end of the line for him if he failed.

Kouros was with the surveillance team watching Demosthenes' apartment when the first message was intercepted. It set off a mad scramble: Andreas sent a male-female team dressed as tourists running off to photograph everyone around the square across from the Arch; two cops watching Demosthenes' apartment were ordered to drop everything and follow him; and Kouros was told to get back to headquarters immediately.

By the time the Syndagma to Omonia message came through, two more cops in plainclothes were sitting in a blue OTE telephone repair van next to the Arch. They were told to hustle over to Syndagma and follow the suspect, now wearing a black and white PAOK cap.

They saw Demosthenes running toward the metro entrance and followed him to Omonia. That's where they almost lost him. He was headed out of the station but unexpectedly turned and went back in, trapping the two cops on a crowded, ascending escalator. By the time they started back down, Demosthenes was out of sight. They split up to look for him and, when the message came through that he was headed to Piraeas, only one cop was close enough to catch the train.

Andreas kept his fingers crossed they wouldn't lose him in Piraeas. No way to get more people from his unit there in time, and he couldn't risk involving local cops. They weren't trained for this sort of thing. Then he saw the next message: Larisis. What a break. Demosthenes was headed back north and into their waiting arms.

A new team picked him up at Larisis and followed him to Omonia.

There was no new message at Omonia. Demosthenes was in the middle of the platform looking around. Maybe the meet was here? Finally, a new message, Kifissia was the next destination. Perfect. They followed him to the new platform. One cop walked to where the car behind Demosthenes would board, the other to where the car in front of him would be. Neither wanted to risk spooking him by getting too close. There would be plenty of time to move closer later.

Kouros stuck his head into Andreas' office. 'We lost him.'

'*What!*'

Kouros stepped inside and closed the door. 'He got off at Victoria.'

'Victoria? I didn't see Victoria on any message.'

'Me either.'

Andreas smacked his fist on the desk. 'Someone must have made contact with him on the train.'

'That's what Angelo thinks. He saw a man bump into him while the train was stopped at Victoria. Seconds later, Demosthenes was gone.'

'Why didn't someone follow them?'

'Christina tried. It all happened so fast. She'd just moved into his car from one in front when she saw Demosthenes trying to get off. She tried getting to the door but he pushed her out of the way, she tripped and . . . well, by the time she got to her feet the doors were closed.'

'And what the hell was Angelo doing while all this was going on?'

'He was in the car behind, watching Demosthenes through the door.' Kouros looked down at the floor. 'Said he'd been watching the hat. When he didn't see it he got out and pushed into Demosthenes' car. By the time he found the hat on the floor and figured out what happened, the train was moving.'

Andreas stared out the window. He was angry but didn't want to show it. 'Pretty slick.'

'More like plain dumb luck.'

Andreas gestured no. 'I'd call it something else. Old-fashioned, simple magic. He got them focused on the hat, not the man, and into the rhythm of expecting both to show up exactly as they'd been conditioned to expect. All it took was an instant of distraction and—' Andreas slammed his hands together. '*Poof!* Surprise, all gone.'

Andreas leaned back in his chair. 'I can guess why they called you and not me.'

'They know you don't kill the messenger.'

'Not until now. So, what *do* we have on the mysterious man on the train?'

240

'They didn't get a good look at him. There wasn't any reason to notice him.'

Andreas put up his hand. 'If you know what's good for you, stay as the messenger. The guy who bumped into Demosthenes was the first person to have any contact with him since he showed up across from the Arch – *and you're telling me that's not a reason to notice him.*' His anger had escaped.

Kouros looked away from Andreas and started biting at his lip. 'I get your point.'

Andreas picked up a pencil and tapped it against his cheek. 'Good. Now, as you were saying.'

Kouros swallowed hard. 'All Angelo remembered was that the guy was very short.'

'How short?'

'Less than five feet and very broad-shouldered, but not like a dwarf or a midget, more like a Sardinian.'

Andreas tapped the pencil to his forehead and shook his head. 'What the fuck are you talking about?'

Kouros looked at Andreas but started shifting weight from one foot to the other. 'I had an Italian girlfriend. She was from Sardinia. She was short, less than five feet, but I'm not that tall, so it was fine and—'

Andreas snapped the pencil in half. '*Yianni!* Please, get to the goddamned point.'

Kouros took a quick breath. 'She told me she wasn't used to being with such a tall man. Most of the men she knew from Sardinia weren't much taller than she. She said it's a national trait.'

Andreas rubbed his eyes. No reason to be taking his frustration out on Yianni. This mess was no more Yianni's

241

fault than his own, or just as much. 'Okay, let's assume your old girlfriend was right and they've made contact. Now what? They could be bombing Parliament for all we know.'

'We're covering all the apartments. When he shows up we might hear something.'

'You mean *if* he shows up.'

'Why, do you think he knows we're on to him?'

'I doubt it. But this Efisio is one cautious son of a bitch. My guess is this metro tour was all his idea. If he feels threatened, no telling what he might do.'

'So, what do we do?'

'Not much we can do but wait to see what turns up. Demosthenes or his body.'

Demon got into the Fiat, Efisio slid onto the seat beside him, and the car pulled away. Demon's heart was racing. He wondered what this little man with the burning black eyes would do next. His size was deceptive. Efisio was at least twice the size of a massive pit bull and larger than a giant rottweiler. Efisio held out his hand. 'Give me the phone.'

Demon did as he asked. 'Why?'

Efisio tore off the back, pulled out the battery and SIM card, rolled down the window, and tossed out the parts piece by piece. 'In case someone's tracking you. Now, take off your clothes.'

That didn't surprise Demon. He'd do the same thing. Can't be too careful about a stranger asking you to do something nasty. He pulled off his shirt. 'I'm not wired.'

'We'll see. Now the pants, shoes too.'

242

A few minutes later Demon was dressed again. He thought to keep track of where the driver was headed but decided it didn't matter.

'So, tell me about the forty million.' Efisio had switched to English, Demon assumed so the two in front wouldn't understand.

'Your English is very good.'

'The forty million.' Not angry, not pleasant either.

Demon decided not to waste more time on grease. 'I need you to kidnap very valuable property.'

'Must be very important to be so valuable.'

'They're children, two, of a very rich man.'

He nodded. 'How much do you want of the forty?'

'Me?' Demon sounded surprised. 'Nothing. It's all yours.'

Efisio stared at him for a full minute. 'If you don't want money, it must be power.' He stared some more. 'Or you're crazy.'

Demon shrugged. 'How soon can you do it?'

'Depends whether you care how sloppy we are.'

'As long as the mother is left behind alive.'

'To convince the father to pay?'

Demon nodded. 'You should know that they're expecting something like this.'

'Most today are.'

'This one particularly so.'

'I see. Is that why you're not using your people?'

Demon could tell he was guessing. 'Yes, I cannot risk any of mine getting caught. Too politically sensitive.' That was bullshit but seemed what Efisio wanted to hear.

'Where are the targets?'

'They're with their mother. On a boat.'

'Where's the boat?'

'Don't know, somewhere in the Mediterranean.'

'How big is the boat?'

'Two hundred forty feet.'

'We'll find it. What's the name?'

'The people or the boat?'

'Both.'

'The family's Kostopoulos, the boat's the *Ginny Too*, named after the mother.'

'Never heard of them, but I never paid much attention to Greece. First time here.' Efisio had turned chatty.

Demon wondered why. 'Really? From how well you knew your way around the metro I thought you were a native.' He smiled.

Efisio laughed; it was forced. 'I have friends who do. They're the ones to thank. I only got on the metro when you came back to Omonia. They waited for me to find you on the platform before sending you the last message. The hat was their idea, too. Made it easier for me to spot you by that Arch and for them to keep an eye on you. It was my idea to toss it. For the same reason.'

He smacked Demon once on the thigh. 'So, my friend, let's talk about the down payment.'

Demon expected that, too. 'You still haven't told me how quickly you can do it.'

Efisio nodded. 'We're fast. The moment there's an opportunity, we take it. Figure within twenty-four hours after we locate the ship. Sooner, if it's in port.'

'That works.'

'Good. So, I think 10 percent up front is fair.'

'I'm sure you do.' Demon paused to smile. 'But I want you to do the job, not just take four million and maybe decide the rest isn't worth the risk.'

Efisio didn't react angrily. He must be used to this sort of negotiation. 'I have an alternative offer. No money down. Just give me Anna.'

Demon knew she would come up; he just didn't expect it this way. It was a tempting offer: if he turned her over, he wouldn't have to raise the down payment. Too tempting in fact. If he went for it, Efisio was likely to think he was full of shit. All talk and no money behind him. Efisio was likely to take Anna and do as he promised – to her. Then simply disappear. No, Demon had to keep these negotiations confined to money. Just enough to show he's for real, not enough to show he's desperate.

'Like I promised before, in due time. We're talking now about money.' Demon's tone was all business.

Efisio stared, more like glared, but did not change his tone. 'So, how much?'

'Two hundred thousand.'

Efisio shook his head no. 'That's not even one percent.'

'What's the going rate for a one-day snatch?'

Efisio smiled. 'So, you know about our business?'

Demon nodded. He didn't, but he'd read about European businessmen kidnapped in the morning and back home in time for dinner. Assuming the ransom was paid.

'Okay, three hundred thousand.'

'Deal. How do you want the money?'

Efisio reached into his pocket and pulled out a card. 'The address on the back is in Athens. You deliver the down payment there. As soon as you do, we get started. On the

245

other side is a bank account. Wire the balance in and we let the kids go. Simple.'

'Expect the down payment tomorrow.'

Efisio stared at Demon again, then shook a finger in his face, but not in a menacing way. 'You're not crazy. No, you are far too dangerous to be crazy.'

The driver pulled over to the curb and stopped.

'This is where you get out, I believe,' said Efisio.

Demon looked around. They were on Patission Street in front of the main entrance to the university. How the hell did he know? Or was it just coincidence? Then he thought, of course, Efisio must have traced him here from his call to him this morning.

Demon said goodbye, opened the door, and got out. But before he could walk away he heard Efisio calling, 'Wait.' He'd slid over and rolled down the window. 'Sorry but I meant to say, "Thank you, *sir*."'

There wasn't a touch of sarcasm to the emphasized 'sir.' Demon was so impressed he smiled and nodded.

Efisio smiled, too, but all toothy, like a shark. 'Or should I have said "thank you Demosthenes Mavrakis."' The glare was back.

And Demon's smile was gone, along with the black Fiat.

20

Demon was angry with himself. He'd been sloppy. All these unanticipated problems were no excuse. He had a goal to achieve, and soon. He must be more careful. He had no ID with him so Efisio didn't get his name from anything in his clothes. They knew before he got into the car, which meant they'd photographed him. Probably at the Arch, and while he was bouncing around Athens on his little metro odyssey they were showing his picture around the university until someone recognized him. Simple.

But there was an upside to Efisio's bit of theatrics: it let Demon know the son of a bitch was watching his every move. Another example of why it never paid to lose your temper. Efisio could have followed him straight to Anna, which was exactly where Demon was headed at the moment.

'Shit.' He mumbled the word aloud. 'I can't see her anymore.' He decided to go home to the apartment listed in the phone book. They probably knew about that one by now anyway. He would miss her. With Anna he never had to pay the political rhetoric price one endured to screw Exarchia hangers-on. She never even complained when she got pregnant. But, what the hell, giving her up was his price for being careless. He took it as a learning experience. Which reminded him: time to raise tuition for Zanni Kostopoulos' next lesson.

'He's in the apartment, Chief.' It was Yianni.

'Anything new?'

'Not so far. He got back about ten minutes ago. No phone calls, only rock music and bathroom sounds.'

'Enjoy. But stay on your toes. He's definitely going to do something, and I'm guessing today's big run-around has him a lot more careful. Don't let him sneak out a back door on you while you're listening to a concert.'

'Will do.'

Andreas hung up and looked at his watch. It was almost nine. *My god, I haven't called Lila!*

He grabbed the phone and dialed.

'Hi, it's Andreas.'

She laughed. 'I recognized the voice.'

He thought to apologize quickly, before she started in on how inconsiderate men were. 'I'm so sorry that I didn't call sooner but—'

'Darling, I understand completely.'

He wanted to say, 'You do?' but decided to keep his mouth shut.

'And I can't believe you took the time to send me those beautiful flowers.'

Here it comes, the sarcastic build up to World War III.

248

'And with such a lovely note.'

Andreas decided to speak, 'Lila, I know how you feel—'

'No, you don't,' she sniffled. 'You've been so nice, so understanding, and then . . . to remember to send me flowers . . . with so much on your mind.'

Andreas made a tactical decision. 'I'm glad you liked them.' And held his breath.

'I loved them.'

They spoke for twenty minutes about everything but the case. He let her know they'd talk about that in person.

The last words Lila said before hanging up were: 'Can't wait to see you. I'll call you tomorrow when I get back. And again, thank you for the flowers. I can't tell you how much they meant to me.'

He put down the phone and looked out the window. It wasn't like he was lying. He would have sent her flowers . . . if he'd thought about it.

But who sent them? And why? No one knew she was there but – then it hit him, Tassos knew. That bastard was teasing him. No, not Tassos; he wouldn't think of sending flowers any more than Andreas would. Besides, he'd already let on that he knew about Lila and the hotel. Sounds more like something Maggie would do. But how did she know about Lila . . . and Mykonos? He leaned back and shut his eyes, but only for an instant. He sat straight up and called Maggie at home.

'Hello.'

'When did you speak to Tassos?'

'Do you ever start a conversation with a simpler question, like "Good evening, Maggie. How are you?"'

'I don't have time for this.'

'It's about the flowers, isn't it?'

Andreas was fuming. 'Yes. Well, in part. What did he tell you?'

'Not as much as this conversation is.'

He could see her smile through the phone. '*Maggie!*'

'Okay, he didn't call me. I called him.'

'Why?'

'What did you expect? You told me he was asking about me. That meant he wanted to talk to me.'

Andreas didn't understand the logic, but somehow he knew she was right.

'Okay, so what did you talk about?'

'Nothing about the case, I assure you.'

'Just tell me.'

'None of your business.'

He drew in and let out a breath. 'Okay, tell me the part that is my business.'

'Fine. He said he bumped into you on the plane from Mykonos and got the impression you met someone there you liked but didn't have time to see her. I asked for her name and where she was staying.'

'That's all he said?'

'Yes, that's all *he* said.' She snickered.

'Uhh . . . what about the note?'

'What about it?'

'What did it say?'

'I miss you desperately. Marry me.'

'Maggie!'

'Sorry I had to leave. Hope you understand. Kisses, Andreas.'

He paused. 'Thank you. That was very nice of you.'

'You're welcome.'

'So, when are you going to see Tassos?' He knew that was inevitable.

'He'll be in Athens tomorrow.'

'That's quick, he must be interested.'

'Let's hope, but he won't have time to see me, he's catching a plane.'

'To where?'

'Didn't say, but my guess is Italy.'

Andreas' pulse jumped. 'Why do you say Italy?'

'Because I offered to cook dinner. He said he couldn't make it for dinner, that he had to catch a plane but lunch was open. I said I had to work. He said "too bad" because it looked like he was going to be eating only pasta for a while. See what I give up for you.'

'Thanks, Maggie,' and he hung up.

Andreas picked up a pencil with his right hand and studied it. Then he talked to it. 'What are you up to, my old friend? Are you with the good guys or the bad guys? Or haven't you decided?' His thumb was in position to snap the pencil to pieces. 'Do I trust you or don't I? Should I or shouldn't I? To press or not to press, that is the question.'

Andreas compromised. He threw the pencil against the wall and went home.

Demon posted a typical Facebook message on the 'wall' of an innocent account holder who had agreed to be a friend of Gertrude Louise. The account belonged to a celebrated member of Parliament with thousands of Facebook friends, most of whom the member didn't know. But politicians didn't say no to someone asking to be their friend. Of the thousands of other friends who might read his message, Demon only cared about the one with a computer instantly alerting him to any Facebook postings by Gertrude Louise.

Demon sat staring at his computer, waiting for a reply. He reread his message:

I have a once in a lifetime marketing opportunity
that requires printing 300,000 fliers by tomorrow.
Please, only respond with the name of a printer who
can do it tomorrow. It's either tomorrow or never.
Thanks, Gertrude Louise.

Demon wondered when he'd hear back. If the Old Man wanted results he'd have to pay. Demon didn't mention the forty million because it wasn't relevant, and the whole mess of them wouldn't pay that much for their cause anyway. Their commitment had a financial price tag: three hundred thousand euros maybe, forty million no chance. The big payoff would come from Kostopoulos. Damn well better. Otherwise, Demon was fucked. But he wasn't worried. Kostopoulos had the money and no choice but to pay, assuming he had a soul. Demon was willing to take that gamble. He wasn't sure he'd take the same bet on the Old Man.

'Ping.' The message he was waiting for:

Printers are hard to find on such short notice.

'Arrogant bastard.' He said the words aloud. Demon's immediate reaction was to reply, but he didn't. His first message said it all. Either the Old Man came up with the money or he didn't. Demon couldn't do anything more

252

about it. But if he didn't pay and Kostopoulos learned who was behind his son's murder, the Old Man and a lot of others would damn well wish he had.

The more Demon thought about it, the more he saw a potential upside to Kostopoulos killing the Old Man and a few of the others. It would galvanize the rest into rallying behind him. Then he'd deal with Kostopoulos, assuming Kostopoulos didn't take him out first and that Efisio was satisfied with Anna as his consolation for no three hundred thousand euros.

On balance, Demon decided to pray that the money turned up by tomorrow.

It was easy finding Tassos' flight but not so easy finding him. Andreas finally caught up to him in the airport security office, sitting around a card table arguing over soccer with two cops.

'Afternoon, Tassos.'

Tassos looked surprised. 'Andreas. What are you doing here?' He paused. 'Maggie.'

Andreas smiled. 'Glad she surprises you, too.'

Tassos grinned. 'Always has. So, to what do I owe the honor of this visit?'

Andreas looked at the two cops. 'Could you guys give us a few minutes?'

Andreas waited until they left. 'I think the time for bull-shit has passed. Why are you flying to Milan?'

'You don't want some witty answer, do you?'

'No.'

'Our mutual friend is sending me.'

'I hope you're talking about Kostopoulos.'

'Who else?'

'Why Milan?'

'Now you're getting a bit too personal.'

Andreas leaned forward. 'Personal is receiving bits and pieces of your wife and kids cut off with a tree-pruner.'

Tassos' eyes narrowed slightly. 'What are you talking about?'

'That's the way it's done by these guys.'

'What guys?'

'The ones who soon will be asking a forty million euro ransom from Kostopoulos.'

'Is this for real?'

'Picked it up from phone calls. We think we found the link between the muscle and the brains.'

'I won't bother to ask who the link is because I know you won't tell me, but I can't believe these guys are dumb enough to pull this shit while they're in the middle of negotiations with Zanni. They stand to make a lot more than forty million. At least they think they do.'

Andreas shook his head. 'Different guys, brand new ones. Give me who's negotiating with Zanni and I'll give you what I have on the new ones for you to worry about.'

Tassos paused. 'Greece's usual suspects from the drug trade. Albanian mobsters teamed up with home-grown Greek bad boys. They work together a lot. No surprise.'

'That's like saying they're AEK fans. Too many of them. Give me a name.'

'I take offense to your using my soccer team for the comparison.'

'It's the best I can say about them.' Andreas grinned.

'So, tell me a bit more.'

Tassos loved to horse-trade, but this time Andreas didn't mind, because he intended to tell him what he knew anyway.

No way he'd let Tassos fly off blind into this mess. 'They're Italians, specializing in kidnapping, living in exile away from Italian authorities somewhere in the Balkans. We have a first name for one, Efisio, about five feet tall, late thirties. Here,' Andreas handed him a photograph and pointed. 'We think this one is Efisio. It was taken yesterday.'

'That's it?'

'Fuck you.'

Tassos grinned. 'The one negotiating with Zanni is tied into the Greek-Albanian crew behind the Angel Club in Athens.'

'Since when are Albanians involved in the Angel Club?'

Tassos smiled. 'Consider it a simple case of consumer fraud. Albanian drugs are the kind of street shit stepped on and sold to druggies around Omonia and Exarchia. It wholesales for about one-half the price of the Angel Club boys' homegrown Greek stuff. So, the guys behind the Angel worked out a deal where they exchange one kilo of theirs for two of the Albanians, then sell it in the club as their own pricier stuff. Most of their customers can't tell the difference between vodka and gasoline. Makes it a no-brainer and doubles their profits.'

Andreas shook his head. 'Greeks, the most adaptive entrepreneurs in the world. Anything else?' said Andreas.

Tassos pressed on the table and stood up. 'No, just thanks, my friend. I appreciate the heads-up.'

But Andreas knew something else was coming. 'What is it?'

Tassos smiled. 'Something you won't want to hear, but since you asked.' He put his hand on Andreas' shoulder. 'If you found the link, why not just take it out and call it a day.' He dropped his hand.

Andreas was angry. 'And forget about all the other bastards involved?'

Tassos shrugged. 'Whether you cut off the head or sever the spine it's the same result. Hard for one part to regrow the other.'

'What about the ones who killed his boy? What bullshit analogy do you have for letting them go free?'

'Don't worry about those two. Yeah, I know about them. They weren't from Greece. It was supposed to be just another quick in-and-out job for them, just like the other times they were asked to teach a banished family a lesson. Too bad for them they became a nonnegotiable deal point. No names, no deal. Their negotiator blinked, we have the names, and like I said, don't worry about those two.'

Andreas didn't have to ask why. 'But what about the bastard who heads this whole thing? The one who thinks he can decide who has the right to live here and who will die for staying when he says "leave." He's the reason Zanni's son is dead.' Andreas pointed a finger at Tassos. 'You know that as well as I do.'

'Who's talking about letting him get away?'

Andreas smacked his hands together. 'Now I get it. Kostopoulos intends to take care of him in his own way. Screw the police. Who needs them? Just hire your own cops, and justice is whatever you decide. Mind telling me how that makes Kostopoulos any different from *he who decided* killing the kid would make the world a better place?'

Tassos shrugged again. 'No one is trying to play God. We just have different views. Look, I'm a realist. There's no way we're ever going to get them all, unless they have

256

a membership list, which we damn well know they don't. So, all we can hope to do is find the head. And once we do, I don't care who takes him out, as long as he disappears. That will scatter the rest until some new psycholeader appears. Hopefully, a very long time from now.'

Andreas had heard Tassos' views on that subject before and knew it was a waste of time to argue. 'Any idea who the big man is?'

'None worth sharing. It might confuse your instincts.'

Zanni must be spinning out one new paranoid theory after another – and Tassos had to listen to them all. 'Okay, I'll take your word on that, but I expect you to tell me as soon as you think you have a lead. You're still a cop, and this is a police investigation.' Andreas knew he might as well have said that last line in Chinese for all the effect it was likely to have on Tassos.

'You sound like your dad.'

Andreas took it as a compliment.

'I better head to the gate. I just want you to know we actually are on the same team, no matter how differently we look at the rules.'

'If only life were that easy.'

Tassos smiled and patted Andreas on the shoulder. 'Anything else to tell me?'

'Just be careful. Like I said, these guys are kidnapping pros. The one in the photograph, Efisio, originally came out of the viscous Sardinian crews from the nineties.'

Tassos blanched. 'My god. That's where I'm headed, connecting through Milan to Cagliari in Sardinia. How could they know?'

'Know what?'

'Ginny Kostopoulos and the children are on a boat off Sardinia!'

It was early afternoon and still no word on the three hundred thousand. Demon was pissed. He left his apartment for a coffee at Exarchia Square but was in no mood to engage in the mindless political rhetoric that came with it. Not that they didn't have a point; they just couldn't stop making it over and over again. He left and went back to the same apartment. He didn't dare go to another. He sensed he was being watched. None of that mattered. *As long as he got the money*.

Tassos made the plane, but a lot of angry people were on board waiting for him. He'd delayed them a half-hour. That was how long it took to fill in Andreas on the purpose for his trip – to verify that appropriate security was in place for Ginny and the children – and to advise Zanni that events were moving quickly in an unanticipated direction. Tassos pressed Andreas for the name of the link, and Andreas insisted on knowing who headed the conspiracy operation. Andreas said he wouldn't tell, and Tassos swore he didn't know. They parted shaking hands and promising to let the other know 'anything important.' Andreas only hoped it was good news, and soon.

He called Lila from the car, and they spoke for most of the way back to his office. Not about the case or even about each other, just about things. Little things, silly things. He liked the way she made him feel. He hoped he wouldn't blow it.

'Got to go, I'm back at headquarters.'

'Will I see you tonight?'

'I'll try.'

'That's not the answer I wanted to hear.'

He laughed. 'Okay, but I can't promise when.'

'I don't care when. Bye, kisses.'

The smile on his face held up until he saw Kouros sitting on his couch.

'Did you catch up with Tassos?'

Andreas sat behind his desk. 'Yes, he's off to Sardinia to meet Mrs Kostopoulos and her kids on their boat. Can you believe it – Sardinia!'

'You think it's a coincidence?'

'Don't know, but if it isn't, someone has a leak the size of the Korinth Canal. Remember that guy you tailed to the airport? From what Tassos said, he's probably part of an Albanian mob working with locals out of the Angel Club.'

'That fits with what I have so far from the two who followed him when he landed. He headed straight for the Albanian border. They're still with him but don't have much to tell. Strangers there stick out like the Panathinaikos mascot at Olympiakos soccer practice. Can't get too close.'

'Tell them not to take any chances.' He paused. 'I think *others* will be dealing with that problem.'

'Others?' Kouros nodded with a grin. 'I like that.'

He's sounding more like Tassos every day, thought Andreas. 'So, what's up with Demosthenes?'

'Not sure, our guess is he's waiting for someone to get a message to him, by e-mail.'

'Can we intercept?'

Kouros gestured no. 'Wish we could.'

'Why do you think he's waiting for an e-mail?'

'He hasn't been on the phone as far as we can tell since he returned home last night. Don't know if he's been text messaging on his mobile, but we did pick up typing sounds right after he got in. Later there was a "ping," like the sound you get from your computer when there's a message. Ten seconds later, we heard the only words from him since he got back: "Arrogant bastard."'

'Sounds like he's pretty pissed at somebody.'

'Anxious too. He only went out once, to one of those anarchist coffee shops by the square near his apartment. He didn't stay long. Was back in less than thirty minutes.'

Andreas nodded. 'I think you're right. And my guess is as soon as he gets whatever he's waiting for he's off like a rabbit. I want to be ready for him this time.' He pointed a finger at Kouros. 'No more excuses or stories about disappearing hat tricks.'

Kouros stood up. 'Understood.' He left.

Andreas wanted to go back to thinking about Lila. But that would have to wait.

Demon finally got what he wanted. Almost.

If you still need a printer, try Kolonaki. Might have availability.

He couldn't believe the Old Man was making him put on a dog and pony show. Maybe the anarchists at the square had a point: 'We all work for "the Man" no matter how independent we think we are.'

Demon walked up the hill to Kolonaki mumbling a lyric from Bob Dylan's Sixties' anthem: 'The times they

260

are a-changin.' He made no effort to conceal where he was headed. As far as he was concerned, anyone following him was welcome to know. His revolutionary and drug-dealing constituents valued Demon's connections with the Athens power elite. If anyone else were interested, good luck at using whatever they thought they found. The rich could take care of themselves. And the Old Man was very, very rich.

On a side street just off Kolonaki Square, Demon paused outside an elegant old mansion that looked to be a museum. It could have been, but wasn't. It was home to the Kolonaki Club, Athens' most exclusive private club. No one but members and their guests were allowed inside. Ever.

Demon's name was on a list of expected visitors, and immediately he was shown upstairs to a private room. He was surprised to see that the Old Man was not alone.

'Hello, Demosthenes, do you know my old friend, Sarantis Linardos?'

'Of course I do, everyone knows the publisher of *The Athenian*. An honor to meet you, sir.'

The Old Man patted Demon on the back and pointed him to the center of three well-padded and broken-in leather armchairs. The room was furnished in heavy mahogany furniture, bookshelves lined with tracts from another era, Oriental rugs, ornate silver and bronze fixtures, and wealth. Demon did not miss the point of picking this place for the meeting: we have it, you don't.

'Demosthenes is Thanassis Mavrakis' grandson.'

Linardos nodded and smiled as if he didn't already know that. A subtle way of making Demon feel he actually might belong here. They sat in a row, like see-no-, hear-no-, and speak-no-evil monkeys.

'Sarantis, Demosthenes says he is in need of a considerable sum of money in order to resolve a rather messy and unexpected situation involving a family I know you're familiar with.'

Why the charade? The Old Man certainly told him all this before. No way Linardos didn't know what was coming.

The Old Man looked straight at Linardos. 'I thought it would be helpful for our discussion if you understood a bit more of what's involved.' He gestured to Demon to speak.

Linardos looked as if he wished he were anywhere but here.

'I'm not sure what there's left to tell you, because I don't know what you were told. So, let me cut to the point.' He turned to face the Old Man. 'Oh, by the way, do you think anyone might be eavesdropping or taping us?'

The effect wasn't lost on Linardos, who said, 'Why? What are you planning to tell me?'

'Just the truth? Do you want to hear it?'

'Now, now, Demosthenes, behave.' It was the Old Man.

'You called this meeting, and I've asked a question. Is it safe to talk or not?'

'You're the one who needs the money.' The smile on the Old Man's face was not pleasant.

'And you're the ones likely to die if I don't get it.'

Linardos bolted up in his chair. 'I don't take kindly to threats, young man!'

Demon pointed at his chest. 'From me? No way. I'm talking about the dead serious threat the two of you face from the man whose son recently turned up murdered in a dumpster.'

262

Linardos looked as if Demon had just stabbed him. Demon paused to let his words sink in deeper. 'My question, although possibly moot by now, remains the same. Is it safe to talk in here?'

The Old Man gestured yes. 'The entire club is swept for listening devices every week, ever since that scandal involving the tapping of our government ministers' phones. One can't be too careful these days.'

'Good. So, what more do you want to hear, other than that if you don't give me three hundred thousand euros, Zanni Kostopoulos will find and kill you.'

'Kostopoulos doesn't know about us.' It was the Old Man.

'If you want to take that bet, fine. Not my problem.'

'Of course it's your problem. You're as much a target as any of us.'

'I had nothing to do with this!' said Linardos.

Demon spoke as if he'd not heard Linardos. 'I don't have as much to lose. Only my life.' He pointed to each of them. 'But the two of you—' he waved his hand in the air. 'When Kostopoulos is done with you, you'll not only be dead, your names will be synonymous with terrorists who murder children. The shame to your families will be eternal. Sandblasters will be working overtime erasing your names from every plaque, every monument, every building . . .' Demon stopped. He liked his argument but thought he might be overselling. Either they'd bite or they wouldn't.

Linardos slouched in the chair, put a hand up to his face, and stared at the floor.

The Old Man answered. 'What makes you think he'd ever find out about us?'

He'd bitten. 'What makes you think he wouldn't? This is Greece. Everything's for sale, and everyone wants to see the big ones fall. Are you telling me you can't think of at least one person who, if given the chance, wouldn't bring you down?'

'Like you for instance?'

Demon smiled at the Old Man. 'I'm probably one of the few who wouldn't, for a couple of reasons. As cavalier as I sounded before about dying, I'd prefer not to die, and bringing you down takes me with you. I need you too much. Almost as much as you need me.'

'You're rather arrogant today, Demosthenes,' said the Old Man.

'No, the word you're looking for is "realistic."'

Linardos drew in a deep breath, dropped his hand to his lap, and sat up in the chair. 'What is it you want, money?'

The Old Man put up his hand. 'Sarantis, that is not what drives Demosthenes. He has a far nobler calling.' There was no sarcasm in his voice, but Demon knew it was there.

Linardos stared at the Old Man. 'And what "nobler calling" justified murdering a boy?'

The Old Man pointed to Demon. 'Tell him.'

So, that's the deal, Demon thought. The Old Man set this up so I could pitch Athens' most influential publisher into joining the Old Man's crusade while he sat back seemingly above it all. That's the carrot. If I pull it off, I get the three hundred thousand.

But Demon saw things differently. This was the opportunity he'd been waiting for to do some recruiting of his own. 'Thanks for the vote of confidence.' There was no sarcasm

264

in Demon's voice. 'The Kostopoulos problem stems from an effort to keep the wrong element from accumulating power in our country. I'm certain I don't have to tell you who they are.'

He looked for a nod from Linardos but received none. 'No matter, you know who I mean. They're the ones you continuously talk about at your dinner parties and study with veiled disdain and envy at all those events you simply *must* attend with *them*. You wish they weren't there, except you need them – if you want their money to hold the damn event. Now do you know whom I'm talking about?'

Demon didn't bother to check for a nod. 'Wouldn't life be easier if we could go back to the good old days where only the *right* families had the money?' Now, the sarcasm was clear. 'Don't act as if you're somehow free of guilt for what we did on your behalf. The boy was murdered. We're all responsible. We all must live with it.' He stared at the Old Man. 'But we cannot continue with these ways of yours.'

The Old Man looked angry. 'We need order and must do whatever is required to achieve it. The Kostopoulos boy's death was necessary. You know that.'

'Yes, but your vigilante method of returning us to the old days isn't working and never will. You can't keep up this potsherd banishment bullshit to achieve your dream. It's now more like terrorism than patriotism and you're running out of patsies who run when you say run. You're left to going after people with balls and the ability to fight back. Things only will get worse if you keep this up.' Demon shrugged. 'Sorry to tell you, but your plan's *kaput*.'

Linardos stared at the Old Man. 'What is he talking about?'

Demon answered. '*I* am talking about this.' He pointed at both men. '*You* and your families are not going to make it. No, not because of Kostopoulos. I can take care of him if you let me, but because you're dinosaurs, unwilling or unable to adapt.'

'I've heard enough.' It was the Old Man.

'Don't think so.' Demon didn't budge from his seat. He looked straight at Linardos. 'What this country needs is leadership, not more terrorists. How many Greeks love their country? Answer, all of them. How many love their form of government? Answer, most of them. How many love their politicians. Answer, none of them; not even their mistresses can stand them. Why is that? Do I really have to tell you? *Because they're all alike.* Name one who ever has gone to prison for corruption? The people have no faith in their politicians and have given up on finding better ones. What I want to give them is hope.'

'You're beyond arrogant.' It was Linardos.

'As I said before: no, I'm realistic. I know what the far left thinks, they know me, and they trust me. I also know how you think. I come from the same roots as you. I'm prepared to do whatever it takes that's best for Greece, for all of Greece. We cannot continue as we are. We must bring about change, but through the system, by making it work for us, not by tearing it apart and bringing it down.' He looked at the Old Man. 'That is how you will realize your dream.'

At that point, Demon's speech morphed into dialog among the three men. It was of the sort he'd engaged in for years, as if training for this singular opportunity. They spoke for hours, and by the time they were through two of Greece's most important men were converts to *his* cause—

266

'Greek children are rioting alongside their parents in the streets. Widespread vandalism, arson, and assaults on police are dismissed by our government as "democracy" in action, and law-abiding Greeks, who once watched such protests in horror and disgust, now call the demonstrators justified! Our countrymen are sick of their politicians and their parties. They want a new beginning and they want it now. They know it can happen, no matter how unrealistic it might have seemed at other times, for they have seen the impossible happen in the United States. A black man elected president. But it requires a fresh leader to emerge, one who can unite the left and the right, the rich and the poor, under one political banner and offer new hope for our beloved Greece' – and the promise of ultimate power for Demon.

The three hundred thousand became a meaningless sum for what they now sought to achieve. The money would be delivered within the hour to the address Demon gave them. A new world was about to begin. Once Demon took care of Kostopoulos.

21

'What do you mean you couldn't get inside?'

'Chief, it's the Kolonaki Club. Nobody gets inside without an invitation.'

Andreas nodded at the phone. 'I know. I'm just pissed.'

'He was inside for over three hours. Can't believe he's a member.'

'Me, either.'

'We photographed everyone going in and coming out. Felt like paparazzi. It was a parade of *Who's Who* in Athens.'

'What are your instincts?'

'Linardos left about twenty minutes after Demosthenes. And we didn't see him go in, so he was inside the whole time Demosthenes was in there.'

'No way that's enough to justify surveillance on Linardos. Shit. So, what's Demosthenes doing now?'

'He's back in the apartment. Humming "the times are a-changin" or something like that.'

'Great, just what I want, a happy terrorist. Let me know if he changes his tune.' Andreas thought it was funny. Kouros just hung up.

Andreas looked at his watch. He promised Lila he'd see her. This would be a good time to start keeping his promises. Besides, Kouros knew how to reach him. Tassos did, too. If he had to.

A man rarely succeeds at convincing a strong-willed woman that he knows what's best for her. Especially when she distrusts his motives. Tassos was having no better success with Ginny Kostopoulos. She called him her husband's 'shill' and said that nothing he said was worthy of her time. She started to listen only when he reluctantly showed her glossy eight-by-ten color photographs of actual body parts cut off by kidnappers and delivered to victims' families to soften them up to ransom demands.

'How dare you show me this garbage? Do you think scare tactics will change my mind? We're safer on this boat than anywhere else in the world. We can go anywhere from here. Anywhere. No one can find us on the open sea.'

Tassos had given up arguing that point. 'Mrs Kostopoulos. I showed you those photographs because that is what these people do. This is the reality.' He tapped his finger on the photographs. 'You cannot ignore this. They did horrible things to your son and will do even worse to you and your daughters if you don't take precautions.' He braced for a screaming tirade. She'd launched into one each time he pressed that point before.

She stared at the photographs. 'I don't believe they know

we're here. It's just a coincidence.' She wasn't yelling. 'The truth is, if you sail around the Mediterranean, sooner or later you end up in Sardinia. And everyone knows about the history of kidnapping here, and elsewhere for that matter. All of us take precautions. Sardinia is no riskier than any other place we sail to.'

That was another point he gave up debating. At least she wasn't yelling. 'You might be right, but the men who are preparing to kidnap your family have roots in Sardinia; that makes it much easier for them to operate here. It's their backyard for god's sake.' Now he was the one heading toward a tirade.

She shook her head. 'We know about them. It is up to you to make sure they don't succeed.'

He shook his head. 'Not while you're in port. You have no mobility. You're a sitting duck here. At least let the captain take us out to sea until we get a better fix on what they're up to. Please.'

She looked at the photographs again. 'Tell the captain I'm tired of Costa Smeralda. Let's sail south.' She walked away, leaving Tassos alone.

He sat down, took a deep breath, and said, 'Thank god.' Then he called the captain. 'Get us the hell out of here.'

'Thank god.' This time it was the captain speaking.

Lila was under the covers, cuddled under Andreas' arm, resting her head on his chest listening to him breath. He slowly ran his hand along her bare hip as he rambled on about the case. He seemed almost numb to the facts until he reached the part about the Kolonaki Club. Anger filled his voice. 'Look at that.' He pointed out her bedroom window toward the Acropolis. 'The symbol of man's greatest achievements. Democracy, literacy, equality—'

Lila interrupted with a giggle. 'For some.'

'The ancient Greeks knew a woman's place. *Ouch*, that hurt.' He rubbed where she'd pinched him.

'Darling, the Kolonaki Club's rules are very strict: only members and invited guests.'

'But these guys are murderers, terrorists. They're antithetical to everything Greece stands for.'

'Or, as some might say, "completely opposite."'

'Stop being a wise-ass. This is serious. We were this close to catching the bastards behind everything and a goddamn club stops us at the door.' He'd pinched a bit of her belly for the measurement.

'Look at it this way, darling: students and revolutionaries have their universities for sanctuary. The Establishment only has the Kolonaki Club.'

He stared at her. 'If you weren't so cute—'

She stuck her hand over his mouth. 'Don't ever call a woman you're in bed with "cute" if you want to stay there.'

He laughed and got to stay a while longer. After breakfast, Andreas left for his office.

Lila left for the Kolonaki Club.

'Morning, Mrs Vardi.' The concierge knew every member by name.

'Morning, Dimitri.'

'What can I do for you?'

'Yesterday, I believe the son of an old friend was here as a guest.'

'Do you know the name of the hosting member?'

'No idea.'

'No problem. What was the name of the visitor? He would be on the list.'

'Mavrakis.'

'Let's see.' He reached under the desk and pulled up a list. 'Oh, yes, here it is, Demosthenes Mavrakis.'

She didn't ask who invited him. She read the two members' names upside down off the list in Dimitri's hand—

'Mrs Vardi, are you all right?'

'Yes, just a little startled at how quickly children grow up. Can't believe he's already coming to the club. Thank you, Dimitri.'

She left the club immediately and walked to the nearest coffee shop. She had to tell Andreas. There was no way he could bring these people down. She crossed herself and whispered, 'My god, my god, my god.'

'Sir, oh, sir.'

'Yes, Dimitri.'

'I'm sorry to bother you but I thought you might like to know that your guest, yesterday, also was the friend of another member.'

'Which guest?'

'The one with you and Mr Linardos.'

The Old Man forced a smile. 'Which member?'

'Mrs Vardi.'

'Lila?'

'Yes?'

'I didn't see her here yesterday.'

'She wasn't.'

'Then how did she know he was here?'

272

'I don't know, perhaps some other member saw him, knew that Mrs Vardi was a friend, and told her?'

The Old Man stared at Dimitri. 'And what exactly did you tell Mrs Vardi?'

'Nothing, sir, nothing at all.'

'Not even his name?'

'Didn't have to, she already knew it, I just checked the list to see if he was here.'

The Old Man paused. 'Did she ask for the names of his hosts?'

'No, sir.'

The Old Man thanked him and gave him twenty euros, a cheap amount for such valuable information. He never thought of Lila Vardi as a friend of the Kostopoulos family. But what else explained her interest in so irrelevant a person as Demosthenes? How did she know Demosthenes was here if he wasn't followed to the club by Kostopoulos' mercenaries and she wasn't then asked to snoop about for names? Demosthenes was right: they must move quickly. He was certain Kostopoulos had their names by now. For he, too, knew how to read upside down.

Efisio never thought Demon would come up with the money. He just wanted to get to Anna. But when the money arrived as promised, she no longer was relevant. At least not for the time being. This job would set him for life. It was not one to subcontract. He must see to it personally. Finding the *Ginny Too* was easy, thanks to all the GPS equipment and websites tracking ships of her size, but when he saw where she was moored he laughed. This almost was too easy. He called a cousin in Sardinia and, within hours, photos of the ship and all onboard appeared on his cell phone. Modern technology was an amazing boon to his business.

He thought of trusting his cousin to run the actual snatch and avoid the risk of being recognized back home; but his cousin wasn't the sharpest knife in the drawer, and for forty million he'd take the chance. Besides, from the way things looked, it all would be over in a matter of days. Forty million for a couple of days' work. Not bad. That's why he was back on Sardinia.

Maggie buzzed through on the intercom. 'Mrs Vardi is downstairs at security.'

'That's a surprise. Have them send her up.'

'Should I leave?' Kouros stood up from the couch as he asked the question.

'No, not unless I give you the signal.'

'What signal?'

'"Yianni, would you please excuse us."' Andreas smiled.

Kouros smiled and shook his head. 'Where was I? Oh, yeah, the asshole hasn't left his apartment since he got back from the Kolonaki Club. He ordered in some food, but all we've heard so far is humming, typing, and music. Seems like he's at peace with the world.'

'Why do I think this guy finding peace isn't a good thing?'

There was a knock and the door opened. 'It's Mrs Vardi.' Maggie let her pass and left.

Lila gave a quick nod to Yianni and went directly to Andreas' desk. She was in front of it before Andreas could stand. 'I must speak to you immediately.'

He looked at Yianni. 'Could you give us a minute?'

'No, he should stay.'

274

Andreas felt a sigh of relief. It was business, not personal.

She sat in a chair in front of the desk and let out a deep breath. 'I just came from the Kolonaki Club.'

Andreas' immediate instinct was to jump out of his chair and say '*You what?*' but he didn't.

'I know that must upset you, but it was so easy for me to do. I'm a member and just casually asked the concierge if a friend was there yesterday as a guest of another member. I wanted to surprise you.'

'You did.' He kept his other thoughts to himself. Like didn't she consider the likelihood of the concierge mentioning their conversation to the other member?

'I was careful, I never asked who he was meeting, just read the members' names upside down off the guest list.'

'Members?' Yianni asked.

She turned to him. 'Yes, two. That way they share the visitor charge. It's not uncommon.' Obviously, she was nervous. Going into arcane, irrelevant details delayed the inevitable point of why she was here.

Lila turned back to face Andreas. She shut her eyes, took a breath, and said the members' names. Then she opened her eyes.

'Jesus Christ.'

'*Fuck us.* Sorry Mrs Vardi.'

'No need to apologize. I thought the same thing when I read the names.'

Andreas ran his hands through his hair. 'Linardos, okay, I get that. Hard to believe, but not totally unexpected.' He paused. 'But the other one . . . *Wow!* Who would have believed that the—'

'Maybe you misread the names? You were reading upside down.' Kouros sounded prayerful.

Lila gestured no. 'That's not a name you misread. And it was *his* name in bold, capital letters.'

Kouros was shaking his head. 'Then we really are fucked. Who's ever going to believe us? Who's ever going to prosecute? Maybe we should just take out Demosthenes and let the rest of them ramble off through their old age?'

Andreas dropped his elbows to his desk and his head into his hands. 'I must admit I never expected this.' He sat up and looked out the window, then over at Lila. 'Thanks. I don't want to think of the mess we'd be in if we didn't know who was behind this.'

She sat straight up in her chair. 'What does that mean? Are you going to let them get away with it?'

Andreas shook a finger at her, but in a friendly way. 'Don't start up with that again.'

She crossed her arms and narrowed her eyes.

Andreas continued. 'I didn't say that and, besides, Zanni Kostopoulos isn't about to walk away from this.' He turned to Kouros. 'Keep doing what we're doing – building our case against Demosthenes. Let's see where it leads.'

He looked back at Lila. 'As for pressing formal charges against the Kolonaki Club kids, that will be decided by someone way above my pay grade.'

She stared at him, then winked.

'Everybody happy now?'

'Oh yeah, perfect. I'm going back to Demosthenes' neighborhood wearing a shirt saying, "Fuck the Revolution." My death will come quicker and less painfully that way. Bye, Mrs Vardi. Sorry, again, about the language.'

Andreas waited until he left. 'You do know what I'm about to say?'

'Something about not taking chances?'

'Not without at least telling me first. Every chance isn't worth the risk.' Though he knew hers at the club clearly was worth it.

Lila's bottom lip turned down into a pout. 'You're absolutely right.' She stood up, walked around his desk, put her lips to his ear, and whispered, 'Is there a lock on your door?'

This one was, too.

22

Dear Gertrude Louise,
A friend stopped by the club today looking for you.
Give a call when you have the chance. Kisses.

Now what? Demon was enjoying the quiet. He'd been working on his plans for the future, preparing for the launch of the new party, his new party. He didn't have time for hand-holding an old man. But he had to; this was *the* Old Man. He reached for the phone but paused before calling. Perhaps they were on to him? Should not risk calling from here, just in case.

The place he had in mind was about eight blocks south-west. He hadn't used that apartment in months. Only went there to get away from everyone. People stayed off that block unless they were desperate to get laid or high or lived there. His building had the obligatory white light above the door and smell of piss in the vestibule. He made a mental note to be out of there before dark.

His apartment was on the second floor – just a room, a table, a bed, two lamps, and two chairs. The water worked sometimes, the refrigerator rarely. He didn't consider it a home. He sat by the table and dialed from a new cell phone number, just in case.

'Hello.' It was the Old Man.

'I understand I had a caller.'

'Yes, an old friend of your family stopped by yesterday and asked for you by name.'

'By name?'

'Yes, and she knows you were our guest. I suspect that very soon each of us will be receiving a personal invitation of some sort.'

Probably to die, Demon thought. 'How did she get my name?'

'Don't know, but I assume from our mutual friend on Mykonos.'

Shit. Kostopoulos was onto him. 'What's her name? I think I should look her up.'

'Yes, that is a very good idea. Lila Vardi '

He remembered the name, vaguely. 'Describe her.'

'Better yet, buy this week's *Hello*. There's a story on her and the museum where she works – with photographs.'

'How convenient.'

'Yes. Please do give her my best when you see her, which I assume will be soon.'

'Will today do?'

'The sooner the better.' He hung up.

Demon did not move from the chair. He heard shouting from the next room. A hooker and a client arguing over the price for some special pleasure the john had in mind.

These are the people who will rally behind me, who will believe I share and understand their pain, that I can lead them to a better life. Let me get elected, and I promise I'll take care of them. I'll take care of *all* of Greece's garbage.

He went back to thinking about Lila Vardi. Ms Vardi is a threat. She's also the perfect vehicle for another sort of message to Kostopoulos: this is what happens to those you send against us.

No reason to use his regulars for this. They'd want too much, and learn too much. He'd give it to local scum from the neighborhood. No, make that a nearby neighborhood, one where he wasn't known. Who knows. If she's pretty enough they might even cut their price.

'What's he doing now?' It was late afternoon and Andreas had been waiting for Kouros' call. His last one didn't make Andreas happy. They'd followed Demosthenes to an apartment on one of Athens' worst streets and had no way of knowing what went on inside.

'Angelo, Christina, and I are with him. He bought a magazine at a newsstand on Sophocleos by the Athens Market and headed down Sophocleos toward Pireos.' One end of Sophocleos Street was known as Greece's Wall Street, but Demon was headed toward its other end, and a 24/7 market for virtually every other sort of vice or crime you might have in mind.

'He just bought two strung-out, junkie-looking guys a souvlaki. The three of them are arguing back and forth.'

'About what?'

'Can't tell. Wait a minute.'

Kouros didn't speak for two minutes. Andreas wanted

to say, 'What's happening?' but he knew Kouros would tell him if he could. Andreas hated it when his old chiefs wanted updates in the middle of a fight. It got his phone all bloody.

'Okay, I'm back. He was looking this way so I started talking to a hooker. Man, are they ugly down here. Whew. Anyway, Angelo told me he saw Demosthenes shake hands with the two guys and give them the magazine.'

'He gave them the magazine?'

'Yeah, they opened it up and took out some money.'

'Why didn't he just hand them the money? No cops around there, at least none who would care.'

'For sure. Wait a second.' This time it was a second. 'I have an angle on them off this window and . . . what the fuck . . . all three of them are looking at the magazine. Demosthenes is pointing to something.'

'Can you make it out?'

'No way to see what he's looking at, too far. But the magazine looks like . . . yes, it's *Hello.*'

'*Hello*? What are they doing with *Hello*?'

'Demosthenes maybe, but other two definitely aren't the *Hello* type. Guarantee you they're into the big tits, wide-open crotch, beat-off in the public toilet sort of stuff. But they've got a serious conversation going on about something in that maga – gotta run, Chief. They're splitting up. Angelo, you and Christina stay with the new guys, I'll take Demosthenes.'

The phone went dead. Andreas rubbed his eyes, then stretched. He pressed the intercom button. 'Maggie, do you have the latest issue of *Hello*?'

'Does the sea have water, the sky clouds?'

'I take it that's a—' before he could say 'yes' Maggie was coming through the door with the magazine.

Maggie dropped it on his desk. 'Some of us have work to do.'

She left him smiling. He looked at the cover. What were they looking at and why? Had to be something bad. Andreas opened to the first page and started turning through the magazine. Never realized how many worked so hard to get their pictures in here, while so many the magazine would love to feature worked even harder to stay out.

There was a story on the Kostopoulos family headlined, 'Where are they?' It was filled with rumors and empty of new facts. But it had pictures of everyone in the family. This was a possibility, he thought, but dismissed it as unlikely. No way, after everything with the Sardinians, Demosthenes was tossing amateurs into the mix. Besides, all of the family was out of Athens and, if they somehow reached Mykonos . . . Andreas smiled at the thought of the two street guys tangling with Zanni's little army, especially the major.

He kept turning pages. There were photographs of a lot of people he recognized and a lot more he didn't. Then he saw Lila. She looked so beautiful. He couldn't believe she actually liked him. Loved him from what she said this morning. What can she possibly see in me? What can I possibly offer her?

'Stop looking for problems. Believe her you idiot, and go with it.' Andreas was talking to himself.

He turned more pages. There was one of Linardos at some benefit, and another of the Old Man at the same benefit. Could be one of them, maybe both. Andreas stared at their photos and wondered what reason Demosthenes had to go after those two. He might get away with one falling victim to a random, tragic, street crime, but two? No way anyone would take that as coincidence. It would trigger an enormous investigation from every imaginable media and government arm. Demosthenes must be going after only one, but which one? And why?

Demosthenes didn't seem upset after his meeting with the two. Even happy. No, what Kouros said was 'at peace with the world.' What happened between then and now that has Demosthenes out hiring street scum who'd cut a throat for ten euros? Amazing, today he wants them dead; yesterday it was drinks at the Kolonaki Club. Guess the old adage is true—

Andreas stopped in mid-thought; his chest seized up, a chill shot through his body, his head started spinning. He thought he'd puke. '*Lila!* My god, they're going after Lila!' He talked to himself, trying to force his way out of whatever was happening to him. 'So, this is what they call an anxiety attack. *No fucking way, asshole!*' Andreas slammed his fists three times on the desk, stood up and headed out the door. '*No FUCKING WAY!*'

They had to hurry. The guy with the magazine said she worked over by the Acropolis and they must be there in thirty minutes. Fastest way was the metro. They ran. Had to get to Omonia – from there it was three stops to Akropoli station. That was their only chance to make it on time. The guy said she wasn't expecting it, and they'd get triple what he'd already paid if they did her today. If they caught her alone it was easy. With people around it would be tougher, but they still could do it. Just a quick bump and stab and she'd be dead before anyone knew what happened.

They hoped she was alone, though, and took a walk. They wanted to find a place to have a little fun with her first. The magazine guy said he didn't care what they did to her, as long as she died. They really wanted this pretty uptown lady to take a walk.

Andreas tried reaching Lila everywhere he could think of. She wasn't answering her mobile. He tried her at home, but she wasn't there, and although the maid thought she was meeting friends for lunch, she didn't know which ones or where. He called the museum, but no one picked up. All he got was a message saying it was closed today. He sent a text message warning her, and prayed she got it. He jumped back and forth between calling and text messaging. Not a word back. Andreas was desperate.

He kept trying to get through to Angelo and Christina. The investigation no longer mattered. He would order them to stop those two immediately, no matter what it took. But he couldn't reach anyone. He called Kouros.

'Chief?'

'Where are Angelo and Christina?'

'No idea, they told me the two guys were headed into the metro at Omonia and they were right behind them. Probably still underground with no signal. What's up?'

'They're after Lila.'

'My god.'

'Grab that bastard Demosthenes and find out where he sent them.'

Kouros didn't answer.

'*Did you hear me?*' Andreas shouted.

'I can't, he's somewhere inside the university. I couldn't follow him in. We're watching the gates for when he comes out.'

'*Fuck the constitution. Just find him!*' Andreas screamed and pounded his fists on the steering wheel. He'd been driving around without any idea of where to go. He was breathing heavily. 'Yianni, please. We've got to find him. They're going to kill her.'

'I'm going in now. I'll call you as soon as I have him.' Kouros paused. 'And I'm praying, too. Bye.'

Where can she be? Andreas never thought he'd see a worse moment in his life than his father's suicide. But this was worse, far worse. At eight years old there was nothing he could do to save someone he loved, but now he could. And yet he couldn't. He was left to dialing phone numbers – 'Angelo, Christina, for god's sake answer me' – and prayer. Andreas pulled the car over to the curb and stopped. He shut his eyes and bowed his head. 'Please, dear Lord, don't let anything happen to Lila, I beg of you, please.'

Angelo and Christina hadn't stopped running since the two men with Demon took off from Sophocleos Street. The men never checked to see if anyone was running behind them, so they figured the two were high. The cops caught their breath on the train, but the moment they reached the metro stop by the Acropolis the running started again. The cops were thirty yards behind them at the metro station, but the distance widened as they passed the new Acropolis Museum, and they were closer to forty yards apart by the time the two men turned left onto the Dionysiou Areopagitou pedestrian

285

promenade. It was part of the wide walkway that ran from the Ancient Agora on the west, past the Odeon of Herodes Atticus and Ancient Theater of Dionysos at the base of the Acropolis, to the plaza across from Hadrian's Arch on the east.

Angelo and Christina reached the pedestrian road just in time to see the two turn left onto a side street. Their communicators had been vibrating wildly since they came out of the metro station, but there was no way to slow down to answer them. They turned the corner onto the side street running at full speed, but stopped abruptly and pulled back around the corner. The two men were halfway down the block, on the east side of street, but they weren't running. They were walking toward the corner, looking back and forth. One pointed to a break between two apartment buildings on the other side of the street, but they didn't cross over; just kept heading toward the corner.

'This must be the place they're looking for. We better wait here. If we start down that street they'll make us for sure.' Angelo nodded toward Christina's communicator. 'Let's check in.'

Christina pressed the respond button and instantly heard their chief's voice. '*Where are you?*'

'On Dionysiou Areopagitou, a few blocks from the Akropoli metro station. The suspects are on a side street heading south toward Rovertou Galli. I think this is—'

Andreas' voice was deadly serious and loud enough for Angelo to hear him. 'Christina, listen carefully, those two are about to murder Lila Vardi, a white female, thirty-five, short black hair, approximately your height and weight.

286

Stop them immediately. Deadly force is authorized. Do you understand?'

Christina didn't answer. Angelo and she were too busy running toward the two men. The men had reached the corner, crossed to the west side, and started back up the street toward a dark-haired woman standing on the sidewalk looking at her cell phone.

Lila had been smiling all day. Why not? She'd finally met a man who put her first, or at least tried to. An American friend once joked that the Greek woman's greatest positive asset was her beauty, and that her greatest negative was her men. She couldn't wait for her friend to meet Andreas. That should change her mind.

The museum was closed today, but an hour and a half ago a major, old-money donor interrupted her lunch with friends with a call insisting they meet immediately at the museum to discuss a new gift. It was an hour-long, all phones off, listen-to-my-brilliance monologue by a very boring man. Thankfully, it was over. She still might be able to catch up with her friends for coffee. The restaurant was nearby, off Dionysiou Areopagitou.

She was a few feet from the museum's front door, headed toward the quiet side street around the corner, when she remembered her phone was off. She found it in her purse and pressed the power button. At the corner she turned left. The pedestrian road was only a hundred yards away.

Lila heard her phone beep to signal it was on, and beep again to signal missed calls and messages. She checked them as she walked. Andreas had called almost a dozen times. She smiled and thought, how sweet. She really did love him. She took a quick look at her messages. There were a half-dozen from Andreas. She sensed something must be wrong and stopped to read the first one:

Killers are after you. Stay where you are. Do not go outside. Call me immediately.

Lila never got to make that call. There was a shout, something struck the back of her head, and she was unconscious before hitting the pavement – lost to what happened next.

Christina and Angelo had pulled their guns when one of the men gave a quick jerk of his hand toward the pavement and brought it back up holding a fully expanded, steel baton. Christina shouted 'Police,' but the man swung it anyway. The woman dropped to the pavement.

The two men stood next to her body, as if not sure what to do or aware that police with drawn guns were running at them. Then, like cockroaches in the light, they bolted; heading south and turning right at the corner.

Angelo raced after them, pointing to Lila as he passed her. 'Take care of her.'

Christina dropped to her knees next to the body and felt for a pulse. She called for an ambulance using the code for officer down. It seemed Lila's only chance.

If there's one place in Athens where you're likely to find a cop when you need one, it's around the Acropolis. And a guy with a gun and a badge chasing two men and yelling 'Stop those bastards' soon had several pairs of fresh coplegs running them down. Three uniformed cops caught up to the two over by the Prisons of Socrates. One of the men held a knife and the other the steel baton, but both dropped their weapons the instant the cops drew their guns.

Five seconds later Angelo caught up to them. He stopped only long enough to say thanks to the cops, then turned and drove the side of his steel semi-automatic square into the face of the one who swung the baton, and twice more before the guy went down. The other one he kicked in the balls hard enough to drop him to the ground; then kicked each of them enough to break a rib or two. It was not the most-tourist friendly scene to witness. But Angelo didn't care. These bastards had tried to kill his chief's girl-friend. The chief never told him or Christina, but everyone in the unit knew. And that made her family.

He turned and looked at the three uniforms. 'Call an ambulance for this garbage, but take your time.' Then he ran back to Lila.

By the time he got there an EMT team was putting Lila on a stretcher. She was unconscious, and Christina would not let go of her hand. 'I'm staying with her. Tell the chief we'll be at Evangelismos Hospital.'

'Anything else?'

Christina walked beside the stretcher as they carried her to the ambulance. She looked down at Lila and squeezed her hand; then looked up at Angelo and mouthed – but did not speak – the words: *Tell him to hurry. It doesn't look good.*

23

It all was a blur. Andreas couldn't tell you where he was or how he got there. But he was sitting outside an operating theater in some hospital somewhere waiting to hear whether Lila would live or die. Or something in between. He wasn't alone. Her parents sat next to him. They were nice people. Gentle people. The mother cried, the father tried not to. Andreas stared straight ahead at nothing.

He had no idea how much time had passed when the surgeon finally came to tell them the news. They did what they could to repair bleeding onto her brain. No idea of the extent of the damage. No idea when she would regain consciousness. Should know more in seventy-two hours. There was nothing more left to do than pray.

Andreas thought he'd said goodbye to Lila's parents but wasn't sure. He remembered leaving the hospital and walking past his car. He just kept walking, wandering. He stopped in front of one church, then another. He went into neither.

He'd already said all the prayers he intended. Now he was thinking about other things, and a church was not a proper place for those thoughts. He kept walking until he stood on Alexandras Avenue across from GADA Headquarters. He wondered whether this was any more appropriate a place for what he had in mind. He didn't care. He crossed the street and went inside. Demon was about to get his wish: the times are a-changin. Andreas intended to see to it personally.

By the time Kouros spotted Demon he knew about Lila. He tried calling Andreas to find out if he still wanted Demon picked up, but Andreas didn't answer. Kouros decided only to watch him. Demon was sitting in the middle of a busy first-floor university hallway and didn't look to be going anywhere. They could grab him later, off-campus, where an arrest wouldn't set off student riots and end Kouros' career.

Hours passed and Demon hadn't moved. He just sat in that hallway reading a book. Every once in a while he looked at his watch and peeked into a nearby office. Three young female cops rotated through the stakeout. It looked less suspicious that way. All any of them had to do was stand still for a moment, and someone hit on her. That sort of *kamaki* conversation could go on indefinitely without attracting attention.

Kouros was out of sight, in an empty office in a hall around the corner from Demon, when his cell phone rang.

'Yianni?' It was not a voice Kouros recognized, yet he knew it was his chief.

'How's Lila?'

'They'll know something in seventy-two hours.' Andreas

spoke without emotion. He sounded numb, or in a trance. 'What have you done with Demosthenes?'

'We're watching him. He's inside the university sitting in a main hallway. I think he's waiting for a phone call.'

'Does he know we're onto him?'

'Don't think so.'

'I think I know who he's waiting to hear from, but those two guys won't be making any calls for a quite a few years.'

'I heard. Angelo told me. That's why I didn't grab him. Figured I'd wait to see what you wanted me to do.'

'You did the right thing. Let's keep him running around out there. Get back to the office as soon as you can get away. We've got things to talk about.'

Kouros assumed they were things Andreas didn't want to discuss over the phone. 'As soon as he leaves, I'll head back.'

'I'll be here. Nowhere else to go.' The phone went dead.

Kouros took a breath and wondered how he'd hold up if something like what happened to Lila ever happened to— 'God forbid,' and crossed himself.

Demon was tired of waiting for the junkies to call. Either they'd done the job or they didn't. Good thing he gave them a university number; if the fools got caught, there was nothing to link them back to him but their word. And little good that would do them.

He watched two pretty girls toy with some young guys hitting on them. He decided to see Anna. Yeah, that meant Efisio would find her for sure. But so what? He'd have to get rid of her soon anyway; the kid, too. Couldn't have a hooker and her bastard son tied to him any longer.

★ ★ ★

Andreas spent fifteen minutes explaining to Kouros what he had in mind. It wasn't complicated, just risky. Sort of like setting off a nuclear explosion inside a cookie jar and hoping no one noticed it was your jar.

Kouros' only question was whether he could use that Laurel and Hardy line again. 'I don't want to think of the mess we're in if this goes wrong.'

'I don't want to think about what happens if it works.'

'When do you talk to Tassos?'

'After he deals with the Sardinians. If he can't . . .' Andreas rubbed his eyes, 'and they snatch the family, there's no chance of pulling this off. None.'

'When do you think we'll know?'

'Don't know, but my guess is soon. Nothing we can do until then, except keep an eye on the cast of characters.' Andreas looked at his watch. 'Do me a favor, will you, and drop me off at the hospital. I left my car there.'

'Sure.'

'Any more word on Demosthenes?'

'Just that he went to Anna's and back to his apartment.'

'Probably led Efisio's boys right to her. Keep an eye on her, too. No other woman's going down because of that miserable bastard.' Andreas clenched his fists. 'So help me, god.'

A strange prayer for what he had in mind.

It was a beautiful day to be on the ocean. All the blues of the sea against the pale blues of the sky ran in one direction, and the greens, whites, and tans of southern Sardinia's shoreline in the other. The *Ginny Too* traveled south, passing near enough to shore to see the ancient watchtowers that once served to send word of invaders from the sea. Some say the sea was never friendly to this island and that was why so few chose to live by its edge. Today, it was building codes that kept construction inland and away from corrupting the beauty of this shore.

They dropped anchor a few hours before sunset off the town of Pula, just south of Sardinia's capital, Cagliari. Two inflatable boats, tenders to the *Ginny Too*, immediately left for shore. One held five men, and the other carried two children, a woman, and two men. The one with all men reached the dock first; four jumped ashore and the fifth moved the boat to idle nearby. Three of the men ran toward the parking lot at the end of the dock, the fourth helped the woman, children, and one man out of the second boat.

As soon as all were ashore, the boats sped back to the *Ginny Too* and the people hurried toward three all-black Hummers idling in the parking lot. The party from the second boat got into the middle Hummer, two men jumped into each of the others, and the three sped off from the port.

They wound through the local streets in crisp, military-convoy fashion. At a main road they turned left, and at another turned right toward Is Molas. Two miles later, in the middle of a modern, campus-style science and technology research center, they turned left onto a dirt road and into the enchanted 270-square-mile Sulcis National Park. A mountainous place of rock and granite, filled with holm oaks and centuries-old cork forests, it was as wild and beautiful a place as one might imagine within view of the sea.

Ten minutes later, just over the crest of a hill, a gate blocked the road. One man got out and opened it, while another scanned the road behind them. Within thirty

294

seconds they were moving again, deeper and deeper into the Sardinian forest.

'Can you believe how dumb those assholes are?' Efisio sounded on the verge of orgasm. 'They have no idea what they're doing.' He was holding court for the four others in the Jeep. Another five men were in the Jeep behind him.

'They're acting like tourists on holiday.' He rolled his hands as he spoke. 'Cruising so close to shore you could drive alongside them almost all the way down from Porto Cervo. And, now, they're on a dirt road heading into the middle of a forest.' He shook his head. 'Whoever's in charge of their security is an idiot. Or an amateur who thinks a Hummer makes them safe.' He patted the rocket propelled grenade launcher lying across his lap. 'This should make those Hummers really hum.'

Everyone in the Jeep laughed.

The driver said, 'I know where they must be headed. It's a farmhouse inn about two miles from where we turned onto this dirt road. This is the only way in. And the only way out.' He smiled.

Efisio also smiled. 'Amateurs.'

S'Atra Sardegna was a beautiful place to eat, everything organically grown and raised. But Tassos wasn't headed there for the food. Once Ginny agreed to take the fight to the kidnappers, Tassos made sure the *Ginny Too* was visible from shore. That's how the professional soldiers on board picked up two Jeeps shadowing them down the coast.

The soldiers also arranged for the drivers and Hummers. Tassos was wary of bringing locals into their camp – blood being blood, as they say – but the major called and convinced him to trust them. The men on board worked for the major, and the ones in the Hummers weren't locals; they were ex-Italian Special Forces who helped clean up the island in the nineties and loved Sardinia so much they stayed. He'd 'worked with them before' and could 'vouch for them.' Tassos certainly hoped so, because the plan was tricky enough without having someone betray them from within.

There was no sign of the Jeeps since a half-mile after the gate. His guess was they'd set up an ambush to catch them on the way back. That was the smart play. His was smarter. The only part he really didn't like was bringing Ginny and the kids along. But in these days of high-resolution digital photography, dressing someone up to look like the family wouldn't fool anyone. At least not with the potential imposters he had to work with.

The inn was just up ahead. Time to get started. The first Hummer moved over so the second could pass. All three stopped. Tassos got out. The family and driver proceeded to the farmhouse. All four would check into a room and wait for word. If word didn't come by a certain time, a helicopter would lift the family out to safety, or try to. And that was the easy part of the plan.

Efisio was getting edgy. It was way past sunset and still no Hummers. Aside from some old, fat farmer in a beat-up pickup truck, nothing had come from the direction of the farmhouse in hours. It was almost ten, and there was only a sliver of moonlight to see by.

He set up at a spot where the road climbed and narrowed to barely wide enough for a Hummer to pass. His men were deployed behind boulders running down from him on his side of the road. On the other side of the road, the right side coming up from the inn, was a steep drop and certain death to anyone in a tumbling vehicle.

It was perfect. Like shooting fish in a barrel, which was precisely why Efisio was here and had the only RPG launcher. This was neither a fish hunt nor target practice. He planned on taking out the front of the first Hummer. That would block the rest. His men and their AK-47's would shoot out the tires of the other two. A Jeep was in position to block any attempt to retreat down the hill. Every man was instructed not to shoot to kill until the family was located. He wasn't about to screw up a forty-million-euro payday by killing a target.

Once they had the kids, everyone else was dead. There was no reason to keep them alive, except, of course, for the very pretty wife. He took another look at her on that camera that caught them getting into the Hummer. Maybe he could have a little fun with her before sending her back to plead with her husband to save their children. Why not?

'Efisio, do you hear that?' It was a muffled shout from the man furthest down the hill followed by the unmistakable roar of a big engine.

'This is it, get ready. And no one shoots at anyone until we know where the family is. *Understand!*' There were mumbled responses but Efisio knew they'd heard him.

Flashes of bouncing light intensified and came more frequently. The Hummers would be here any minute. Efisio positioned himself behind a granite boulder in such a way that he could nail the first one at point-blank range and still have cover from the explosion. It was forty yards from where he was to where the first Hummer would appear. He'd fire when it was ten yards away. No way he could miss.

The first one came roaring around the turn, headed straight for him with blinding roof lights angled front and left covering every inch of ground it approached. Efisio took careful aim and prepared to fire the instant those first lights appeared in his sights.

But that never happened. Every light went off, every sound stopped – except for a single slamming door. That's when Efisio realized there was only one Hummer and – '*Shoot, shoot to kill! It's A TRAP!*' he screamed.

But they'd lost their night vision to the Hummer's blinding lights and fired wildly into the dark in the direction of the slamming door, giving away their positions to five men flanking them from above with unimpeded sight and night vision goggles. The kidnappers' spray-and-pray approach to marksmanship did not serve them well in this fight. Three died instantly from precisely placed sniper rounds. Six others were badly crippled from less accurate but more than adequate bullet placement. The tenth, and only uninjured kidnapper, dropped a grenade launcher and fled up the road away from the Hummer the moment the firing started.

Efisio could hear his men's screams. He was frantic. These were no amateurs. He had to get away. He ran on fear and adrenaline without stopping. He had no idea where he was, but when he heard no sounds and saw no lights behind him he felt calmer. He had to get his wits back. He had to get out of here.

There was a farm gate up ahead. He remembered seeing it coming in. Something to do with food for the inn's restaurant, one of his men had said. Parked next to it was the pickup that passed by earlier. It looked like the driver was asleep inside. He crept closer and heard snoring. What a break. He flipped open his stiletto and moved up along the driver's side. One quick jab to the throat through the window and that fat farmer was gone.

Shit, the driver's window was closed almost to the top. No problem; he'd just pull open the door and stick the blade in his neck before he knew what hit him. Efisio grabbed the door handle and yanked.

'Surprise.'

That was the last word Efisio heard before the shotgun went off in his face.

Within an hour every trace of what just happened was gone. The major was right about those guys. The dead kidnappers disappeared, the crippled found their way to the welcoming arms of Italian police, and no one said a word about the unscheduled celebratory fireworks festival in the park.

Tassos was particularly happy that none of his men was hurt, though the one who drove the Hummer and pulled off the distracting door slam did catch a ricochet in his ballistic vest. Tassos was sorry he missed the actual battle, but he knew he was too old for that sort of thing. He was far better suited these days to supporting roles, like scout, backup – and old, fat farmer in a pickup truck.

24

Andreas fell asleep in a chair next to Lila's hospital bed, where he'd been holding her hand and talking to her. He'd read somewhere that might comfort her, help to bring her back. He didn't talk about anything in particular; just whatever came into his head. Andreas missed her.

He sensed light in the room and slight pressure on his shoulder. He opened his eyes. It was Lila's mother.

'Morning, Chief Kaldis.'

He stumbled to get up. 'Morning, ma'am.'

'Thank you.'

'For what?'

'For being here for our daughter.'

Andreas nodded. He wanted to say all of this was his fault, but didn't. He had a tough enough time as it was dealing with the guilt, and he couldn't bear the thought of turning her parents against him, too. He promised himself to tell them some other time.

'The nurse said there is a message for you at her desk. The caller said to give it to you when you woke up.'

'Thank you.' He put out his hand. 'Goodbye.'

She took it and looked in his eyes. 'This is not your fault,' and kissed him on both cheeks.

Andreas left quickly. He didn't want her to see his tears. Like daughter, like mother.

On the way out he picked up the message. It was from Kouros.

'Hi, Yianni.'

'How's Lila?'

'No change. Thanks for asking. What's up?'

'Tassos called this morning. He's been trying to reach you all night. I told him what happened and he said he'd pray for you both.' Yianni paused.

'That's nice of him.'

'Good news. Efisio and his boys are no more.'

'That's terrific. What happened?'

'Tassos made me promise I'd let him tell you himself. He sounded like a rookie talking about his first collar. Really excited.'

Andreas felt a slight grin, his first since . . . 'Can't wait.'

'But you better hurry, before it starts sounding like a winning version of three hundred Spartans fighting a million Persians at Thermopylae. And since Tassos says he was the only Greek in the fight, we know who's getting the King Leonidas part.'

Andreas laughed. 'And there's no one to challenge his story.' He paused. 'Thanks, Yianni.'

'For what?'

'For making me laugh. I'll call him right away. And, if

he says it's a go with the plan, we hit the Angel Club. With luck, this afternoon.'

'Sounds good.'

'What about Demosthenes?' Every time Andreas said that name, his thoughts cursed the man to hell.

'He's still in his apartment. Nothing different; no calls, no visitors, just typing sounds and humming.'

'I guess that means he hasn't heard what happened in Sardinia?'

Kouros paused. 'You're right.'

'Not sure who there is to tell him. Possibly Anna, if someone calls to make her day by saying Efisio's dead, but my guess is she hates Demosthenes as much, if not more, than she did Efisio. Doubt she'd tell him.'

'Do you think the Sardinians will come after her?'

'It seemed pretty much a personal thing between Efisio and her. No reason I can think of for any of them to care about her now. But keep an eye on her anyway. At least until we see how this Demosthenes thing plays out. My guess is he's her biggest threat. No telling what that asshole might do.'

Andreas was standing next to his car by the time they hung up. He decided to wait and call Tassos from home. He needed Tassos' help if his plan was to get off the ground, and he wanted a shower to put some distance between his praying here and talk of vengeance there.

All Andreas had to say was 'hello' and Tassos was off and running after a brief, but sincere, inquiry into Lila's status.

Tassos' telling of his epic tale took almost an hour. They joked and laughed through much of it in the bravado style cops use to help process the many fears and dark memories that surround events, even great successes, which so easily might have ended their lives.

'How did you know it was Efisio coming up to the pickup?'

'I didn't. One of the Italians on our side radioed me to say they found a grenade launcher without an operator. Whoever got away had to be pretty nasty, because he brought the only RPG to the party.'

'They had some heavy weapons.'

'Yeah, but no match for our guys' professionalism. They had the pickup truck and sawed-off shotgun waiting for me by the farmhouse, and after I radioed the location of the ambush they told me where to park the truck and wait. They said anyone who escaped was likely to be running like a madman and, by the time he reached me, be past his adrenaline rush.'

'How thoughtful of them to make it easier for an old, fat farmer like you to handle an uninvited visitor.' Andreas laughed.

'I knew I shouldn't have told you that part.' Tassos laughed.

'So, how did you know he was one of them?'

'I was inside, leaning against the window, looking back up the road in the side view mirror. He kept creeping up as if he thought I was sleeping. So, I started snoring. Then he pulled a knife, I pulled a shotgun, and the rest is history. Didn't know until later he was Efisio. One of the wounded identified him. From his clothes.'

Andreas started clapping. 'Bravo, bravo, great job. I'm sure the Kostopoulos family was happy.'

'Who knows with those people? They think it's your job to turn water into wine and only complain when you don't.'

Andreas chuckled. 'So, let me tell you where we are.'

'You mean there still are bad guys out there?'

Andreas ignored the sarcasm. He knew it wasn't directed at him. He told Tassos everything he knew about Demosthenes, the Angel Club, and Demosthenes' meeting at the Kolonaki Club. When Andreas named Demon's hosts—

'You *must* be kidding me! The Old Man's involved?'

Andreas answered flatly. 'Don't know. All I'm certain of is Demosthenes is the link between whoever wanted Kostopoulos' son murdered and the actual killers. The Old Man and Linardos met with Demosthenes at the Kolonaki Club. Only someone from the club could have told Demosthenes that Lila mentioned his name in connection with that meeting, and Demosthenes hired two low-lifes to kill her.' He crossed himself.

'That's never going to convince a court the Old Man and Linardos were involved.'

'No shit! It doesn't even convince me.'

'So, what are you saying?'

'I want to be convinced.'

'How do you propose doing that?'

Andreas spent the next fifteen minutes telling him.

'That's a pretty interesting plan. Do you really think it's going to work?'

'If you convince Kostopoulos to work with us, I think we have a better than fifty-fifty chance. Especially after that fiasco in Sardinia.'

'You know, once I tell Zanni all these things and mention names, there's no telling how he might react. He could

304

send his little army off on vengeance missions like the Israelis after the Munich Olympics.'

'I know how he feels, believe me, but I don't know what else I can do. Sure, I can go after Demosthenes and let the big boys get away. But don't you think Kostopoulos has a right to know the facts? After all, it was his son who was murdered, and the only chance I see of proving who was behind it is *if* Zanni cooperates. Either we get them on tape admitting to everything, or there's not a snowball's chance in hell of touching one of them in court.'

He heard Tassos breathing heavily. 'Okay, but I'm still worried about how he'll react.'

'Let me put it this way. If he goes after Demosthenes he'll lock horns with me, big time. And he doesn't want to do that, fucking army or not. He has no reason to go after Linardos or the Old Man on what we have now, unless he's insane.'

'That's one thing he's not. Bitter, angry, vengeful, yes. Insane, no.'

'Fine, then tell him if he wants to know who was behind his son's murder, this is how to find out, and the only way to prove it to a court. Otherwise, tell him to see a shrink, put the tragedy behind him, and get on with his life.' Andreas paused. 'Maybe that's the best advice after all.'

Tassos cleared his throat. 'I'll talk to him and let you know.'

'Well, make it soon, because I've got to put the Angel Club boys in play.'

'I'll try. That's all I can promise. Take care. Give Lila a kiss for me.'

Andreas stared out the window. He decided to go back to the hospital and wait for news. Pray it was good.

Demon was waiting for a simple, one-word e-mail from Efisio: DONE. But there was no word from that psycho and no word from the druggies. That didn't surprise him. Demon long ago gave up on expecting society's irresponsible scum to act otherwise. The only thing that ever worked with them was money. They always were on time for payday.

Demon decided to go back to the university for an hour or so to give the druggies another chance to call. If they got to Vardi today, they'd be calling for their bonus money. Efisio presented a different problem. Demon and his new political allies faced potential all-out war with Kostopoulos, but he knew Efisio couldn't care less about their problems. He didn't need Demon any more; the ransom demands and negotiations could be directly with Kostopoulos. No middleman required.

Demon needed to know the status of the kidnappings, and he needed to know now. Not when Efisio got around to telling him. If he didn't have an e-mail from Efisio by the time he got back to his apartment, he'd call him. No, Efisio might not take his call. Anna would make the call. That's a call he'd take for sure.

'Maybe we should call ahead, make sure Giorgio is there?'

Andreas drummed his left-hand fingers on the dashboard. 'No, he's used to us kicking in his door, not knocking on it. That might make him suspicious.'

Kouros nodded. 'Are you surprised Kostopoulos agreed to go along?'

306

'Tassos can be pretty convincing.'

'How are we going to get the Old Man to admit all this shit on tape?'

Andreas turned his head and looked out the side window. 'I'm working on it.'

'If we don't, there's going to be war. I can't see Kostopoulos letting them get away with killing his son and then trying to take out the rest of his family.'

'Look at those kids over there, the ones playing in the park. Nice to have a family.'

Kouros gave a quick glance toward Andreas. 'I was talking about war.'

'I'd rather talk about peace.'

They compromised and spoke about soccer.

At the Angel Club, they were met in the vestibule by the same two bouncers as greeted them the last time. Andreas smiled. 'Excuse me, gentlemen. Is Mr Giorgio available to see us?'

The bigger of the two glared. The smaller one spoke. 'I'll check,' and went inside to a phone.

No one else moved or said a word. They just waited for the man to return.

He called out from the doorway. 'He'll see you now.'

The four walked together to Giorgio's office. Giorgio was inside, sitting alone, and Andreas suggested he kept it that way. Giorgio told the bouncers to wait outside.

'Okay, so what's so private?' Giorgio seemed indifferent.

Andreas didn't bother telling him to shut off whatever recording device he was using. Guys like him always ran one, hoping to catch crooked cops demanding bribes, to keep them in line if they later got greedy. Andreas wanted all this on tape so Giorgio could play it back for whoever made the real decisions.

'I got a call this morning from a Captain Cacace of the Italian Police. He said Zanni Kostopoulos told him to call me.'

Giorgio shrugged. 'About what?'

'I asked the same thing. He said last night some local boys over in Sardinia took a shot at kidnapping Kostopoulos' wife and kids.'

Giorgio blinked twice.

Andreas shook his head. 'Didn't work out too well for those boys. They ended up either dead or in jail. All ten of them. He wanted to know if I might know the guy who hired them to do it. I didn't, but I thought you might.'

'Me? Why me?'

'Remember that girl in here with the Kostopoulos boy the night he was murdered?'

Giorgio nodded. 'Yeah.'

'The captain told me that one of the guys in the kidnapping crew was her ex-boyfriend.'

Giorgio shifted in his chair.

'Yeah, and the same guy said they were hired for that job by someone who contacted them through her.'

'What's the name?' It was Giorgio's first show of interest in anything Andreas had said.

'Nobody I ever heard of.' Andreas pulled out his notebook. 'Mavrakis, Demosthenes Mavrakis. You know him?'

Giorgio looked straight ahead at the wall. 'Never heard of him.'

*   *   *

'Hello, is Efisio there?'

There was a brief pause on the other end of the line. 'Who's calling?'

'Anna, Anna Panitz.'

'Been a long time.'

'Yes. I know, but I must speak to Efisio. It's very important.'

'He's not here.'

'Do you know where he is?'

'Back in his village, in Sardinia.' The speaker let out a breath. 'The funeral is in a couple of days.'

'What funeral?'

'His.'

Demon grabbed the phone. 'Dead. He can't be dead! What happened?'

Anna heard a hum on the other end of the line, but Demon kept yelling into the phone.

'The line's dead. They hung up,' she said.

Demon threw the phone against the wall, then swung around and slapped her face. 'It's your fucking fault.' And stormed out of the apartment.

Anna touched her fingers to where he'd slapped her. Despite everything else Demon had done to her, this was the first time he'd hit her. She swore to herself when she fled Efisio that no man ever would strike her again.

It was time to move on.

Andreas was in his office with Kouros when the call came in from the cops covering Anna's apartment. They played what they caught on tape. Andreas bit at his lower lip while he listened, and Kouros seemed to be holding his breath.

When it came to the part where Demon stormed out of the apartment, Kouros threw his right fist in the air and yelled, '*Yes!*'

Andreas smiled. They listened to the tapes again and hung up.

'First good news in a long time. The son of a bitch is worried.' Kouros pumped his fist again.

'Wait until the Angel Club boys figure out Demosthenes' decision to hire new muscle cost them a mega-payday with Kostopoulos.'

'Has Kostopoulos told them yet?'

'Tassos said the next time the negotiator calls, Kostopoulos will tell him everything's off because of *their* attempt to kill his family in Sardinia. That, together with our little visit to Giorgio, should tie everything together for them very nicely.'

'They will be pissed. Do you think they'll kill Demosthenes?'

Andreas gestured no. 'Doubt we'd be that lucky. This is a business problem for them. As much as they might want to whack him, he's the only one who can convince Kostopoulos they had nothing to do with Sardinia. At least that's what I'm hoping they'll do.'

'Otherwise, he's dead.'

'And we lose. Oh, well, too bad for Demosthenes.' Andreas smiled. 'That would really upset me. Especially the painful, drawn-out way they'd do it.'

'I can tell you're all broken up at the possibility.'

'It's up to Kostopoulos now. If he pushes the right buttons, we've got Demosthenes working overtime on saving his ass from his former buddies.'

'What about the Old Man and Linardos?'

Andreas gestured no. 'The most that muscle has on them

is Demosthenes' word that they're involved, and I doubt they put much value on his word these days. Besides, the Old Man and Linardos are too powerful for them to go after. It would bring down the wrath of Greece's powers that be for attacking one of their own and shatter whatever business arrangements those mob guys must have with some of them.'

Andreas stretched. 'On the other hand, Demosthenes desperately needs the Old Man's help to get to Kostopoulos. Otherwise, what's Demosthenes? A nobody, a less than nobody. "Hi, Mr Kostopoulos, I'm the one who hired the people who killed or tried to kill members of your family, but trust me when I say the ones who killed your son had nothing to do with Sardinia."'

Kouros laughed.

Andreas frowned and shook his head. 'Demosthenes can't think that's going to work. He must know his only chance at getting to Kostopoulos, and living, is if he convinces the Old Man to intervene directly with Kostopoulos.'

'Why would the Old Man do that? What does he have to gain coming out of the closet at this point in his life to announce he's a terrorist? And not just a terrorist, the *head* terrorist.'

'That's the wing-and-a-prayer part of the plan. I've no idea what will do it. I'm leaving that up to Demosthenes. We've motivated him. Let's hope he can do the same for the Old Man.'

Maggie stuck her head in the office. 'Yianni, those cops from up north called, the ones you had following the guy you tailed to the airport. They said he's on the move again. He's back over the border into Greece and headed to the airport. They'll call you as soon as they know where he's headed.'

Kouros turned to Andreas and smiled. 'Care to bet where Demosthenes' old buddy is headed?'

Andreas clapped his hands together. 'Let the games begin.'

The message was 'Be outside Kato Patissia metro, 9 a.m.' Another metro ride to another tough neighborhood. Probably another unpleasant car ride, too.

Demon's mind wandered to thoughts of his future and of private drivers to whisk him to such places. He knew he could never put these sorts of meetings behind him. He would always need these types. Now, to convince them they still needed him.

He looked at his watch. Nine-fifteen. Where is he? The answer came in the form of a taxi pulling up beside him. 'Taxi, mister?'

'No, I'm wait—'

Demon got in the back seat. 'Didn't recognize you. Nice touch, no one notices a Balkan taxi driver these days.'

'What the fuck did you do?'

'Beg your pardon.'

'You heard me. Sardinia.'

'Oh, yes. Well, you left me with no choice. What was I supposed to do? The gentlemen I report to made me do it. I wanted you to get the job but—'

'Enough of your bullshit. You've cost us a lot of money. Kostopoulos killed the deal. Thinks we tried to kill his wife and kids. You asshole.'

Demon sounded calm, but his heart was racing. He expected Sardinia was the reason he was here, even

312

anticipated the anger, but expecting something and facing it eyeball-to-eyeball, even through a rearview mirror, were very different things.

'I understand you're angry. But, you've profited quite handsomely over the years from my relationships with very powerful people, people who want to continue working with you, through me, making you more money than you can imagine. This is just a slight bump in the road.' He paused and waved a hand as if swatting away some minor distraction. 'To continue with the analogy, my friend, you cannot imagine the extraordinary opportunities that await us if we just stay on the road we've traveled together for so long, and so prosperously. Trust me.'

'Trust you!' He laughed. 'I'm a simple man, so let me put it to you in simple terms. I don't care about your buddies or connections. You're the one we deal with, you're the one we know, and you're the one we no longer trust. Either you straighten out this shit storm you created with Kostopoulos or – to continue the analogy . . .' he paused to smile in the rearview mirror. 'It's the end of the road for you. Asshole.'

He pulled over to the curb and told Demon to get out. 'Forty-eight hours to get Kostopoulos talking again.' He drove away without voicing another threat. He didn't have to. He'd let Demon off in front of one of the few funeral parlors in Athens.

25

'It's Yianni.'

'What happened?'

'I followed the guy from the airport. A taxi picked him up and drove him to Kato Patissia. The driver got out at a coffee shop and the guy took his cab. He drove to the metro and picked up Demosthenes. They rode around for five minutes, Demosthenes got out, and the guy went back to the coffee shop. The guy and the driver are having breakfast together. Probably cousins.'

'Any idea what Demosthenes and he talked about?'

'No way of telling. Didn't seem to be arguing. When Demosthenes got out, he just looked around and walked back to the metro. Angelo's with him.'

'Damn it. If they didn't put some real heat on him, nothing's going to happen. No pressure from Demosthenes on the Old Man to meet Kostopoulos, no meeting with Kostopoulos—'

'No recording of the Old Man's confession.'

'Shit.' Andreas tried sounding calm.

'Should we bust the guy?'

'For what, borrowing his cousin's cab? Wish we could, but it's too risky. If he gets busted so soon after meeting Demosthenes, his buddies might get nervous, think things are getting out of control, and decide to blow Demosthenes away. What the hell, odds are guys like that don't live very long, anyway. Occupational hazard.'

'I still don't like letting him get away.'

Andreas smiled. 'Glad to hear that. Me, neither.'

'Hold on, Chief. It's Angelo.'

Andreas tapped a pencil on his desk. Keep your fingers crossed, he thought.

'Demosthenes came out of the metro at Evangelismos.'

Andreas' heart skipped two beats, then started racing. 'My god. That's the stop for the hospital. He's going after Lila!'

Kouros spoke quickly. 'No, no, Chief, he's headed in the other direction.'

Andreas didn't say anything for a few seconds. He let his breathing return to normal. 'I guess I'm more anxious than I thought.'

'Who wouldn't be? If it makes you feel better, I think Demosthenes' taxi ride may have done the trick.'

'Why?'

'Because . . . sorry, it's Angelo again.' Ten seconds went by. 'Uhh . . . yeah, because that metro stop is also the one for Kolonaki. And guess where our little Demosthenes is now.'

'Heading for the Kolonaki Club.'

'No, actually he's inside, as of thirty seconds ago.'

'*Yes!*' and two double fist pumps.

'I'm sorry, if you're not on the list you cannot come in, sir.'

'But I know he wants to see me, please call him.'

'I'm sorry, sir, but the rules do not allow us to do that.'

'Do what?'

'Disturb a member when someone appears unannounced claiming to be invited.'

Demon wanted to kill the pretentious bastard. Didn't he realize he was from the servant class? But Demon needed the idiot. 'I understand. Is there a phone I may use?'

'Certainly.' He pointed to the one on his desk. 'Dial nine first.'

Demon dialed without saying thank you.

An operator answered. 'Kolonaki Club, how may I help you?'

Demon asked for the Old Man and waited.

'Yes.'

'It's me, I'm downstairs. Your doorman won't let me in. Speak to him, please.' Demon handed him the phone without waiting to hear the Old Man's reply.

'Yes, sir. Right away, sir.' The man didn't look happy at Demon making him look stupid. Sorts like him believed people who looked like Demon should know their place – somewhere far beneath his. 'Third floor, second door to the right off the elevator.'

Demon nodded and walked to the elevator. He would take great pleasure in watching that guy kiss his ass someday.

'By the way, I'm not a doorman. I'm the club's concierge.'

Demon didn't bother looking back. 'Don't worry. Soon you will be.'

In the elevator Demon closed his eyes and took several deep breaths. This was the most important performance of his life. He must remain calm. He must stay focused. The doors opened, he walked to the second door to the right and knocked.

'Come in.'

Another quick breath and Demon pushed open the door.

'Welcome, Demosthenes.'

Demon gave a quick look around. He couldn't care less about how the room looked; they all looked the same to him here, anyway. He wanted to make sure they were alone.

'I assumed you wanted privacy. We have it.' The Old Man pointed to the chair beside his. 'So, what has you so bothered, my boy?'

Don't let his patronizing get to you. Stay focused. 'We have a very serious problem.'

'Every day brings serious problems.' The Old Man smiled. 'They are what make life interesting.'

Demon nodded. 'Well put. That's why I came to you for advice.'

He patted Demon's knee. 'So, what's bothering you?'

'The operation in Sardinia did not go as planned. The family got away and all of the kidnappers were killed or caught.'

The Old Man just stared.

'Kostopoulos knows we were behind it. The Albanians and their new Greek mob buddies know we tried to go around them. I just received a very unpleasant personal message giving us forty-eight hours to straighten things out with Kostopoulos or we're all dead.'

317

The Old Man shook his head. 'Terrible predicament. I wish this had been handled better. I had such high hopes for you.'

Keep your cool. 'I know, and I wish I hadn't dragged you into this. I'll never be able to forgive myself for having brought all this misery into your home.'

The Old Man pointed to his chest. 'My home? What does this have to do with me? You certainly don't think any of them would dare come after me, or my family?' He leaned forward and showed his teeth. 'And if you think you can scare me by saying you'll talk, forget it. No one will believe you.' He leaned back.

'I know, you're absolutely right. Who in Greece would take my word against yours? But then again, I'm not trying to convince Greeks. Well, at least not Greeks according to your definition. I just have to convince some mobsters that you cost them hundreds of millions of euros and one very hard-assed Greek you don't think belongs here.'

The Old Man shrugged. 'I'll take my chances. As far as Kostopoulos knows, this is something between you and hired killers in it for the money. The others, well,' he waved his hands, 'they wouldn't dare come after me on your word.'

Demon leaned back and stretched. 'You are so right.' Then he reached into his pocket, pulled out a metal object, pointed it at the Old Man, and pressed.

The Old Man sat straight up in his chair. 'What are you do—'

'*Hello, Demosthenes, do you know my old friend Sarantis Linardos?*' It was a tape recorder, and those were the Old Man's words. The tape continued. '*Sarantis, Demosthenes says he is in need of a considerable sum of money in order to resolve a rather messy and unexpected situation involving a family I know you're familiar with.'*

The Old Man put up his hand to Demon. 'Stop.'

Demon didn't, and the Old Man's voice continued on the tape. *'Kostopoulos doesn't know about us.'*

Demon pressed stop. 'But he will, and this is what he'll hear.'

'We need order and must do whatever is required to achieve it. The Kostopoulos boy's death was necessary. You know that.'

Demon smiled. 'But not just him. Copies of the tape of our entire meeting are in envelopes addressed to every political party, newspaper and television station in Greece, plus of course, CNN, BBC, and whatever international antiterrorist organizations I could think of. And, if anything happens to me . . . yes . . . you guessed it, *voilà*, they get them. Frankly, once this comes out, I don't think Kostopoulos will want to kill you. He'll be getting too much pleasure watching you and your family being destroyed.'

Demon leaned over and patted the Old Man's knee. 'If I were you, I'd start considering suicide. If you have the balls.'

The Old Man was shaking. 'You miserable piece of shit.'

Demon smiled. 'Now that we understand each other, would you like Kostopoulos' phone number?' Demon held out a piece of paper. 'Make nice and do whatever it takes to get an appointment to see him by tomorrow. Just remember—' He pressed the button again. It was Demon's voice this time. *'I'd prefer not to die, and bringing you down takes me with you. I need you too much. Almost as much as you need me.'* He clicked it off.

The Old Man's face was so red and his breathing so

rapid, that for a moment Demon feared he might have pushed him into a heart attack. The Old Man glared at Demon, then reached out and snatched the paper from his hand. 'Are you recording this too, or was the other day here a special occasion?'

Demon shrugged and smiled. 'You can't be that surprised, considering how many of your distinguished colleagues in government find their recorded indiscretions making it into the press these days. My personal favorite is that DVD secretly shot by the lover of our prime minister's married fat friend from the culture ministry. Poor guy didn't know what to do, so he jumped out a window. Too bad he picked a low floor. He's lived to see his DVD a big hit on the Internet. But you're smarter; you'll pick a higher floor. As you say, one can't be too careful.'

The Old Man sat quietly for a few moments, then picked up the phone on the table next to him and dialed the number on the paper. He identified himself to the man who answered and asked to speak to 'Mr Kostopoulos.'

'I'm sorry, Mr Kostopoulos is not in at the moment. May I have him call you back when he returns? It should be within the hour.'

The Old Man hesitated. Demon looked at him and mouthed, 'Yes.'

'Yes, that will be fine.' He gave him the number for the Kolonaki Club and hung up.

Demon smiled. 'Good. Now, we just wait.' He looked around the room. 'You know, I'm really starting to like this place. Why don't you propose me for membership?'

The Old Man showed no expression, just stared at the floor.

320

'After all, don't you think I fit in?' Probably more than either of them imagined.

Tassos used the hour going over everything again with Kostopoulos. If Zanni lost his notorious temper . . . Tassos didn't want to think about it. He placed the call, and when the Old Man answered said, 'I am putting Mr Kostopoulos through now, sir.' He pointed to Zanni to pick up the extension.

'Hello, Zanni Kostopoulos.'

'Oh, yes, Zanni, how are you?'

'Busy.'

'I'm sure.'

Kostopoulos didn't say a word.

'I understand there have been several tragic events involving your family, and I thought perhaps we should meet to see if there is anything I can do to assist in bringing all of this unpleasantness to an end.'

Tassos cringed. If Kostopoulos didn't lose it here . . .

'And how do you think you can help?' Zanni was as calm as a falling snowflake – headed toward hell. He seemed in a trance to Tassos.

'Oh, I think I can be very helpful. People trust me. They know that I get things done. Resolve misunderstandings.'

'Let's put it this way. I don't have any idea what you're talking about. Except that you want to talk. If you want to meet, fine. But I'm only going to do it where I feel safe. Understand?'

The Old Man paused. 'Understood.'

'Then we meet here. On Mykonos.'

321

Again a pause. 'As long as I pick the place. I have similar concerns.'

Kostopoulos looked at Tassos. 'Let's agree on a place now. Otherwise we're wasting each other's time.'

'Okay. How about the new Cultural Center, past the hospital coming out of town on the way to Ano Mera?'

'The Gripario?' Kostopoulos looked at Tassos, who nodded yes. 'That works. I'll speak to the mayor and make sure we have the place to ourselves. When do you want to do it?'

Another pause. 'Tomorrow night, around eight?'

Again, Tassos nodded yes.

'Okay,' said Kostopoulos.

'See you then. Goodbye.'

Tassos let out a breath. 'Good job.'

Kostopoulos' expression hadn't changed. '*Unpleasantness*. This is "*unpleasantness*" to him.' Kostopoulos kept repeating the word as he walked out of the room.

A minute later, Tassos called Andreas and told him it was a 'go' for tomorrow. They had a lot to do in less than twenty-four hours.

Everyone did.

26

Tassos promised Andreas to have the Cultural Center wired for sound and video by noon. He was doing it through the place's existing audio and video system. Nothing would seem out of the ordinary; no one would even know it was running. It was the perfect setup.

The first thing Andreas did after hanging up with Tassos was arrange for the immediate transport to Mykonos of his two best surveillance teams – vans, equipment and all. He was taking no chances. If something went wrong inside, they'd be there to pick it up. No way he would let some screw-up allow those bastards to get away.

The Old Man told Demon to go home and get some sleep; that they'd speak in the morning. Demon told him not to even *think* about meeting with Kostópoulos alone. No telling what the Old Man might try to pull on him if he wasn't there to protect himself. They agreed to meet at the

Kolonaki Club at three the next day and leave for Mykonos from there.

Demon decided to see Anna. He had nothing else to do.

He knocked on her door. No answer. He took out the key she didn't know he had and opened the door. He called out her name but there was no answer. He walked around. The place was empty. Then he noticed the drawers were open. Everything was gone. The bitch had run out on him.

Andreas woke up when the sunlight hit his eyes. He still was holding Lila's hand. He looked at his phone. No messages. Angelo and Christina should be in Mykonos by now. He figured the Old Man would be taking a flight leaving Athens around seven at night. But he might take his own plane, or a helicopter. No matter, they'd be ready for him at the Cultural Center.

He called Kouros. 'Hi, how's Demosthenes doing?'

'I'm hoping miserable and horny. He made a late-night visit to Anna's place, but she and the kid were gone, packed up and left. He was pissed. Started throwing furniture around from the sound of things.'

'Where is she?'

'Caught a train at Larisis station, headed north to Thesaloniki.'

'A new start in another city?'

'Hope so, for her sake. We have someone on the train. Just in case.'

'And Demosthenes?'

'Back in his apartment. I'm staying on him.'

'I've got two watching the Old Man. He's still home.'

'Guess things won't get moving until this afternoon.'

'But when they do—'

'I know. We'll be ready, don't worry.'

Andreas did worry. He wanted to be on Mykonos, but couldn't risk it. His presence would be noticed, and if it got back to the Old Man that the cop in charge of the Kostopoulos murder investigation was on Mykonos on the day of their meeting, it was certain to spook him away. At least Tassos was there. Andreas hoped that was a good thing.

At three sharp, Demon was at the Kolonaki Club. Five minutes later, the Old Man and he were in the back of a Mercedes 600 limousine heading toward the airport. The Old Man seemed remarkably calm. Neither spoke.

'He missed the turn.'

The Old Man gestured no. 'He didn't.'

'Sure, he did, the airport is to the right.'

'We're not going to the airport. We're catching the Hi Speed at Rafina.'

'The ferry? Why are we taking a boat?'

The Old Man smiled. 'You'll see.'

Twenty-five minutes later they pulled onto the pier. A man dressed in black fatigues gestured them toward a line of four black Porsche Cayennes. Two pulled onto the boat ahead of the limousine, two behind.

'I thought some prudence was in order. Considering what happened in Sardinia, I wasn't about to go anywhere without equivalent assistance. Oh, yes, I spoke to Linardos about our little chat yesterday, and he checked with his newspaper sources in Italy. It wasn't police. It was mercenaries. You were right about one thing, though: Mr Kostopoulos is a very dangerous man indeed.' The Old Man picked up a newspaper and started reading as if he didn't have a care in the world.

Demon made a mental note to get copies of those tapes and envelopes into the hands of more than one friend. Of all the nuts running around threatening to kill him, this was the one most likely to do it.

It was a slightly less than three-hour trip, and passengers weren't allowed to stay with their vehicles. They had to go above unless, of course, you were part of the Old Man's party. There always were exceptions for him. Demon watched one of the dozen men in fatigues tinker with a pair of headphones. 'What's he doing?'

The Old Man looked up from his newspaper. 'Practicing.'

Demon sounded impatient. 'Practicing what?'

'He's trying to catch signals. He's a counter-surveillance specialist. That's some of his equipment. He can pick up a gnat recording a hum a mile away.' He smiled. 'After your little recording session at the club, you didn't think I was going to make that mistake again, did you? If this turns out to be a setup, I think the operative word is "duck."'

'The Old Man and Demosthenes are on their way to Mykonos, but they're in a black Mercedes limo taking the fast boat from Rafina and traveling with a dozen military types in black fatigues. The limo's surrounded by four black Cayennes. Looks like a goddamned military convoy.'

Andreas hadn't left the hospital. Kouros updated him every half hour. 'I was afraid of something like that. But it's not unexpected. I'll let Tassos know. Anything else?'

'I'm on the boat with them. I tried walking by the limo on the way to the upper deck, but the Cayenne-guys started

326

checking me out, so I didn't push it. I'll try again later. But it won't be easy. I've no excuse for being down there. The boat was full, and they wouldn't take my car. I had to flash my badge to get on as a passenger.'

'Don't worry, I'll have someone meet you when you get in.'

'It's due in at six forty-five p.m., at the new harbor in Tourlos.'

'Okay. Let me know if anything changes.'

Andreas hung up. He hadn't bothered to leave Lila's room. It didn't seem to matter how loud he talked or what he said. He wondered if she'd ever hear him again.

He called Tassos. 'The Old Man is on his way by boat from Rafina.'

'Boat?'

'Yes, the Hi Speed. It gets into Tourlos at six forty-five p.m. Looks like he's trying to surprise you by showing up early.'

'Don't worry. We'll be ready for him.'

'It's ready for *them*. He's traveling with Demosthenes and a dozen guys like Kostopoulos' major. Two Cayennes in front and two in back of the Old Man's limo.'

'What kind of limo?'

'Is that important?'

'Could be.'

'It's a Mercedes 600.'

'Thanks.'

Andreas paused. 'You know, if he's hiring first-rate professional talent, my guess is they'll sweep the place for bugs.'

Tassos didn't sound concerned. 'We're ready for that.'

'How?'

'We just are. Like I said, it's set up to run through the

327

Center's system. It's undetectable. Gotta run – have to get ready for our guests. Bye.'

Andreas hoped Tassos knew what he was doing. But if anything went wrong, it was Tassos' people who would take the heat. That reminded him: he'd better have someone pick up Kouros at the harbor, and tell his own surveillance guys to be careful. This was no time to take unnecessary chances. He didn't want anyone else getting hurt. At least not any of the good guys.

Mykonos' new harbor lay like a chubby-bottom north-to-south 'H' about one mile north of the island's historic old harbor. The western leg of the 'H' sat out to sea, connected to the onshore leg by a hardly noticeable bridge. The distance between the two legs was well less than one hundred yards at the south and no more than forty yards at the north. Cruise ships docked at the seaward northern end of the western leg. The Hi Speed and other large ferries docked and unloaded from the stern at its southern seaward end. The areas between the legs were for smaller craft.

A part of the onshore leg ran alongside and from three to nine feet below the main road into town. It was approximately a quarter-mile long and seemed forever under construction. People were used to it. A giant's sandbox, complete with all the old-time trucks, cranes, bulldozers, and other sorts of tank-tread earthmoving equipment every giant's little boy would love to play with. It even had a set of blocks: car-size concrete ones, lined up along the seaside and used to keep pressure on footings that some day would support the 'soon to be completed' marina.

The loudspeaker blared, 'We are arriving at Mykonos. Drivers please return to your vehicles.'

Demon was sleeping, the Old Man dozing. The Old Man leaned over from the passenger's side of the back seat and said to the driver, 'Did you tell them where we're going?'

'Yes, sir.'

'And how to get there?'

'Yes, sir. I told them to take the back way, up that steep hill next to the taverna across from the stop sign where we come out of the port.'

'Good.' He leaned back and looked at Demon. 'I prefer not to be predictable. Just in case.'

'I understand.'

The boat docked and the rear door began descending. Drivers started their engines.

Demon looked at the Old Man. 'Do you mind if I ask a question?'

'Possibly.'

'What are you planning to say to Kostopoulos?'

'Ah, now that's a good question. And one I'm prepared to answer.'

The Cayennes in front started moving. He leaned forward again. 'Stay close, no more than ten yards behind.'

'Yes, sir.'

The Old Man continued. 'He is a very interesting man, more so than I realized. He has both the willingness and capacity to do whatever he thinks necessary to achieve what he sets his mind to. He is not swayed by emotions or fears. He stays focused. He has the qualities of a Spartan.'

This was not what Demon wanted to know. He did not need a lecture. He wanted to know the game plan. He thought of saying, 'And Spartans helped end the Golden Age of Athens, so now what?' But didn't. He assumed the Old Man was dragging things out to kill time – some bus looked to have traffic backed up coming out of the port.

'I am going to tell Mr Kostopoulos exactly what he wants to hear. He wants to be accepted. He wants glory. He wants prestige. He wants to be among Greece's aristocracy. I will offer him all that. I will offer him everything he's ever wanted. And I am the one man in Greece who can guarantee all of that to him.'

Demon nodded. Those were his goals, too. 'But, what if Kostopoulos doesn't agree?'

They were up to the stop sign, but the bus responsible for the traffic tie-up still blocked the road they intended to take. People were screaming at the bus driver to move. He screamed back that he couldn't move it, that the bus was broken, and walked into the taverna.

'What shall we do, sir?' asked the driver.

'Always problems. Tell the men to go along the sea road, and just past that construction.' He pointed to a large yellow excavator working below the wall next to the road. 'Take the first left up the hill.'

The traffic started moving again. The first two Cayennes sped out onto the main road. The Mercedes started to follow, but a motorcyclist shot up along its right side and cut directly in front of it. The limo driver slammed on his brakes and missed the motorcyclist by inches. '*Malaka!*' the driver screamed. 'Sorry, sir, I didn't mean to swear.'

The Old Man didn't seem upset. 'That's okay, just catch up with them.'

The two Cayennes were a hundred yards ahead. The driver floored it. He'd be up to them in seconds. The two other Cayennes were right behind him.

'To answer your question, let me put it in American movie vernacular, "I'm gonna make him an offer he can't refuse."' The Old Man smiled.

Demon leaned forward to pick up a water bottle on the floor by his feet. He didn't think that was the right way to negotiate with Kostopoulos, but he didn't have the opportunity to suggest a different approach. All negotiations were peremptorily cancelled by the yellow excavator's refrigerator-size steel bucket.

At top speed, the Liebherr 942 excavator cab spins completely around – with claw-tooth bucket extended – in eight seconds. But it only took two seconds for this perfect, some might say golf-like, swing of the bucket down over the wall, into the Mercedes' windshield, through its insides and out the rear glass. The Cayennes plowed into the mess from behind at fifty miles an hour.

But the tall man who jumped out of the excavator, raced thirty yards to the sea, and leaped into a waiting Zodiac was not a golfer. He'd prefer calling it a perfect assassination.

27

Kouros walked off the Hi Speed before the vehicles were moving and hustled on foot toward the main road. Christina was waiting for him there because 'traffic was terrible in the port.' He was three hundred yards from the stop sign when the first Cayenne crept past him. Every window in the convoy had dark glass, but he could make out Demon sitting behind the driver through the less darkly tinted rear window.

About fifty yards from the stop sign, a motorcycle shot out from behind a dumpster ten feet in front of Kouros and headed toward the main road. The cyclist was riding in the dirt on the side of the road, but when the first Cayenne turned right he accelerated so that he arrived at the intersection just as the second one turned and cut in front of the limo. It was a damn lucky thing he didn't get hit – or a very professional move.

Kouros watched the limo and Cayennes tear after the

two in front. The surreal part played out in seconds: the swinging bucket across the roadway, the explosion of glass, the wrenching of steel, the aftershocks delivered by the Cayennes; the tall man running toward the sea and disappearing with a leap into a boat.

That was how Kouros described what he saw to Andreas. The official investigation didn't yield much more.

Headlines screamed, 'New Terrorist Assault on the Fabric of Our Country,' and everyone ran stories venerating the Old Man and his accomplishments. His funeral was delayed by a day, because the Old Man had left instructions insisting there be a public viewing of his body – and that required spare parts from a theatrical supply house in London. It was attended by virtually everyone in Greece who mattered, or thought they did.

Buried in the stories were the fates of the others in the limo. The driver died instantly. The young passenger miraculously survived the bucket. Evidently he was bent forward when the bucket swept through, shearing off everything above him, but was tragically crippled by the impacting vehicles from behind. He was not expected to survive.

Andreas stopped reading the stories. He long ago gave up on 'the truth will out' or 'justice prevails.' He just did his job. And prayed for Lila to survive.

It was a little more than a week later when Andreas received a call from Tassos.

'Hi, I hear Lila is out of her coma.'

'Yes, thank God. About four days ago. Doctors said she's getting stronger every day.' Andreas heard a sniffling sound on Tassos' end of the line.

'That's great. I'm in Athens—'

Andreas interrupted. 'I figured you were from the increased number of smiles on Maggie's face.'

'I'll never tell.' Tassos laughed. 'Do you think it would be okay if I visited Lila?'

'She'd like that.' Andreas paused. 'I'd like that, too. Meet you there in an hour.' He hung up.

He knew how Tassos felt about him. Tassos lost his own son and his wife during childbirth. Yes, Tassos wasn't a cop like his father. But then, Andreas thought, am I? Sure, Tassos had something to do with what happened at the port. Andreas was certain of that. Big fucking deal. In today's world, who knew which of them was doing things the right way? He really should do something about the distance he'd put between them. He knew what Lila would say: it's time to start trusting again.

Andreas arrived at the hospital fifteen minutes later than he said. That would give Tassos all the time he needed to enchant Lila.

'Hi, honey.' Andreas kissed her.

'Ah, the other cop in my life has arrived. You've just lost number-one position to Tassos. I never knew before how much everything you've achieved in life was because of him.'

Tassos smiled. 'Well, almost everything. He did get to you before I did.'

'And a lucky thing for him.'

'Maybe I should leave and give you guys more time alone.' Andreas was smiling ear to ear.

'As a matter of fact, I'm the one who must leave. I have to catch a boat back to Syros.' Tassos leaned over and kissed Lila on both cheeks. 'See you soon. And keep him in line, please.'

Andreas walked Tassos to the elevator. 'So, any more news on our port pancakes?'

Tassos turned grim. 'Don't start with me, please.'

Andreas put up his hand. 'No, no, I'm not going that way with this. Whatever went on there is out of my jurisdiction. Mykonos is your jurisdiction. You're in charge, and I have no interest in what happened other than curiosity. Trust me on that.'

Tassos smiled. 'There's hope for you yet, Kaldis.'

Andreas rolled his eyes. 'Thanks. So, what happened?'

'Bottom line, Kostopoulos did not have as much confidence in the recording equipment as I did. My guess, and it's only a guess, is he was willing to cooperate with your plan and remained cool on the phone with the Old Man because he had his own plans. You should have seen his face when I told him they were coming by boat. He went white as a ghost. The major and his men had been at the airport all day doing God knows what. Kostopoulos took off to find them and that was the last I saw of Zanni until he showed up at the hospital asking to see the Old Man's corpse.'

'Whew.'

'Yeah, he wanted to see all the parts they'd been able to find.' Tassos shook his head. 'As for the scene at the port, that bus blocking the road miraculously started and disappeared right after the . . . what did you call it?'

'Pancake party.'

'So, I leave to your imagination whether the bus was a setup to block the only other way out of the port to the

Cultural Center. And the construction site wasn't supposed to be working at that hour, so the guy running the excavator wasn't union. From Kouros' description, I think we both know who he was, but Kostopoulos insists the major was with him at the time.'

'Neat, very neat.'

Tassos nodded. 'Want to bet whether the ones who actually killed Zanni's son are still alive?' Tassos waved a finger. 'Don't take it. Bad odds on the negotiator, too.'

'What are Linardos' chances?'

'Pretty good, unless Kostopoulos is suicidal.'

'What are you saying?'

'I don't think the Old Man's cronies in this banishment bullshit missed Kostopoulos' message – delivered on a steel bucket inscribed with the head of their leader – that their potsherd days were over. But that created a problem for Zanni. He doesn't know who the others are, but they know who he is. They're probably deciding right now whether to walk away or put a bounty on his head.'

Andreas smiled. 'How much would it take to get the major's attention?'

Tassos laughed. 'That's why I think Linardos is safe. If Kostopoulos goes after him, that guarantees the others will pay whatever it costs to take him out rather than wait around and wonder if he's coming after them too.'

'All it takes is for one of them to get nervous enough to put up the bounty.'

Tassos nodded. 'I think Zanni now realizes that his power-trip bullshit has brought home a curse. My guess is he'll leave Greece and spend the rest of his life looking over his shoulder, trusting no one. A pretty miserable penance.'

'For a pretty miserable guy.'

Tassos shrugged.

'Speaking of penance, do you know what Linardos is doing these days?'

Tassos head-gestured no.

'Playing Demosthenes' guardian angel. He hired the MedEvac unit that airlifted Demosthenes to a private hospital in Athens and is paying all his bills. Kouros tells me Linardos visits Demosthenes and prays. Sits by his bed and actually prays.' Andreas paused. 'But the prayers aren't working. His doctor told Kouros that if he survives it will be as a mind trapped in an utterly useless body.' Andreas paused again. 'Like being buried alive and forced to silently watch the rest of the world walk over your grave until the day you die.'

Tassos let the thought drift away before speaking. 'You'd think he'd want Demosthenes to die, to get rid of the last bit of incriminating evidence.'

'Makes you wonder what will happen if Demosthenes dies.'

Tassos shook his head. 'Can't imagine Linardos is worried about anything Demosthenes has on him. The Old Man is a martyred national hero, and no politician wants to tarnish that image by letting this story get out. It just might get the people wondering who in government can they trust.' He paused, then rolled his left hand in the air. 'As far as the media are concerned, they're no different. If they go after Linardos they're going after one of their most respected own – with a story guaranteed to make enemies of some of Greece's richest and most powerful families. Besides, God knows what shit Linardos has on his colleagues in the Greek press.'

'Yeah, but there's always the foreign press.'

Tassos smiled. 'Spoken like a true Greek. But, as much as we like to think they do, the rest of the world doesn't give a damn about what goes on here. Unless something is burning, Greece doesn't make the international news. Even then, not for long.' He shook his head again. 'No matter what coverage this gets outside of Greece, the story is dead here because *everyone* wants it to go away. Linardos knows that. My guess is he's not praying out of concern over what might happen to him if Demosthenes dies.'

'Then, why? For his granddaughter, for Greece?'

Tassos spread his arms and looked up as if asking for an answer from above. 'Who knows? Both could use some heavenly intervention.' He let his arms fall to his sides and looked back at Andreas. 'Maybe it's just guilt for whatever part he played in all this, or simply a matter of thanks that he's not the one who'll end up living out the rest of his days on a slab. My guess is it's a bit of both.'

Andreas shrugged. 'Well, we keep track of everyone in and out of Demosthenes' room. Sooner or later, something will break and,' Andreas pointed up to where Tassos had been looking, 'god willing, we mere mortals might get an answer.'

'Or he dies and you find out faster.'

'That's the easy way.'

Tassos winked. 'I know.'

Andreas laughed. 'And so you sum up our differences, my friend.' They embraced and said goodbye.

Andreas still was smiling as he walked into Lila's room.

'Happy, stranger?'

'Very.'

'Come over here and hold my hand.' Her eyes were wet.

'What's wrong?'

'Nothing. I'm terribly happy, and hope you are too.' She kissed his hand. 'I have something to tell you. The doctors spoke to me this morning. They're still running tests. They're not sure yet about the extent of the damage—'

Andreas' heart jumped. He prayed it would be good news.

'But they wanted me to know they were very hopeful.'

Thank god. He squeezed her hand.

'Only one test is unequivocal.' Lila stared into Andreas' eyes. 'I'm pregnant.'

Watch out for the next novel by Jeffrey Siger
Coming soon from Piatkus:

AN AEGEAN
PROPHECY

St John wrote the apocalyptic Book of Revelation
over 1900 years ago in a cave on Greece's eastern Aegean
island of Patmos. When a revered monk
from that holy island's thousand-year-old monastery is
murdered in Patmos's town square during Easter Week,
Chief Inspector Andreas Kaldis is called upon to
find the killer.

Andreas's impolitic search for answers brings him
face-to-face with a scandal haunting the world's oldest
surviving monastic community. On the pristine Aegean
peninsula of Mount Athos, isolated from the rest of
humanity, twenty monasteries sit protecting the secrets
of Byzantium amid a way of life virtually unchanged
for more than 1500 years. But today this sacred refuge
harbours modern international intrigues that threaten
to destroy the very heart of the Church . . . in a
matter of days.

978-0-7499-5236-5